Golden Promises

A Single Father Romance

Maya Alden

"The heart was made to be broken."
—*Oscar Wilde*

"Love is not something you go out and look for. Love finds you, and when it does, ready or not, it'll be the best thing to ever happen to you."
—*Anonymous*

"The only thing we never get enough of is love, and the only thing we never give enough of is love."
—*Henry Miller*

Playlist

I Want to Know What Love Is — Foreigner

Take a Chance on Me — ABBA

Can't Help Falling in Love — Elvis Presley

Ain't No Mountain High Enough — Marvin Gaye & Tammi Terrell

Un-break My Heart — Toni Braxton

You're Still the One — Shania Twain

Make You Feel My Love — Adele

Come Away With Me — Norah Jones

Halo — Beyoncé

I Knew I Loved You — Savage Garden

Bleeding Love — Leona Lewis

I Choose You — Sara Bareilles

Say You Won't Let Go — James Arthur

A Thousand Years — Christina Perri

I Will Always Love You — Whitney Houston

Chapter 1

Alejandro.

I t had been six months since I'd had sex and celibacy did not suit me.

It wasn't because I was busy at work or life or anything else that caused this sexual deprivation; it was a *woman* I couldn't shake off. Her taste was in my mouth—sweet and spicy, like chocolate and cinnamon. I could hear her husky voice when she was aroused, especially when I put my hands on her. *Alejandro*, she'd whimpered when I cupped her breast through her clothes.

I'd kissed her and touched *one* of her breasts like I was in fucking high school, and she had me so hot that six months later, I wanted no one but her.

I'd seen her for dinner two months ago in Fresno, but that was too close to where I lived. I didn't bring a woman home or close to home. I didn't mix sex and family. My priorities were simple. My son Silvano, who was eleven, came first, *always*; my family came next, and my business came last. There was no room for a woman. And what did I need a woman for? Sex? Well, that I could get hassle-free. I was Alejandro Santos, the CEO of one of the largest farms in the United States West Coast—and I'd been told I wasn't hard on the eyes.

I traveled a lot for work, and it was easy to find another road warrior who wanted sexual relief without complications because if they seemed *the type* who tried to complicate matters, they weren't *my type*.

Now, *this* woman, chocolate, and cinnamon was complicated up the wazoo. *Dios mío*, she was driving me crazy.

It wasn't like I hadn't tried to get rid of her. I had.

I tried to sleep with other women, but I couldn't close the deal. It was almost like if I kissed another woman, I'd lose her taste, and I was addicted to the memory of it. Is this how a forty-two-year-old man behaved? *No.* But I couldn't help myself. This had never happened before.

Since I practiced Ashtanga yoga, I tried to meditate her the hell out of my head. It hadn't worked.

I buried myself in work. That became a more significant problem because whenever I was in a hotel room for the night, I was tempted to call her and see if maybe she'd open to at least phone sex, anything at all, to hear her voice again calling my name.

I volunteered to help during my son's school trip to the Downing Planetarium in Fresno. The other parent was a devoted mother who gave me a stern look whenever I checked my email on my phone. I wished Maria had been with me because it would have been tolerable.

I went camping with Silvano to Mono Lake and at night wondered if she'd like to lie with me and watch the stars.

So, yeah, I was fucked because it looked like I didn't just want to have sex with Maria Caruso. I wanted a relationship with her, and I didn't have time for that.

However, I was getting desperate, so I asked her to have dinner with me when I was in Los Angeles for a meeting. I'd hoped she'd invite me to her place or come to my hotel—but she suggested a restaurant *close* to her house in Silver Lake.

I met Mateo for a drink at the Intercontinental Hotel's lobby bar on the seventy-first floor. Mateo and Raya Silva had become family since my mother, Paloma, had introduced us to the woman she'd helped in Boston when she was a young girl. My mother used to work at a women's shelter. It was at Mateo and Raya's wedding reception that I'd fucked my life up by dancing with the elegant woman who made my cock hard by just taking a sip of champagne and laughing that made me think of fairies and fucking pixies, books I'd read to my baby sister Isadora when she was little.

There was something about Maria that made me want to muss her up. I wanted to run my hands through her soft and silky straight hair. I wanted her lipstick to be smudged. I wanted to see a beard burn on her cheek, a hickey on her neck...I wanted to brand. *Yeah*, so she brought out the alpha male in me, someone I hadn't seen in a long time.

"Raya and I are thinking of getting a place close to you guys," Mateo told me.

I smiled. "Why not use one of the cottages on the

farm? Or we can give you a piece of land if you want to build a place."

Mateo stared at me like I'd grown a second head.

"What?" I asked.

"Are you saying we could build a home in Golden Valley?"

Golden Valley was our family estate, where we built homes for the family over our acres of land. The rest was used for farming and raising some cattle for personal use.

I nodded. "You're family. Isadora has reserved her piece of land by the lake—if you want that, you need to discuss that with her. Currently, she's living at the main house more because Mama and Papa want her to than her need for privacy. Aurelio has a place, it's closer to the forest. He likes his privacy. I'm sure we can find something that could work for you."

Mateo closed his eyes for a moment and took a deep breath. When he opened his eyes, I was surprised to see them bright with emotion. "I can't tell you how much your offer means."

I put a hand on Mateo's shoulder. "*Mi hermano*, you're family."

He nodded and smiled widely. "Raya is going to flip."

Mateo and Raya had not grown up with parents or any semblance of a family. I could not imagine how barren that life could be. My family was vital to me —I'd do anything for them. I was fifteen and Aurelio had been ten when Papa met Paloma—and our lives changed. We'd immediately become a family.

Paloma became Mama, and now I thought of her as my mother. I couldn't remember my own, who died a year after Aurelio was born, but it wouldn't have mattered. Paloma's big heart was impossible to resist. Isadora was born three years after they met; I'm sure if you counted the months, Mama was pregnant before the wedding. Isa was our adored baby sister. I changed her diapers, bathed her, and held her when she cried like a baby. She was almost like my child. We couldn't be closer.

My son Silvano might not have a mother, but he had the most loving family around him. He spent more time in the main house than in our place, which was a ten-minute bike ride.

I was fortunate. And I was happy that Mateo and Raya were now family as well—and we could share our good fortune with them. Through Mateo and Raya, we'd also become close to Declan and Esme Knight, their beautiful baby girl, Mireya, and Dec's cousin, Judge Forest Knight and his beautiful wife, Daisy. As well as Maria and her brother Mark, a neurosurgery resident at UCLA.

"Just call my office. My assistant, Mercedes, can set you up with a walk-through and introduce you to our architect. We'd love to have you live close by. You won't mind leaving the big, bad city?" I waved a hand at the view of Los Angeles, sparkling lights, and high rises.

"No. Raya and I want to…well, keep an apartment here, but we want a quieter life. Dec and Esme couldn't leave the city, and I get it. There's energy here."

I waved a hand at the bartender, watching the clock. I was meeting Maria in forty-five minutes at Silver Lake.

"Can I get an espresso?" I requested.

"Isn't it early for coffee?" Mateo wondered.

"I have a dinner thing, and I'd like to stay awake. I left

Golden Valley at four in the morning, so it's been a long day," I explained.

Mateo narrowed his eyes. "Who are you having dinner with?"

"None of your business."

"And here I thought we were family."

I sighed. "I have Mama and Papa, and let's not forget Isadora, who I believe spies on all of us."

"I noticed you were dancing with Maria Caruso at the reception."

"That was six months ago and weren't you busy that night? It was *your* wedding reception," I remarked and looked at my watch again as the server brought me my espresso.

"You need a ride to Silver Lake, *mi hermano*," Mateo teased.

I took a sip of the dark coffee. "I have a son, Mat. I can't do relationships."

"I don't agree, but it's not my place to tell you how to live your life—and I have learned that this is a journey every man must take on his own." Mateo drained his beer and stood up. "Just so you know, Maria wants a relationship. She wants the picket fence, the two and a half kids and the dog. And she fucking deserves it. That girl has a big heart and brains to match."

"You warning me off her, Mat?" My tone was tighter than I'd expected it to be.

Mateo shook his head. "No. That's not part of my job description. I just wanted you to know a little about my friend Maria."

"I appreciate it," I thanked him sincerely, but didn't add that I didn't want to marry the girl. I just wanted to fuck her brains out. But considering Mateo's "friend" comment, I didn't think it would be appropriate to mention that.

Chapter 2

Maria

"**I** don't know what to wear," I wailed as I walked around my closet, facetiming with my brother Mark. He was trying to stay awake at home as he'd just completed a double shift in the pediatric NICU, where he was doing a rotation.

"Sis, you have every piece of clothing ever created with a designer label in your closet." I heard him yawn. "Can I go to sleep now?"

"No. I need you to tell me how I look. I need five minutes." I put a dress on and modeled it for him.

"Damn it, Maria. You look good no matter what you wear..." he paused when he focused on me in a red silk sheath dress, "This one gives out high-class escort vibes. Maybe you don't need to show him your nips on your first date."

"Second date... third because the wedding reception

counts as one. We met in Fresno for dinner a while back." I walked away from Mark's line of sight and let the red high-class escort dress slide off my body. "So that was the second date. This is the third."

"Then make sure not to wear your skanky underwear."

"I don't have any skanky underwear, thank you very much," I snapped and put on another dress. "What about this?"

Mark sat up on his bed and nodded appreciatively. "Virginal. I like it."

"Oh no. I want to have sex tonight, Mark. I don't want to look virginal."

"Which would also be false advertising," Mark commented dryly. "You look nice in white. Keep the dress. Tie the hair up...that loose bun thing you do. Wear heels. He's tall enough, so you don't have to hunch. Now, I'm going to get some sleep before I have to go back to the hospital and attend surgery for a little person with a big brain problem."

I blew him a kiss. "Thanks, Mark. Sleep well, baby bro."

The dress was a typical Victoria Beckman, simple, designed to elevate my silhouette far beyond any shapewear could. It was a slim midi-dress with a square neckline and a front cutout along the waist. I put on nude pumps and pearl earrings and, as Mark suggested, wore my hair in a loose bun. I kept my makeup simple, as I always did. Having too much always made me conscious, so I did the basics: tinted moisturizer, mascara, blush, and lipstick. I was a spicy perfume girl, and my go-to was Tom Ford's Jasmin Rouge, which perfumed me with a burst of jasmine and ylang-ylang and a whisper of cinnamon.

I looked at myself in the mirror and shrugged; well, I looked good, or at least good enough. *Was I dressed too corporate? Should I have worn something more boho chic, like my friend Esme? But I didn't do boho chic. It was important to be comfortable, to look comfortable. Right?* I wanted to call and ask Esme how I looked, but I knew Alejandro would not appreciate anyone finding out that we were *seeing* each other if that was what we were doing.

When he'd called to say he'd like to take me out for dinner and I didn't want to sound completely promiscuous, I'd told Alejandro that I'd meet him at a restaurant. It was a five-minute walk from my condo, which was a good thing because my heels were not made for walking long distances.

When I got there, he was already inside the restaurant. Check punctuality off on the checklist.

I could see him through the glass windows. He was going through his phone, his face serious. Alejandro Santos was *handsome* with a big H. Last time we had dinner, he wore a suit. That night at Mateo's and Raya's reception, he'd worn a suit. Today, he wore a white dress shirt, the sleeves folded, and jeans. Businessman in repose.

Not wanting to be caught eye-fucking my date, I stepped away from the window and stood under the warm glow of simple A above the door of my local Italian restaurant. I took a deep breath and opened the door and was immediately greeted by the inviting aroma of soulful Italian cuisine. I'd chosen the restaurant so I could *indicate* how I wanted to end the night without being too forward. I wanted this to go well. For the first time in my thirty-two years, my heart was galloping at the idea of spending an evening with a man.

I liked Alimento's food, as well as their minimalist, casual interiors that exuded a relaxed ambiance, making it the perfect setting for an intimate dinner. The friendly hostess who knew me smiled at me. "Welcome back."

I waved to Alejandro. She turned to look at him and grinned broadly, and then turned to me. "*Nice.*"

"Wish me luck." I couldn't keep the smile off my face.

"The way you look, no luck is needed." The hostess winked at me.

Alejandro rose as I walked to the cozy table. We looked at each other awkwardly for a moment, unsure how to greet one another. A hug would be weird. A kiss, forward. A handshake, ridiculous. I decided to be forward. I brushed my lips against his.

"Hi," I whispered.

His eyes hooded for a moment, and then his mouth was on mine, gently coaxing a breathless kiss so I could taste him, and he could taste me. I moaned softly as he deepened the kiss, but suddenly, he froze and pulled away.

"Not here," his voice was harsh.

He stepped around me and pulled my chair for me. My lips felt like they were on fire, and I was disoriented for a moment. If this man could arouse me like this with a kiss, if we ever made it to having sex, I might combust.

We settled into our seats. I picked up the menu so I wouldn't stare at him. He did the same. "This is one of my favorite restaurants in Silver Lake. I hope you'll like it."

"No reason not to," he replied, not looking up from the menu.

I didn't like his tone. Something seemed to have turned a switch *off* inside him. The last time we met in Fresno, we had fun. He'd been charming, and the sizzle was enticing. Today, with that kiss, we'd sexually charged ourselves to where my thighs wanted to fall apart and allow him in.

"Alejandro," my voice came out in a whisper.

He looked up at me. His eyes were dark, dilated, and he wore a snarl I hadn't seen before.

"I need a minute, *Duquesa*, to...*fuck*..." he panted. "The way you look at me. I want to pull you on to me and make you ride me."

My mouth went dry. No one, but no one, had ever spoken to me like this.

"Or go down on my knees and taste you." He set the menu down and held up a hand that wasn't steady. "I'm shaking like this is my first time in my father's car."

I smiled, wanting to lighten the mood. "What kind of car?"

He closed his eyes for a minute and grinned. "An F150."

"Plenty of room in the back."

He took my hand in his. "What kind of wine do you like, *Duquesa*?"

He started calling me *Duquesa* almost immediately. When I'd asked him why when we met in Fresno, he'd seduced me with his response.

"You look like royalty...and every time I look at you, I'm not sure if I should genuflect and tug my forelock or

go down on my knees to taste you, to make you scream."
I blushed like an ingénue and lowered my eyes to look at the drinks menu. This man pushed every one of my buttons.

"I'm partial to red. They have a nice wine from Sicily that I can recommend if you like red. It's rich and intense."

A server came by then and asked what we'd like to drink. I looked at Alejandro and he grinned. "Order away. I'm in your hands."

"Still water okay?" I asked. He nodded.

"A bottle of still, please, and we'll have the 2019 Arianna Occhipinti Il Frappato."

"Excellent choice," the server said. "Do you have questions about the menu?"

We both said we were still browsing.

"Why this wine?" he asked.

"The winemaker is a woman, Arianna Occhipinti. I like that this is made with a grape that we don't know well in the US, frappato. The wine is spicy, earthy, and bright. The taste is complex. It's a long wine."

He leaned back and looked at me. "You're a sensuous woman, Maria. You live with all your senses. It's very... erotic." I licked my lips then, and his eyes narrowed. "You're having quite an impact on me, and I can't understand it."

"Well, the feeling is mutual," I confessed.

Before Alejandro could say anything, a server came and filled our glasses with water. The floor sommelier followed the server with our wine. He knew me and welcomed me back.

"I'm thinking that I need to keep this wine in stock.

It's become one of your favorites, *eh?*" The sommelier said in his Italian accent.

"Thanks, Francesco. I appreciate it."

He expertly opened the bottle, removed the cork, and sniffed it. He set the cork down and poured me a taste.

I sipped the wine and closed my eyes as the taste of cherries, strawberry and autumn leaves filled my senses. I handed my glass to Alejandro, a challenge in my eyes. "Would you like to try as well?"

He took the glass and turned it to where there was a small smudge of my pink lipstick. He drank from there, and a shiver ran right down to my pussy.

"Delicious," he said, looking at me. I wasn't sure if he was talking about the wine or the taste of my lipstick. But with the way he said it, probably the latter.

Francesco poured the wine for us and left.

Just as Alejandro was about to say something, our server came back, and I sighed in irritation. I should've asked him over to my place and cooked him a meal. Then we wouldn't be disturbed by eager servers and the Somm every five minutes.

As if he sensed my irritation and understood it, Alejandro put his hand on mine and smiled. "What's good here?"

"Everything." I watched his hand on mine and felt the warmth of it. I'd never had a physical reaction like this to any other man, and I was thirty-two years old, so there had been several men in my life.

"Order for me," he commanded.

"We'll start with the chicken liver *crostone* and scallop crudo. I'll have the tortellini *en brood*, and he'll have the *radiatori*."

Alejandro handed his menu to the server, his eyes on me.

"Maria, I will not pretend there isn't a connection between us. You can feel it, and god knows I can feel it. I've been hard ever since you walked in here."

I flushed. This man had a mouth on him.

"And I bet you're wet. Aren't you?"

I nodded, feeling completely out of my depth.

"The sex between us will be...well, amazing. *And* I want you. *But* I'm not looking for more than that. I have a son. I have a demanding job. I don't want a wife, girlfriend, or partner."

I felt like he smacked me. "I don't think I've indicated to you I want to be your wife, girlfriend, or partner. And you have some nerve."

He grabbed my hand as he saw I was getting ready to flounce out of there.

"Please, don't be angry. I *want* you like I have not wanted another woman. Since we kissed fucking six months ago...I've not had a woman. And I never go that long. But all I offer is sex. I can't be anything more. I'm not saying this because I think you're expecting these things for me, I'm telling you this because..." He ran a hand through his hair, "Hell, because I had a drink with Mateo before I came here and he—"

"Played big brother, did he?" Understanding dawned, and I was amused.

"Something like that."

"If you had a drink with my *actual* brother Mark, he'd tell you, make sure she orgasms, treat her with respect, and you're good."

Now it was Alejandro's turn to be taken aback. Oh, yes, yes, I said the word orgasm.

"How many orgasms would I need to give you to make sure you're...ah *good*?"

I frowned. "Like...one. I mean, an orgasm...ah... what? Why are you smiling like that?"

"Ever had more than one when you had sex?"

I sighed. "Now, who's being cocky? It's not always easy to have an orgasm during sex without some...you know, mechanical help."

"I don't know. Are you saying you use a vibrator while you're with a man to come?"

I looked around to make sure no one heard him, and he laughed. "Are you embarrassed, *Duquesa*?"

"Yes," I whispered. "I...I'm not used to talking like this."

"Or having multiple orgasms without a battery-operated device," he teased.

Chapter 3

Alejandro

What the fuck are you doing, Alejandro?

 I'd come with every intention to let her know dinner was great, but I wasn't the man of her dreams, just of her wet ones, and could give her nothing but a few rounds of sex. Usually, this was not an issue because I indulged in one-night stands and no phone numbers were exchanged.

So why was I flirting with her? I didn't have a problem with dirty talk—but I never did it in a restaurant. And here I'm asking her if she's wet and like a shy bird, she nods. *Doesn't she realize what a challenge she is?*

Tall, elegant, and almost fairy-like, Maria Caruso was perfect. Today, she wore a white dress that cupped her breasts, her round ass and she *should* look sexy and maybe even slutty in that dress, instead she looked formidable, sensuous, and untouchable.

The zipper of the dress was in the back and my fingers itched to unzip, unhook, and bare her to me.

I remembered Mateo's words: *Maria wants a relationship. She wants the picket fence, the two and a half kids and the dog. And she fucking deserves it. That girl has a big heart and brains to match.*

Sure, her blood was heated as mine was...damn it. I wanted her.

"Don't knock battery-operated boyfriends. Every self-respecting woman has one or a few." Maria sat back as the server came to our table with our small plates of chicken liver and scallop crudo.

We veered away from sex even though the heat remained between us. Maria was the CEO of Caruso Investment Bank. She was well-read, well-traveled and highly intelligent. It was hard to have a poor conversation with someone like her.

"It's been busy with all the attention on life sciences since the pandemic," she told me when I asked her to tell me more about her company. "We're working with a *very* interesting gene therapy company right now, helping them become publicly traded. We're facilitating their IPO."

I'd done my research on Caruso, a premier elite investment banking advisory firm that worked with life sciences and biotechnology companies to facilitate IPOs, capital raising, mergers and acquisitions, and provided expertise in complex financial transactions. She had a reputation of being smart and tenacious as an investment banker and CEO and knew how to pick a winner. Unlike her father, who'd retired a couple of years ago, she refused to work on hostile takeovers and had increased Caruso's charitable profile to the benefit of the company.

I told her what I was working on. As the CEO of one of the largest farms in the country, a big part of my job was helping to make sure that Golden Valley successfully navigated the many regulations related to environmental stewardship and labor practices. I spent a lot of my time talking to politicians and agriculture boards. As a privately owned farm, we didn't have to worry about the stock market, but we had to worry about local communities, suppliers, buyers, regulatory agencies, and industry associations.

"Luckily, Aurelio deals with the day-to-day farm operations, including planting, harvesting, irrigation, pest control, and livestock management," I told Maria as we drank coffee at the end of our meal and a *very* entertaining evening. She was smart, interesting, and interested.

She let me pay for dinner—and I say *let me*, because this was her turf, and she easily could have asked the server to never bring the bill to us; but she already knew that it would be important for me to assert some sense of stupid alpha male masculinity.

We stepped out into the summer freshness of a Southern California evening. I *wanted her*. I couldn't have her. Not after seeing who she was. Mateo was right. This woman was made for a relationship—for true love and picket fences.

"Maria," I began, and she looked at me with her wide brown eyes, soft and *fucking* enchanting. Yeah, here I was thinking words like *enchanting*. I was losing my mind. I bent to brush my lips against hers, gently. A benediction, a thank you, no more.

She got the message. "Alejandro," she murmured.

"I *want* you," I said simply. "*But* I won't take you. I'm sorry that I called you and asked to meet you. It was wrong of me. Please forgive me. *And* I promise this won't happen again. I'll try my best to make sure you never have to see me again."

She licked her lips, and I almost growled like an animal scenting his mate. *She has to stop doing that,* I thought.

"Okay." Her voice was small, like I had shrunk her with my words. I probably had. Rejection was rejection —and regardless of how much I said I wanted her, I was telling her that whatever we were thinking of starting was over before it began.

"You know Mateo and Raya, and they're family. I... *never* play close to my family, Maria, and that's what this would be. The last time I had a relationship was...*never.* I married my son's mother because she was pregnant, not because we were dating and in love."

She nodded, and I could see the hurt in her eyes. It made me feel like an *asshole.* But it was better to hurt her now with a gentle rejection than later after we'd fucked like rabbits, after I'd tasted her, felt her wetness, and let her come around my cock, which was hard as stone. I wanted to see her mouth open and scream with pleasure. This elegant duchess, spread, bare and wanton for me.

"I'm sorry. I shouldn't have led you on."

Her eyes flashed with irritation now. "I don't give a damn, Alejandro."

She turned and walked away. Her ass was a fucking dream as it swayed. *Would she let me take her in her ass? Enter that lush pussy from behind? Stop it, Alejandro, you're going to die of blue balls at this rate.*

I pulled out my phone and texted my driver to pick me up. I should never have called her. I should never have met her in Fresno. I should never have kissed her six months ago. Because now I knew how she tasted and smelled; and I didn't think any other woman would do.

Get over it, Alejandro, and move the fuck on.

Maybe I could find a road warrior in the lobby of the Intercontinental, I thought as I got into the Escalade. I could ride a nameless, faceless body and find release. Yeah, that's what I was going to do, have sex with another woman and get Maria Caruso out of my system.

Chapter 4

Maria

I walked into my house, closed the door, and leaned against the door, feeling drained. I sank to the floor. I raised my knees, hugged them, and rested my head on them.

I'd met this man *three times*. Just three times and my heart was broken when he rejected me. I didn't believe in love at first sight and all that nonsense. I was a practical adult. I believed that love happened slowly— not like this. An explosion inside my chest.

I fell in love with Alejandro! And wanted desperately to be with him. This was what falling in love felt like. Screw those idiots who said falling in love was amazing. It wasn't amazing. It hurt like a *motherfucker*.

When I first saw Alejandro at Raya and Mateo's wedding reception, I knew he'd be someone important in my life. There had been an explosion then. A recognition. Things that I didn't use to believe in.

Mark and I were running late because I had an emergency call with the board that Saturday. I had paid as little attention as I usually did to how I looked. I wore a simple Schiaparelli column dress made of hammered mahogany satin. I didn't have to worry about accessorizing with jewelry as the neckline of the dress was bound by a gold collar. The dress was as comfortable as it cut on the bias, draping down to expose a leg through the slit in the front and hanging low on my back. I'd blow-dried my hair that morning, so I let it loose in dark curls around my shoulders.

According to Mark, I looked like a warrior princess. I felt harried and walked straight to the bar after congratulating Raya and Mateo.

He'd been there, leaning against the bar, talking to a boy who looked just like him.

"I think a quarter of a glass of champagne should be appropriate. Data shows, drinking alcohol in regulated environments with supervision decreases unsafe drinking activity in the future," *the young man proselytized.*

Alejandro grinned. "That study was for kids who were older than eighteen. I know of at least fifteen case studies that show that because your cerebellum is still developing, it is vulnerable to the toxic effects of alcohol. Once you're past the age of nineteen and your cerebellum is cooked, you can drink and make an ass of yourself."

"If I was born in wine country, I'd be drinking wine since I was two years old," *the young man persisted.*

"This ain't the wine country, mi hijo. And Silvano, you find alcohol bitter."

Silvano made a face. "It's just that I'm wearing a suit and I want to feel grown up. Holding a glass of lemonade makes me feel like I'm eleven."

"You are eleven."

And that's when Alejandro noticed me. He smiled lazily.

I looked at the young boy and said, "When I was your age, I'd ask the server to pour Sprite into a champagne glass, so I'd feel like I was drinking like the grownups. I also didn't like the taste of champagne then."

The boy considered me. "Do you like it now?"

"Yes, I do," I beamed.

The boy contemplated what I said seriously and stated, "In a clinical study, they found that older people appreciate complex flavors, such as wine because their saliva can detect smokey and peppery flavors. Young palates are not developed because our brain wants us to eat food with a higher amount of carbohydrates so we can grow properly."

"I'm older than you, so that explains why I like good champagne," I ventured. The boy was charming.

"In which case, Papa, you should get this nice lady a glass of good champagne."

Alejandro turned to the bartender who'd listened to our conversation. I was quickly supplied with a glass of champagne; and the young man was given Sprite in a champagne glass.

"I'm Silvano. I'm eleven years old." He held out his hand. I shook it.

"I'm Maria. I'm thirty-two years old."

"This is my father, Alejandro Santos and he's very old," Silvano informed me. "I'm going to go dance, Papa, since you won't let me drink. It was nice meeting you, Maria."

"Oh my god, if only I were younger, I'd be madly in love with your son," I joked.

"If you were any younger, I'd feel like I was robbing the cradle...when I ask you to dance." Alejandro held out his *hand, and I put mine in his. We left my hardly-touched champagne glass at the bar and he pulled me in his arms to the slow and sexy,* Make You Feel My Love *by Adele.*

"Bride or groom," he asked me. He made sure there was distance between us as propriety demanded.

"Both," I told him. "I knew Esme Knight through my brother Mark; and then we got close to their whole Boston gang of friends."

"Boston?"

I nodded. "Forest studied law and was interning for a judge; Dec and Mateo met in Harvard; Daisy was at Tufts, and she knew Dec from LA. And Raya worked at a bar. Esme met my brother Mark in Seattle. He was studying medicine, and she was finishing her masters in social work."

His hand shifted and grazed my bare back. "And how about you?"

"I didn't go to Boston. I went to Stanford."

"Did you? When?" He pulled me closer.

I told him, my heart hammering.

"I studied agriculture at UC Davis—and then did an MBA at Stanford."

Well, aren't we all just very well-educated, I thought.

"You're very young."

"Excuse me?"

"I'm ten years older than you," he murmured, his eyes looking deeply into mine. "I don't know why I'm talking about fucking universities because..." and then as if it struck him, he chuckled, "You're Maria Caruso."

"Yes."

"I know of you."

"I know of you," I replied in kind. As soon as Silvano had mentioned his father's name, I knew he was the oldest

Santos, the CEO Of Golden Valley. He had an eleven-year-old son, so he wasn't a child himself—and I'd guess he was in his early forties, which he confirmed. I always liked older men. There was an ease about them. I felt their maturity matched mine.

"You're extremely beautiful." Now we were setting propriety on fire as the music changed and the DJ played a speeded-up version of Un-Break My Heart. *His hips moved against mine and he groaned as I came closer so he could smell me.*

"I...I think you're very handsome." I hadn't felt this gauche since I was a high schooler trying to make it with a college student.

His smile made him beautiful. He had dark blue...blue-gray eyes. His hair was dark, with a sprinkle of gray on his sideburns. His skin looked like he spent time in the sun and his hands didn't feel like those of a pampered CEO.

"My mother has a beautiful garden," he whispered, his breath moist against the shell of my ear, making me shiver. "Could I interest you in a walk?"

I nodded, unable to speak. I was a CEO. A tough businesswoman and I could barely hear his words over the hammering in my heart. No man and I mean no man, ever had me tongue-tied and hormonal—both things Alejandro Santos had achieved with absolutely no effort. Did he do this a lot? Take a woman out at a family party? Were we going to have sex? Had I shaved my legs? When was my last bikini wax?

He put his arm on the naked small of my back and walked me away from the festivities into the gardens where the music filtered gently. The massive garden was lit with twinkling lights and our destination appeared to be a gazebo by a white oak tree.

As if he could read my mind, he said softly, "The effect we have on each other is mutual, Maria. My hands feel as clammy as yours do."

He held my hand then, and we walked to the magnificent wooden handmade gazebo nestled within Paloma's vibrant and lush garden, like children, excited to have made a new friend. As we got closer, I could see that the gazebo's wooden framework was fashioned from rich mahogany and cedar, radiating warmth and authenticity. The surrounding lights flared against the deep reddish-brown hues of the wood, which contrasted softly with the surrounding greenery, creating an enchanting visual contrast.

"This is beautiful," I remarked as we walked on the weathered stone path, leading to the gazebo's open platform, providing a vantage point from which to appreciate the garden's breathtaking beauty.

The gazebo had benches and a gas fire pit for cool nights. Alejandro pressed a button, and the fire flared up. In its warm light, I could see the intricate carvings etched into the wooden pillars and railings. Delicate patterns of cherry blossoms, bamboo leaves, and flowing streams creating an atmosphere of tranquility and serenity, paying homage to the surrounding garden's natural beauty.

"This is something else."

"I come here every morning to do yoga."

The inner sanctum of the gazebo was roomy, and I could see Alejandro meditating here. "What kind of yoga?"

"Ashtanga. It keeps me centered. I need centering."

"Why?" The white oak leaves rustled, making me feel like we were the only two people in the world. The people and the music of the wedding reception seemed far away.

He didn't answer but pulled me into his arms. "May I kiss you?" His lips hovered over mine and I could smell pine and leather.

"Yes," I breathed.

He took advantage of my open mouth and swooped.

Now, I've kissed before. I'd had sex with a select few partners. I had one long-term relationship that lasted eight months and the sex had been pretty good. But this kiss, this was not a kiss, this was an erotic exploration of our mouths, of our tastes, our moans, and groans, our essence.

He nibbled my lips, taking his time before letting his tongue wander inside my mouth. His hands on my hips pulled me against him so I could feel his erection. We both moaned when my hips shimmied. I couldn't help myself. This had never happened before, this perfumed eroticism, this need that came out of nowhere. I was Maria Caruso, and I was the Snow Queen, calm and unruffled. And here I was, panting. Actually, panting and rubbing my pussy against his hardness. What was happening to me? I tried to pull away, but he gripped me harder, and that caveman technique would have gotten any other man a knee in the nuts, but he got a gasp out of me.

"Open, let me in," he roughly demanded as he angled his mouth so he could go deeper, taste me, and force me to taste him.

His hand moved up from hip and cupped one of my breasts through the hammered satin of my dress. My nipples hardened, and he squeezed as he kissed me. His mouth wandered across my jaw and licked the sensitive skin below my left earlobe.

"Alejandro." I was now shaking with arousal.

"Yes."

"Stop," I stammered.

Immediately, he raised his head and looked at me, his hand on my breast, teasing the nipple.

"Yes," he agreed. And then, reluctantly, he stepped away, his hands in front of him to show me he wasn't touching me any longer.

"What was that?" I asked helplessly.

Alejandro chuckled in self-deprecation. "The best fucking kiss of my life. What was it to you?"

"I don't know." I felt panic rise within me. This was not how Maria Caruso behaved.

"We should get back to the party," he smiled tightly.

"Yes." I took a step and stumbled on my heels; my legs felt like jelly. He put a gentle hand around my waist.

"I got you."

The hammering on my door snapped me out of my reverie. I removed my shoes and stood up, annoyed at the intrusion.

"Maria, open the door."

I froze, one hand on the handle of the door and the other holding my nude pumps. It was Alejandro.

Chapter 5

Alejandro

I didn't want to have sex with some woman I picked up at the lobby bar of the Intercontinental. I wanted Maria. God damn it! And damn me to hell.

She opened the door, and I saw tears in her eyes. *She'd been crying.* Fuck!

I stepped inside and closed the door behind me. She looked at me with fear—as if waiting for me to hurt her again. I'd met this woman three times in my life and I could hurt her? And she could crowd my thoughts to the exclusion of everything else? The alarm in my head said *warning: complications ahead*, blazing in neon signs with loud sirens.

I pulled her to me and pushed her against the door. The shoes she was holding dropped onto the hardwood floor with a small thud.

"I want you," I got out the words before I slammed

my lips against her.

Finesse, Alejandro, come on, show this elegant woman some fucking skill and don't go in at ramming speed.

I slowed the kiss, and the world went into slow motion. Every suck, lick, and slurp was enhanced. Her hands in my hair felt like they were spiking me with electricity. My hips held hers in place, my erection against her stomach, throbbing, keeping pace with my raging heartbeat.

"You want me?" I bit her bottom lip, the one she licked all the time when she was thinking about what to say.

"Yes," her voice was shaky.

Good, I thought. She was as affected as I was because my hands weren't steady. *Dios mío!* My heart was hammering against my ribs.

"How much do you want me?" I demanded, brushing my lips against a satiny cheek, working my way to her earlobes, and licking around the pearl earring she wore.

"Alejandro," she moaned.

"You like that." I sucked on the skin below her earlobe, and she cried out in pleasure. I bit gently and then licked to soothe the skin.

My jeans went from comfortable to tight a long time ago and now my cock was pleading to be freed.

"I want you very much," she finally answered my question, looking into my eyes with her brown ones, dark with mystery and desire.

"Show me," I barked.

She looked down at my crotch and then slumped down on her knees. I watched her fumble with my belt and zipper. It took her time to unbutton and unzip, but

I didn't help her. I wanted her to reveal her sensuality, show me how she made love.

The tip of my erection was swollen, angry, throbbing, leaking. A pink tongue licked the precum off me and my hands immediately went to her hair, holding her closer to my cock.

"Open, *Duquesa*," I murmured, "And, eyes on me, baby."

She opened her mouth, and I slid inside, looking into her honey soft eyes that were saying things to me I didn't want to hear but was desperately happy about all the same.

I pumped in and out of her sexy mouth, holding her head. When I gently hit the back of her throat, her eyes watered. "Is it too much?" My words came out in a suffocated breath.

She shook her head.

"You can take more?"

She nodded.

Her pink lips around my cock were more erotic than anything I had ever experienced. This refined woman was on her knees in front of me—she was letting me own her and nothing had ever been this heady and overpowering.

"You want me to come in your mouth, Maria?" I asked because I was getting close after six months of celibacy, six months of fantasizing exactly about this.

She nodded and pulled away.

"What is it, baby?" I asked.

"I've...never done that," she panted. "So...I don't know how to do it."

I smiled. "Make me come in your mouth?"

"Yes," her voice was husky, sexy.

"Let me fuck your mouth, baby. Will you let me?"

"Yes, please," she said primly, and I think my cock swelled some more.

"This time is for me," I growled. "Next time I promise to make it up to you."

I held her head still and closed my eyes as my orgasm began deep in my balls and worked its way all the way through my spine to my brain. I exploded and my cum leaked out of her mouth. She couldn't swallow it all and I pulled out because it was, as she said, her first time making a man come in her mouth. More cum flowed from between her lips onto her white dress. She looked defiled, and I felt like fucking a Viking conqueror. Maria brought out the alpha male in me, who I hadn't seen since I was a young man.

She wiped her mouth and looked bewildered. "I always thought it would taste...well, terrible. It doesn't."

Her honesty unraveled me. She wasn't trying to appear sophisticated as so many women I was with did...or maybe they were more experienced than her. *Warning, Alejandro, she may look like a fucking duchess but with sex, maybe she wasn't as experienced as what you're used to.*

I helped her stand and then picked her up in my arms. She slid a hand around my neck and looked at me. "Was it okay, Alejandro?" she asked nervously.

"Like fucking heaven." I couldn't resist her moist lips and kissed her, tasting her, myself. "Bedroom, *Duquesa*."

She pointed toward her hallway. I'd expected her to be heavier—she was nearly five feet ten inches tall, but she wasn't, she was just right. *Just right for me! Fuck!*

Her bedroom was just like her. It smelled like her and felt like her, elegance and charm, passion, and innocence.

White bedspread, white blinds, colorful paintings, neat and tidy. Again, she made me want to muss her bed up, her up. And I had. She looked thoroughly debauched as I let her stand. She looked down at my cock, still half erect, hanging out of my jeans. I took my pants off and stood naked in front of her while she remained fully dressed.

I laid down on her bed, leaning against the headboard. "Darling, could you take that dress off... *slowly*...you know like I was going to leave two big ones on your bedside table after you're done."

Her eyes widened, and I bit my smile. She looked like she was ready to throw something at me. My right hand went to my erection, and I stroked myself. Her eyes watched me and whatever she was feeling at that not-so-subtle *be a stripper for me* request dissipated.

"Two big ones? I think what's underneath this will need a lot more than that." She winked at me, and her hands went to the back of her dress. She turned around, giving me a view of her absolutely perfect ass.

"Alejandro," she whispered. "Can you unzip me, baby?"

It was the baby that did it. I scrambled out of bed and pulled her zipper down. She held her dress to her chest.

"Now go back," she ordered. Our roles had reversed, and I was weak with pleasure.

Slowly, oh so slowly, she turned around and let the white dress fall. Then, with a shimmy of her hips, the dress pooled at her feet. She kicked it aside. Underneath her dress, Maria was a vision. She wore a matching lacy skin-colored bra and panties, so sheer and delicate that they looked like her skin.

I slowed stroking my cock because the way she looked, I was about to come again in my hands like a teenager.

"Nice. Now, take off that bra, baby, and show me your tits," I commanded.

She did as I asked. Her breasts were beautiful. The tips were dusky dark rose and a perfect handful. She wasn't big like some women, and neither was she small —*a good C cup,* I thought. Her breasts were lush, and I wanted to suckle them, see if I could make her come just like that.

"Are you wet, baby?"

She nodded.

"Then take your panties off and show me."

She bent all the way down and all the blood from my head went straight to my cock. *Fuck! Maria Caruso knew how to do a striptease.*

Her pussy was bare. I didn't have a preference. But her smooth kitty was made for licking, made to see my cum leak out of her.

"Put one finger inside you and show me how wet you are."

She put a finger in and pulled it out, glistening with her juices. I groaned. "Wet your nipples with your juices and come here."

Her nipples were erect and wet. She stood in front of me. I leaned over and licked one and then the other nipple. "You taste delicious."

I grabbed her ass and pulled her closer to me. "Put

your leg up on the bed." I patted her left leg.

"Alejandro." Her essence was now flowing down her thighs that shook. She was desperate.

"I know, baby. But do as you're told, and I'll give you what you want."

She blushed, and I was enamored. She put a leg up, her pussy open for me to see. I ran a finger across her slit and she jerked.

"Hold still, Duquesa." I put my lips on her. I licked and tasted her. Her hands were in my hair as she ground her pussy against my mouth. She was so close. I could smell it on her.

I caught her by the waist and threw her down on the bed. I crawled between her legs, shoved her thighs on my shoulder, and lifted her, cupping her ass so I could stick my tongue deep inside her. That's all it took. She came, moaning, screaming, her body shaking hard. I didn't let her go down easily, I continued to lick her clit and bit it gently, so she'd ride a higher wave even before she was all the way back to earth.

I left her for a moment and found my jeans. I pulled out my wallet and found a condom. I showed it to her. She nodded.

I never went into a woman bare. After Anika got pregnant with Silvano, who I never ever regretted, I didn't take a chance. If a woman was ever getting pregnant by me again, and that was not a possibility, it would be because we'd agreed to have a child together that we'd raise as parents who lived in the same fucking house.

"Come inside," she whimpered when my erection hovered at her entrance.

I slid inside her and everything inside my brain

slammed to a halt. Sex was fun. I had a lot of it. This wasn't sex. This delicious intensity, this feel of homecoming, this was something else, something I'd *never* experienced before.

I couldn't understand myself and I let my body take over so I could go back to the familiarity of fucking a willing, wet, and wanton woman. But each time I stroked in, her hips tilted up and I felt my balls scream for release.

Christ! This woman was potent.

When I came, she came with me, her body tuned to mine. I had to barely suckle on a nipple and gently stimulate her clitoris to bring her to orgasm.

"I'm glad I came back because, baby, you have a magic fucking pussy," I ground out as I felt my release approach with such ferocity as if I hadn't just come inside her mouth.

This woman was dangerous, the alarm bells inside my head announced as I poured into the condom, resenting that barrier, wanting to have felt her bare, raw, skin against skin, life against life.

I forced myself to pull out of her. I lay on my back, catching my breath. I turned to look at her; her eyes were still closed, her chest going up and down as she got enough oxygen inside her lungs. She looked like a Botticelli painting, beatific, satisfied, and serene.

I felt something inside my chest ache.

What had I done?

Chapter 6

Maria

He woke up before I did and left me a note. A yellow sticky note.

Had to go into the city. Pick you up at noon for lunch. –A.

It was nine in the morning.

I'd slept in, I thought, smiling. Of course, I had. We'd spent a good part of the night touching, tasting, and exploring. Just the thought of all the things we did and said had me getting aroused all over again.

I picked up my phone and found a text message from Mark, asking me to call him when I woke up.

"So?" he asked.

"I had the most amazing sex of my life," I gushed.

"Good for you," Mark responded, and I could hear him yawn.

"Do you ever wonder if it would've been easier to follow in dad's footsteps and work at Caruso? I promise you'll get more sleep."

"Sleep is for wusses," Mark said in a big bad wolf tone. "Maria, I love you, babe but you know this guy is not available, right?"

"You always know how to rain on my parade," I joked and then because this was important, I added, "I don't have a choice, Mark. I'm in love."

There was a long pause before my brother spoke again, "Well, that sucks."

"Thank you. Anyone else would say, oh, how wonderful."

"Falling in love is not wonderful—it sucks energy, your life, and everything that's good inside you. I don't recommend it."

Mark had just broken up with his boyfriend who'd moved back to Seattle. He wasn't heartbroken per se, but lonely. They'd been together for several years, so the heartache was real.

"He ended the evening by telling me he wanted me but wouldn't have me and then came over." I picked up the sticky note and admired his brusque handwriting. "He's taking me to lunch today, probably to dump my ass."

"You think so."

I sighed. "I'm hoping he won't, but his repertoire is pretty much, come here, go away. And he doesn't live here, Mark. I'm not going to bump into him when I have lunch at the Ivy. He's all the way in Golden Valley and—"

"You'll enjoy him while you can and—"

"And cry my heart out, eat some ice cream, and fried

chicken."

"I'll come by with the chocolates and red wine."

"And we can watch all the breakup hits," I smiled. Mark was four years younger than me, but we were each other's best friends. Well, Mark also had Esme.

"Maybe Drago can join us," Mark suggested.

"You know he's straight, right?"

"I just want to eye fuck him and he makes a mean martini."

I didn't have many friends—it came from working *very* hard and not going out enough. But I had Drago Horvat, my high school sweetheart and now friend. With an athlete's body, he looked like a disreputable Hollywood actor.

A Detective in the LAPD, Drago and I were too similar to have made it. We were both driven, ambitious, single-minded when we had a project in hand, and loyal to a fault. I hadn't been in touch with Drago for several months because he was working undercover, and he couldn't tell me where. But he knew I was worried, so I got text messages from unknown phone numbers with lines from Alfred Tennyson's Ulysses, a poem we'd studied together in high school. Last week, I got a message saying: *One equal temper of heroic hearts.*

A Croatian detective who enjoyed poetry and was as earthy as they came. It surprised people who knew us that we were friends. Many people assumed we were lovers, and we had been; in fact, Drago had been my first and I had been his.

I wish I could reach out to him now—but he was off the grid, and I wasn't expecting a message for at least three days, as I got one the day before.

I didn't know how to handle what I was certain Alejandro was going to say to me at lunch. Something along the lines of, *this was fun, let's not do it again.*

I'd be stoic, I promised myself as I put on a Stella McCartney linen cutout halter-neck dress decorated with blue flowers. I paired the dress with my favorite and comfortable Prada crochet wedge sandals and a baby blue Jacquemus bag. I didn't look overdressed like I'd spent too much time getting ready for him, but I looked good enough that he would regret walking away from me.

I looked at the slender Bulgari watch on my wrist. It was eleven forty-five. I was ready, but I knew he would get here at noon. This was a man who was punctual. He didn't like to be early or late.

My phone rang and my smile widened as I answered.

"Mama, are you back?"

"Ten minutes ago, and your father is driving me up the wall, so I locked myself into the studio and called you."

My mother, Judith Caruso, was a famous artist and her paintings hung in museums around the world. My father had left Caruso to me and retired—but he wasn't a happy retired man, but then he'd never been happy. We tolerated our father to make our mother happy. My parents had recently gone on vacation to Turks & Caicos.

"How's Dad?" I asked because I knew she needed to talk about him.

"Threatening to come back to work."

"He doesn't have a job here," I remarked dryly. "You know, if he so badly wants to do something, send him to Safe Harbor." This was a women's shelter that Esme ran, and Caruso Investments supported. Daddy didn't believe in charitable works. People had to be self-made, according to him, which was a lot of bullshit as my grandfather had come to the United States from Mexico with money his father made selling crude oil. Money had been in the Caruso family for generations. None of us were self-made, except maybe Mark.

"How are you, Maria?" My mother has always changed the topic from my father to *anything* else.

"I'm good." I looked at my watch and smiled at the prospect of seeing Alejandro again, soon. "I'm seeing someone."

"Really? Tell me all about him."

I gave her the highlights.

"You've met his son?" she asked. "You know in these situations you're marrying the whole family."

"*Whoa*, mama. I've met this man exactly three times in my life."

"But, baby, you like him. I can hear it in your voice. Bring him home for Sunday dinner tomorrow night."

I chuckled. "I don't want to bring him home yet. Let's say I'd like the man to know me before he met Daddy. All this is moot because he's here in five minutes and he's going to dump me."

"Dump you? What's wrong with this boy?"

"*Man*, Mama. He's forty-two years old."

"Asshole. You tell him that no one dumps my baby girl."

"I will, Mama." I saw an Escalade stop in front of my condo. "I have to go, Mama."

I stepped out of my condo and Alejandro came

toward me, a smile on his face. *Maybe he won't dump me after all.*

I stopped in front of him and lifted my lips to brush against his; he moved ever so slightly, so I got his cheek. *Then again, maybe he will.*

Chapter 7

Alejandro

I didn't drive when I was in LA. It was easier to get a car and driver; so I could get work done or make calls. It also came in handy when I wanted to spend time with a beautiful woman without worrying about traffic.

"The concierge at the Intercontinental recommended Nobu in Malibu," I told her.

"It's a lovely restaurant with a beautiful view."

She looked like an angel and once again reminded me of a Botticelli painting, this time the *Minerva*. She had a delicate face with a bone structure that meant she'd be beautiful forever, even when she was older. Her silky hair cascaded around her face, hair I had pulled at when we made love.

Maldito infierno, Alejandro, sex, not making love.

"I'm sorry I didn't wake you when I left this

morning."

I curbed the desire to hold her hand. Nothing good would come of it. I shouldn't lead her on. I was taking her to lunch to make a clean break. I couldn't resist her last night, and the problem was I couldn't resist her now either. I wanted her. I wanted to roll up the privacy screen and make her ride me. My cock could already feel what she'd feel like, remember what she'd felt like. But I didn't have a condom. I had not brought one on purpose so that I wouldn't touch her.

"That's okay." She was looking out of the window as if everything around her was so much more interesting than me.

"Thank you for last night."

Now, she turned to look at me, amusement in her eyes. "Alejandro, it was mutual. You don't have to thank me. Or do you want me to thank you?"

You can do it on your knees, Duquesa.

"Of course not. Any plans for the weekend?"

"You mean after lunch with you?"

I nodded.

"My parents came back from a holiday. We always have Sunday dinner at their place. My mother insists. She invited you if you were free." She was a trained executive; she knew how to keep her emotions out of her voice, but I heard a tremor.

"I'm going home tonight," I whispered.

Our conversation resumed once we got to the restaurant, as if I hadn't once again rejected her. Because I had. She invited me to her parents' home, and I'd not said things like another time, rain check or some other polite nonsense.

The host knew her, which surprised me. "Would you rather we'd gone elsewhere?"

"No." She laughed, and I heard that fucking fairytale tinkling of bells when she did. "I love Nobu. I used to come here a lot when I lived in Malibu. But then I moved to Silver Lake."

We ordered and as we ate, I felt an ease that I hadn't in a long time. I rarely talked to women I had sex with. I talked to my family, some friends, people at work, but never lovers because there had been mostly only one or two-night stands since Silvano was born.

"Do you miss the city when you're all the way in Golden Valley?" she asked me.

"No," I replied honestly. "I love Golden Valley. I couldn't imagine living anywhere else. I travel for work, but I like to be home as much as I can."

"Who takes care of your son when you travel?"

"My mother."

"You *really* think of Paloma as your mother, don't you?"

I smiled as I always did when I thought about the woman who'd entered my life when I was fifteen. We were lucky, all of us, to have found her. She'd changed our lives, brought so much love and laughter into our home. And she'd given us Isadora.

"You know when you think of your family, you smile. You look happy," she observed.

"I am. My family is *very* important to me."

After lunch, we continued to dance around the main topic of conversation: *what happens next.*

We sat in the car outside her condo. "Why don't I make it easy for you?" she suggested after three minutes of interminable silence. "It was a great evening and a wonderful lunch, but we won't be doing this again. Am I right?"

It had never been difficult for me to make it clear to a bedmate that this is all it was. It had never been problematic to walk away. But I was reluctant this time.

I took her slender hands in both of mine. She'd painted her nails pink. She wore a beautiful ring with a diamond butterfly on it. Everything about this woman was elegant. She made me want things I wasn't supposed to have.

"I more than enjoyed our time together. You're amazing." I looked at her face, the hope in her eyes almost deterred me. "And I have trouble keeping my hands off of you. But you've noticed that from the very start. The minute I saw you, I wanted you under me, I wanted to be inside you."

She squirmed. "Are you dumping me or arousing me?" she whispered.

I let go of her hands. "You are everything I want in a woman. Smart, beautiful, sexy as fuck...the best lover I've ever had."

She waited for me to get to the point.

"I live in Golden Valley. I have a son. I work all the time. I find time for sex—I don't believe in celibacy. You're the first woman I've slept with who I've had a meal with in...well, over a decade. And—"

She put a hand to my lips, and I kissed her skin, licked to taste her one last fucking time.

"I feel a lot when you're around and trust me, it's disturbing and scares me as well."

I took her hand in mine. "What are you scared of?"

"Of getting hurt. And you?"

"Of hurting you."

She choked out a gasp at my words and pulled her hand away. "Then don't hurt me."

"Baby, I'm too old, too damaged, and just not what you want in a man. I don't want a relationship. I don't want to disturb my son's life."

"Paloma became your mother," she said. "Don't you —"

I didn't let her continue because she was drawing a false equivalency.

"Silvano is a fabulous kid. He has a *very* high IQ, which means he's smarter than his old man and most people around him, maybe except Mateo. I don't have *time* for a relationship," I told her honestly. "If you were the kind of woman who'd say, *let's hook up whenever you're in town*, it would be one thing. But you're not that woman. And in any case, sex with you is dangerous."

Her eyelashes swooped down so I couldn't see her eyes.

"I want you, Maria. But—"

"Not enough," she cut in and gave me a small smile.

I sighed. "I have a request. Please do not mention this to people we know. I...my family is nosey, and it will start a conversation at home that I'd much rather not have."

Her eyes went stormy.

"No, baby, not because what we did is something I'm ashamed of. I never sleep with a woman close to my family, ever. And..." I was at a loss for words.

She leaned closer and brushed her lips against my cheek. "Bye, Alejandro."

I watched her leave the car; and waited for her to open her door and go inside.

There, I'd fucked up the best thing that had happened to me in a long time. And now the question was, how long would it take to stop tasting and smelling her? *Mierda!*

Chapter 8

Maria

Life went on even with a broken heart. When Cher asked, "Is There Life After Love," well, yeah, there is but it's a little sad and a little dark.

Inherently, I was a cheerful person. I was an optimist but losing Alejandro just after I found him had left me bruised.

"Okay, spit it out. It's Christmas. You love the holidays and here you are moping around," Drago demanded when we met for a drink at Library Bar. He'd just finished his undercover assignment and had a new scar on his hand, which he refused to explain.

"I'm not moping around," I protested. "I'm even drinking a happy holiday beer."

"Maria," Drago used his *stop beating around the bush, bitch* tone.

"I think I have a broken heart," I muttered.

Drago's eyes got as wide as they physically could. "I was undercover for like six months; and you're telling me you fell in love and broke your heart in that time?"

A woman walked by us then and smiled at Drago. He was a big guy, all muscle, and a face that looked like it came straight from one of those mafia romance movies. *But* I was sitting next to him. How did they know we weren't together?

"Hey. I'm sitting here." I was two beers down otherwise, I'd never have done it.

The woman looked immediately contrite and skedaddled away. "Now, you're moping around *and* being a cock blocker."

"You want her?"

"Normally you play wing woman. Tell me about this paragon of virtues you fell in love with, and he turned into a turd from hell and broke your heart."

I laughed at his description of my situation as he wanted me to.

"I met *him* at Raya and Mateo's wedding reception." I told him everything. Well, I didn't go into detail about the sex because I wasn't that crass, but I told him everything else.

"I don't get it. He's a single father, fine, but single parents have relationships." Drago waved to the bartender to get a refill.

"He apparently doesn't do relationships. According to Raya, Alejandro's wife was a piece of work. But that was eleven years ago. I think he doesn't want to be tied down. Likes his freedom. Likes to fuck around like some other people I know."

Drago leaned back on the plush barstool. "My

lifestyle doesn't really permit me to have relationships, Maria. You know that. I see cops getting married and then I see them getting divorced; and all I can think is, no thank you. Sex, I like. This whole let's live together and gouge each other's eyes out when we're sick of one another, I can do without."

"Not all marriages are like that. Esme and Dec seem happy. Raya and Mateo are happy. Daisy and Forest... well, I'm not sure what's going on there."

"I like Mateo and Dec," Drago affirmed. He'd met them for a drink along with Mark. Drago knew Forest well because they'd worked together in LAPD many years ago. "Mateo is some genius though, isn't he? It's just the way he talks sometimes."

"Yeah, his IQ is off the charts," I agreed. "As is Alejandro's son's."

"I don't know, Maria... I respect him not wanting to lead you on, but he came over and fuck you when he knew he shouldn't because that *was* leading you on. Some men cannot fall in love—and you want love."

I pouted. "The sex was amazing. Why can't we *just* hook up now and again?"

"Because every time you do, it's going to break your heart all over again," Drago stated. His eyes flashed suddenly, and he watched two men as they came into the bar. As the men got closer, he seemed to relax.

"Detective Horvat," one man held his hand out.

Drago shook it. "Benny, how are you, man?"

The other man almost genuflected. "Wow! I've heard so much about you, sir. I'm Officer Nelson, sir."

"Nice to meet you, Nelson."

"Great work on the—"

"Guys, it was great to see you. I look forward to meeting you at the station," he interrupted them, his head tilting toward me. The men nodded stiffly. They sat down at the other end of the bar.

"I know you're a vice cop, Drago. You didn't have to be rude to them."

He shook his head. "I don't want you anywhere near the garbage I deal with."

"Why?" I was baffled.

"Because you're Maria." He stroked my cheek and then brushed his lips against my forehead. "And I love you."

I leaned, so his forehead touched mine. "I missed you," I whispered. I pulled away to look at him, "Are you done doing undercover work for a while?"

"Maybe forever," he assured me. "I have to testify in a trial and after that it'll be near impossible for me to go undercover. I'm thinking of moving to homicide."

"That would be a promotion, right?"

"Yeah. Keep your fingers crossed—" his eyes became cold again, "Do you know that guy?"

I turned to look at who he was talking about and everything inside me froze. "Tha...that's him."

"That's the guy?" Drago was amused. "Man, if looks could kill, I'd be riddled with bullets."

"Yes. I..." I raised a hand and waved.

He nodded but didn't wave back. "Oh, looks like Mateo is with him," Drago mentioned and raised his glass.

Mateo and Alejandro walked up to us.

"Hey, man, Drago. Good to see you." Mateo and Drago did the man thumping on the shoulders thing and introduced Alejandro to Drago, who immediately laid it on thick.

"You know my girl, Maria?" he asked Alejandro.

"Yes," Alejandro replied tightly.

Drago then ignored Alejandro and focused on Mateo. "I hear you managed to find Raya. I'm sorry I wasn't around to help when things were happening. Forest mentioned he handled things."

"Oh, he certainly did. The guy is a badass." Mateo laughed. "Maria, are you coming to Esme and Dec's party? I'm trying to convince Alejandro here to stay an extra day and join us."

I looked at Alejandro and felt a shiver run up my spine, the same spine that Drago had slid his hand over. I wanted to ask him to cut it out and stop trying to make Alejandro jealous, but Drago would not listen, anyway.

"I'm thinking about it."

"Baby, I can be your date." He purred the *baby* out.

Mateo looked at Drago and me suspiciously but said nothing. Alejandro's phone pinged then, and he looked at the screen. "Excuse me." He walked out of the bar, and I slumped.

"Oh, stop it, Drago," I admonished and shook his hand off my back.

Mateo looked at both of us speculatively. "What's going on?"

"Did you see how Alejandro was ready to kill me?" Drago thought it was hilarious that my ex-lover wanted a piece of him.

Mateo nodded, now amused.

"Stop. I'm sorry, Mateo. Alejandro doesn't want anyone to know," I apologized.

Mateo laughed. "Men are morons."

"What?" I asked, perplexed.

"I said the same thing to Raya and man, did I pay for that. I'm lucky she let me back into her life and damned lucky she agreed to marry me."

"*Some* men are morons," Drago countered.

"Especially you." I punched Drago on his shoulder. He took my fist and brought it to his lips. Before I could say something pithy, I realized we had an audience again. Alejandro was back.

"All okay?" Mateo asked him.

Alejandro nodded. He wore a charcoal gray suit. It fit him extremely well. His blue eyes were piercing. His hair was longer than it had been last time when I had slid my hands through them as he'd tasted me, and made me orgasm.

I straightened as the thought struck me and his lips thinned.

"How's Silvano?" I asked Alejandro.

"Good."

"He's great. That kid just got into a UCLA program for STEM kids. He's going to be here the first week of January," Mateo grinned. "He's going to stay with us. We're very excited."

"That's wonderful," I exclaimed. "You must be so proud."

Alejandro nodded and looked at Drago. "Mateo tells me you're a detective."

"Yeah. LAPD."

"Drago is going to get a promotion soon. He's moving to homicide." I was excited for my friend.

"That's great, man." Mateo clapped him on his

shoulder. "I know Mark's been worried about you and so has Maria. I'm assuming this will put an end to your undercover stints."

Drago nodded. "Maria has no business worrying. She gets a message from me at least once a week."

"Thank you, Drago for letting me know you're alive."

"Is that safe?" Alejandro demanded.

"Yeah, it's safe," Drago retorted.

I felt like I had to keep the peace. "He sends me lines from a poem we studied together in high school."

Drago put an arm around me and brushed his lips against mine. I pinched him surreptitiously. He was taking it too far. "We're high school sweethearts."

"Were," I asserted because Alejandro looked like he was going to rip *someone* a new one.

"I have an appointment," I lied smoothly, looking at my watch. "So, gentlemen, I'm going to say goodbye." I got off my barstool and gave Drago a warning look in case he was planning to indulge in some more PDA to piss Alejandro off.

I kissed Mateo on his cheek. "Say hi to Raya. How's Daisy, do you know? I know Forest's senate hearings are coming up soon."

"She's okay. Check in with her, will you?" Mateo gave me a hug and whispered in my ear, "Tell Drago to back off or Alejandro may rip his head off."

I nodded at Alejandro and walked out into the cool LA December night. I was fumbling with my phone to get an Uber when I felt him next to me.

"Are you going home, or do you have another date?" he demanded.

I was going to say, *none of your business*, but it would

be impolite and just because he was being an ass didn't mean I had to be one as well.

"Home," I smiled. "It's nice to see you."

"Were you fucking him when we were together?" His hands were in his pockets like he was struggling to keep them from going around my neck.

"We were a one-night stand months ago. Who I see and not see is none of your business." Politeness be damned. No one spoke to me like this.

His jaw tightened.

"He's a friend, for god's sake. One of my closest. I told him about you, which was why he was giving you a hard time. Okay? Not that I thought he could."

"Why? Last I checked I was a perfectly normal red-blooded male."

"Who's slept with god knows how many women since we were together. You rejected me, or have you forgotten that?" I opened the Uber app and was astounded when he took my phone away.

"I have a car. I'll drop you off."

"No, thank you. Give me my phone back. You're behaving like you have some rights over me, which is delusional."

"How would you feel if you knew I was seeing another woman when we were together?"

"Hurt, but I would have no right to demand anything from you," I replied honestly.

"I don't give a shit about rights." He grabbed my arm as a car stopped in front of us. The door opened, and he ushered me in. I looked out of the window to see Drago and Mateo grinning like fools.

Men were morons!

Chapter 9

Alejandro

I'd been thinking about her all day. Since I stepped off a helicopter at the private South Park rooftop helipad. It was easier and faster to fly than drive. My plan was to meet with the CEO of a distribution company we were planning to work with and go straight back to Golden Valley.

I didn't want to be tempted by staying the night. I had already deleted her contact information from my phone, so I wouldn't reach out to her. I had also tried to sleep with another woman when I was in DC for some meetings and found that I couldn't.

I was at the bar at the Ritz and the woman who came to sit next to me at the bar was a gorgeous blond. She was a pharmaceutical executive from Boston. She had legs for days and she was *very* interested. I thought I was as well until I thought about seeing her naked and I realized I didn't want her. I wanted Maria.

"Why are you doing this?" Maria asked.

I raised the privacy screen. "Doing what? Dropping you off home?"

She turned to face me. "Why are you so angry with me? What have I done?"

"You've fucking ruined me for other women. I dream about you. I wake up hungry for you," I bit out.

"Alejandro," she said softly, "You can't treat me like this. You can't push me away and then pull me back whenever you feel like it."

I hated that she said that, but it was true. I was treating her abominably. *Mierda!* I didn't know how to be in a relationship with a woman and I didn't want to be in one with Maria. *Pussy was pussy,* I told myself crudely. I could find others.

Like hell!

"You're right," I agreed. "I apologize."

She shook her head and looked out of the window of the car. "You can't do this," she whispered again, and I saw tears flowing down her cheeks. "It's—"

"Oh, baby." I pulled her toward me and into my arms. "I'm so sorry. I never meant to hurt you. Please don't cry."

She leaned into me, her breath shallow as she tried to control herself. She felt fragile in my arms. This gentle, beautiful woman was shaking because of me. I stroked her back and my hand dismantled the chignon she'd tied her up in. I liked her hair loose. She smelled of jasmine and cinnamon as she always did. I kissed her hair, holding her close.

"I smell you in my house," she breathed.

I knew that feeling. I hadn't cleaned the shirt I'd worn when I was with her. It hung in my closet and like a heartsick teenager, I'd inhale her scent or pretend to, because after two months, the smell and taste of her were mostly imagined.

I felt her tears against my dress shirt and my heart clenched. I never meant to hurt her. I was so drawn into myself and what I was going through that I'd neglected to think about how she was feeling.

"Baby, *mi amor*, please don't cry." I moved her so I could see her face. Her mascara was running and yet, she looked terrifyingly beautiful. I kissed her lips, and she shivered against me.

Yes. It was still there, that magic that had drawn us to each other from the start. I didn't know what to do about it.

"Don't," she pleaded. "Don't."

"You're very hard to resist." I looked at her and smiled. I looked out of the car window. "We're at your place."

She nodded. "I fell in love with you."

A woman had never said these words to me when sober. Anika had, but we all knew how that worked out. Her words should have made me want to run for the hills, but they didn't. They made my heart grow a few inches along with my cock.

"I can't see you again. It hurts too much." Her honesty undid me.

"I don't want to hurt you."

She pulled away from me. With her hand on the door handle, she said, "Merry Christmas, Alejandro."

"Maria, let me come inside." *Inside your house. Inside*

you. Please.

She looked at me like I'd lost my mind. "No."

I stroked her cheek. "I thought I was fine and then I saw that asshole touch you, and I couldn't stand it. Ask my family, they'll tell you that it's impossible to make me jealous. But I wanted to rip that guy's head off."

"Drago?"

"That's a fucked up name."

She chuckled. "He's Croatian."

Her eyes were sad, but I could see she felt lighter. "He's an asshole for riling me up on purpose. But I should be grateful because if he hadn't, I wouldn't know how you felt, how I continue to feel."

"Are you going to use my words against me now, Alejandro?" Her fear was palpable.

"No, baby. I'd never do that." *Who did she think I was?*

"I'm not going to be some dirty sex secret of yours."

I closed my eyes and took a deep breath. "I'm sorry I made you feel that way."

"If I let you come inside my home, will you want sex?" Her voice was stronger now, as if she'd figured out how to handle us—good thing someone knew how to manage this situation.

"Baby, I'll always want sex, but I'll never pressure you."

She sighed. "I'm probably making a big fat mistake. Have you eaten?"

I shook my head.

"I was going to open a bottle of Chablis and make myself halibut. Would you like to join me?"

"I'd love to."

I let the driver know that I'd call him when I was

ready to leave. And then I texted my assistant to find me a hotel for the night and requested a helicopter for the next morning. I wasn't being presumptuous, but I didn't want to rush us either. I'd stay the night at a hotel. I'd rather I slept on her couch even if she didn't want me in her bed, but I'd take whatever she'd give me —whatever she could, knowing my limitations.

She left me in her bright kitchen that led to a fairytale of a patio with twinkling lights, a water feature, and comfortable furniture. She had flower beds and potted plants. It was cozy and exactly the way I thought Maria's safe space would feel like. I opened the bottle of Chablis and took it and two glasses outside.

I half reclined on a chaise lounge and looked up at the sky. No stars here in the big city with all the bright lights. In Golden Valley, I could see the Milky Way. But this had its own appeal as well. It was interesting that Maria chose to live in a small condo in Silver Lake rather than a large house in Malibu. She'd also not gone the penthouse route like Declan Knight had. She was a CEO and powerful businesswoman but a homebody at heart.

She came onto the patio and all my thoughts scattered. She had been wearing a blue pencil skirt and a white silk blouse—and looked fucking gorgeous. Now, she wore a pair of tight pants and a white T-shirt. Her feet were bare and there was something erotic about her pink toenails. She looked like she'd stepped out of an edition of vintage French Vogue.

Alejandro, you're losing your mind hombre, if you think her feet are erotic. What? Are you developing a new kink or something?

I held out a glass of wine, and she took it. "Thanks."

"This is a beautiful space."

She smiled. "Mark and I put it together. He complained the entire time, but we had so much fun doing something together. He lives in an apartment and doesn't have a patio, so he comes here."

"Don't your parents live close by?"

"In Beverly Hills," she confirmed. "My father and Mark are...struggling. Daddy never forgave him for going into medicine. A part of him feels he handed over Caruso Investments to the less intelligent child, which is true. Mark is the brilliant one."

"I think you're terrific," I countered. "And you have already built a reputation for being a tough and smart investor with a golden touch."

"Thank you," she smiled and held up her glass. I clinked mine against hers.

"I met Anika, my wife, at a party in Fresno. The farming community is small. Those days I used to date. I was thirty and far less cynical than I am now."

She listened intently. I liked that about Maria. There was a seriousness about her but also a peacefulness. I rarely talked about Anika. It made me uncomfortable, but I had no trouble opening old wounds for Maria.

"She wanted to get engaged and married. I knew she wasn't the one. I told her it was over. We had a goodbye fuck and *voila*, she was pregnant. Apparently, she'd been trying for a while. I found this out later. I don't regret it, I got Silvano out of it and he's the best thing that ever happened to me. I'm grateful for him."

"As you should be." She took a sip of wine.

I held my hand out, wanting to touch her, wanting to hold her light while I told her about the dark inside me.

"I married her. She knew I would. Anika's parents,"

they're good people and they were happy that their daughter was marrying into the Santos family. But Anika wasn't interested in the life I wanted to live. A quiet life in Golden Valley. She wanted the big city...she thought that's what we'd do. She didn't know me very well." I let go of her hand and stood up. "I heard rumors of halibut."

"Then let's make those rumors a reality."

I asked if I could help, and she declined my offer, so I watched her. I sat on a barstool at the kitchen counter. She'd turned on the music and Nina Simone was singing about wanting a little sugar in her bowl.

"Then what happened?" she asked.

I topped our wine glasses. "She had Silvano. She didn't want to nurse him or take care of him. I thought it was postpartum depression. I took care of him while she disappeared for days. I was fine with that. We were a team, my little boy and I."

My demeanor softened as it always did when I thought about my son. "She came to me when he was six months old and said she wanted a divorce; and she'd give me full custody for a couple of million dollars. It wasn't the money that bothered me, we had the money. I hated that Silvano wouldn't have a mother. But better to have no mother than someone like Anika."

Maria stopped what she was doing and put a hand on my shoulder. She brushed her lips against mine. "I'm so sorry."

She went back to prepping our meal of halibut and a salad. She put a frying pan on the stove, her back turned to me. The smell of fish frying in butter filled the air.

This was so domestic, I thought. I'd never had this, not for myself. Sure, Paloma cooked up a storm along with Isadora. Aurelio was worse than me when it came to cooking, he could make coffee and a grilled cheese sandwich but that was about as far as he'd go.

"Before the divorce could go through, she died in a car accident. So, there I was, a widower with an eight-month-old baby. It was a blessing ultimately. Her parents were broken up about it. They moved away and died a few years later. Silvano never got to know them, and I didn't encourage that connection either, didn't want him to find out that his mother didn't want him."

Maria put the halibut into the oven to keep them warm. She gave me the salad bowl and a bottle of homemade dressing. "Why don't you toss this for me?"

"Will do."

She set the table for us outside and turned on the infrared heater as the evening was getting cooler since we were so close to the Pacific Ocean.

We clinked our glasses together. "To the chef."

She laughed. "It's simple. I like to cook, which is a good thing because I don't like to eat out all the time. I keep it simple."

I took a bite of the halibut. "And delicious."

We ate companionably.

"Does Silvano ask about his mother?" Maria asked after dinner as we sat down with espressos and chocolates from a local chocolate shop.

"No. He knows she's dead. He also knows that we were getting divorced. He's a smart kid. And he's a happy kid. He doesn't miss her."

She nodded thoughtfully. "How do you manage his high IQ? Does he go to a different school?"

"It's been a journey. In the beginning, he went to a

regular school but then he got into trouble because he was bored. Now, he does a combination of school so he can develop his social skills and he has university-level Zoom lessons in math and physics, which keeps him grounded." It had taken a while for all of us in the family to get settled into a rhythm with Silvano. It hadn't been easy, but we were doing better every day.

Nat King Cole's rendition of *Unforgettable* filtered through from Maria's house onto the patio. On impulse, I stood up in her fairytale garden and held out my hand. "Dance with me."

Chapter 10

Maria

"It's not good enough for me, since I been with you," Alejandro hummed along with Nat King Cole as he held me in his arms.

We swayed with the music in harmony. His hand on my waist was warm and comforting. My hand on his shoulder balanced me. *How could he not see that we were meant to be together?* The rightness of us came rushing back to me. I had felt this way when we'd danced together that first time in Raya and Mateo's reception in Golden Valley when he'd taken me to his mother's gazebo and kissed me for the first time.

His lips slid across my cheek, peppering kisses.

"You smell like cinnamon and chocolate, *Duquesa*," he whispered in my ear, his breath moist, hot, and enticing.

You smell like my man, I thought.

I ached. I loved this man. I loved everything about him, even his reluctance, his fear of hurting me because he felt he didn't have the time or the space for me. But when it was love, you didn't *need to make space*, your heart expanded and enhanced your life.

I knew why he'd told me about his wife, to explain why he didn't trust easily, why he didn't want to bring anyone into his life. He was protecting his son. Marriages ended in divorce but your responsibility as a parent never ended.

"There is no home plate. You never touch the base, swing the bat, and do your victory dance," I said and when he raised an eyebrow, I explained, "My grandfather, a big baseball fan used to say that."

The song ended and a new one began but we were not listening. We were immersed in each other.

"I want you so much," his voice shook. "I can't sleep some nights because I remember how it felt to be inside you. I remember tasting you. Let me kiss you, Maria."

How could I resist him?

I let my mouth trail to his and we devoured each other as if starved, which we were. When the frenzy slowed, we languidly tasted one another. He nibbled on my lips, found that spot right under my ear that he knew was erogenous to graze gently with his teeth and then soothe with a lick.

I could feel his erection against my stomach. He was hard and I could almost feel him inside me. I was wet, wanting, and ready for him. My desire was throbbing, and I desperately wanted to orgasm *with* him, *only him*.

"*Dios mío*, you're intoxicating." He stepped away from me. His eyes were hooded, dark with desire.

I licked my lips, and he groaned. "Whenever you do that, I want to taste you. Stop doing that in front of me baby. I remember that mouth and how good you looked on your knees sucking me off."

I wasn't used to this onslaught of emotions and tears filled my eyes.

"No, no," he shook his head. "Don't cry. Please. I don't want you to get hurt. Don't you understand?"

"But it does hurt," I sniffled. "Not being with you hurts." I put a hand to my heart.

"Mateo was right. You want picket fences, and you can't have that with me. I don't want more children. I don't want *more*." He closed his eyes and then nodded as if realizing something. "I should stay away from you, shouldn't I? Because every time I'm going to be selfish and greedy, and you're so fucking generous that you'll open your heart and admit that you love me."

I wrapped my arms around me, suddenly feeling a chill. He was doing it again. Leaving. Rejecting. Love didn't mean letting the person you loved hurt you over and over again.

"You think I'm foolish, don't you? Telling you what's in my heart." I felt ashamed that I'd told him, and he'd not responded in kind.

"No. I think you're the bravest person I know." His eyes swam with emotion, and I was taken aback by his sincerity. "I am the coward, the fool, the weak one."

As long as Alejandro was in my life, there would be room for no other. But I also knew that when he wasn't there, I felt half-alive. This was the fourth time I was seeing him—how could the universe have betrayed me like this to make me fall so hard and so fast for a man who could not let go of his past so he could walk into a future we'd build together?

I decided then. I loved him. And for as long as *this*, whatever *this* was lasted, I'd enjoy him. "Give me what you can."

I saw pain flashing in his eyes. "Baby, I won't stay. I never do."

"I'm not foolish." I gave him my best watery smile. "I'm a grown up; and not the woman who believes she can change a man. I don't want you to change. I love you for many reasons and one of them is your commitment to your family and your son."

"I won't even be able to give you those words back."

His integrity pierced through my heart, and I almost doubled over in pain. "I know." So, this was love. Loving and believing when you knew that in the long run, there would be pain.

"Your friend Drago would be right when he said I'd be taking advantage of you."

"It's not taking advantage when I'm walking into this with my eyes wide open."

He came closer to me and wiped a tear flowing down my cheek. He kissed my mouth gently. "I'll see you when I can. I'll try to be there if you ask for me. But I can't introduce you to my family as my woman. I won't do that to them or you."

I wish he'd stop talking. But he was an honest man and honest men wanted to be upfront. I should appreciate that about him.

"And if I'm not able to be there for you when you ask for me?"

He smiled. "There will be only acceptance. You give me what and when you can, and I'll do the same. And when it's over, we'll know."

"What if I want to end it before you do?" *Like that would happen!*

"Like I said, I'll accept whatever you give me—and also that someday you won't want to give me yourself anymore."

I nodded. "I won't share you."

"Oh, baby, since I kissed you all those months ago, you've not shared me—neither physically nor emotionally. I don't cheat."

"Neither do I."

He put his hands on my waist, and I linked my hands around his neck. "There will be one regret I will have. Every night in my bed, I have thought how you'd look lying there, your hair spread over my pillows, your body naked against my sheets. I won't be able to give that to you or myself."

What the hell was I signing up for, I thought. He'd be my fuck buddy.

"We'll make do with my bed," I cajoled.

"I wish I could be more for you."

"You're enough. This is enough." No, it wasn't but it would have to be. I wanted time with Alejandro—my man—the soulmate I'd never thought I'd find.

He kissed me again, deep.

"Make love to me," I beseeched as my blood grew hotter.

"I want to, can't you feel how much I want to?" He pushed his erection into me, and I moaned. "But *mi amor*, not today, not tonight. I want you to think this through and I need to do the same. I'll be back in LA in the first week of January with Silvano. Can you keep a couple of nights for me free then?"

"Yes."

He kissed me again for long minutes and then, as if deciding, stepped away. "Now, I need to leave. I'm already in pretty poor shape."

"Cold shower?" I teased.

"No. I'm going to have the best orgasm in weeks thinking about you, imagining all the things I'm going to do to you as soon as I have you under me again."

I walked him out to his car. He kissed me again like he wasn't able to get enough. Neither was I. I'd be happy to get him naked and inside me, but what he said made sense. Decisions made when your blood was hot could be ones you regretted once the body had cooled.

I knew that wouldn't happen to me. I was in love with the man—that wasn't a heated blood thing; it was a heart full of love thing.

Chapter 11

Alejandro

"**B**aby, *please,*" I groaned, my hand on my erection, her voice in my ear, her face on my phone's screen.

"Alejandro." Her eyes were bright with arousal and embarrassment.

"Show me how wet you are." I stroked myself.

She smiled and shook her head. "I...I can't."

"Baby, after all that we've done for each other, with each other, how can you still be shy?" She charmed me with her reluctance. I wanted to touch her. It wasn't fucking enough to see her on my phone screen. I wanted to smell her. Taste her.

She closed her eyes then, and I knew she was caressing herself, in and out, as I'd asked her to. "Put one more finger in, baby."

"Ah," she moaned.

I stilled my hand on my cock that was weeping for release. Watching Maria lose herself was one of the most erotic things I'd ever seen.

"You are so beautiful, baby," I whispered. "Squeeze your nipple hard. Just like I do. Can you feel that?"

"Oh, god." She tossed her head on her pillow and I all but blew my load as her mouth opened on a gasp and she came.

She looked at me with eyes liquid with desire. She smiled as she came back to the earth.

"That was...wow," she said joyfully.

"I could watch you come all day. Next time I get my hands on you, that's all I'm going to do, make you come again and again until I can't tell where I end, and you start." I started stroking my cock again, looking at her.

She moved her phone and put it between her legs. And that's all it took. One look at her glistening pussy. "Maria," I cried out as I came.

It had become a ritual. Every night, we made love over the phone, desperate to hear each other orgasm, desperate to talk to one another, and hungry to see what we did to each other. I felt like a fucking teenager. I'd never felt this alive before.

My family had noticed a change in me.

My mother pulled me aside after Christmas dinner when I'd been restless, waiting for a message from Maria. She dragged me out to the porch.

"Mama, it's freezing out here," I mentioned. The mountains were already snowcapped, and our part of the world had the winter bite in the air.

"Is everything okay?"

"Of course."

"Something is off, I can feel it."

I kissed her on her forehead. "There's nothing."

"Is it the business? Did we lose all our money? Because that's fine."

I laughed. "The business is fine."

"Is it a woman? Are you in love?"

No. But I'm madly in lust. I didn't want to lie to her, so I just gave her a look that said she was barking up the wrong tree.

"Yeah, I didn't think so," she muttered. "Isa thought maybe something was going on. Alejandro, you know, don't you, that you'll be fine if you fall in love again."

"You just want grandchildren," I teased.

"I have Silvano, and I'm thrilled if that's all I get. But maybe you'd like more children."

I scoffed at that. "I'm forty-two years old, Mama. I think I'm done."

"Oh please, your father was about that old when we had Isa."

I hadn't thought about that. But that was my father, not me. My biological mother had passed away—she had been a warm and loving soul, nothing like Anika. My experiences were not his. I couldn't take the chance of bringing a woman into our lives if she was going to run away and abandon us. I couldn't, wouldn't do that to Silvano. It would upend his life and that was a risk I couldn't take.

"Mama, if I ever fall in love, you'll be the first person I'll tell."

She looked at me with her dark honey eyes. "Promise?"

"Absolutely." I put my arm around her and kissed her hair, urging her back into the warmth of the main house.

"Oh, by the way, did you offer Raya and Mateo land in

Golden Valley to build a home?" she asked.

"Yes. I thought you and Papa would be okay with it."

"We are thrilled," my mother beamed. "You have such a big heart and generous soul. I wish you'd share that with someone."

"I share it with all of you."

"You know what I mean."

"Alejandro, let me love you," Maria had said a few days ago as she'd come, desperate to share what was in her heart. I wished I could say the words back, but I didn't want to lie to her. I liked Maria. She was a drug I couldn't give up. But I didn't love her. Maybe I'd never felt this addicted to a woman before, but sometimes in the past, the sex had been amazing—and instead of a one or two-night stand, we'd had a few weeks together. But soon enough, the demands began: be with me, you're never around, don't you want me, and I'd walk away, clear, and free.

Maria and I were at the start of our relationship. In fact, we'd spent exactly one night together since we met nearly nine months ago. But once the sex grew stale as it always did, what would we be left with? I was hoping for some mutual respect so that when we saw each other as we shared family and friends, we could do it without bitterness.

"I can't believe the things you make me do," Maria exclaimed, once we'd cleaned up and were lying on our beds, facing each other on our phones.

"This is new for me too," I admitted.

"You've never had phone sex before?" She was surprised.

"No. I have *actual* sex and then it's done. There has never been a need or desire for phone sex."

Something flitted through her eyes, but I couldn't catch it over the phone. I had become adept at hearing the change in her tone of voice and could pinpoint when she got angry so I could backtrack to understand why. I'd never cared how a woman felt—except for those in my family.

My concern for her scared me. And when that happened, I avoided her—texted her with an excuse that we wouldn't be able to talk that evening. She never pushed. She never demanded more than I could give. *But* I wanted to give her everything she wanted, seeing her smile was a new hobby. Hearing her laugh lightened my heart.

"I can't wait to see you." She touched the screen with a finger as if stroking my face. She loved me. She'd told me. She'd never said it again. I wanted to hear her say it. What kind of asshole wanted a woman to confess her love to him when he had no means of reciprocating? A selfish *cabrón* like me.

"I'll be there soon, baby." I was counting the days. Everything with Maria was new for me. Had I ever felt this way about any woman? Had I ever had this irresistible need to be with someone? I couldn't remember. I had had my share of teenage heartbreaks and heartaches. But that was a long time ago.

"I want to ask you something." The shyness was back in her voice.

"Ask away."

She licked her lips and my cock twitched. She had me so hot that I could go again and again. And at this side of forty, that was a fucking miracle without chemical help.

She cleared her throat. "I feel...I sometimes feel cheap for doing the things we do."

"What?" I heard what she said, but I had trouble comprehending her words.

"I...nothing. Forget about it. I have an early meeting with Europe tomorrow. We should call it a night. As it is, I'm going to get five hours of sleep." She spoke quickly, wanting to end the conversation.

"Wait, baby. Did you say I make you feel cheap?"

"No," she rejected that immediately. "Not you...me. I...can we forget I said anything? Please."

My jaw tightened as I felt a wave of self-loathing. "Baby, everything we do together is between us. I love seeing you come. I wish I could be there to see your face, taste your orgasm. I wish you were there to taste mine. But if doing this over the phone makes you at any point feel...less...we'll never do it. We can just talk." I didn't want to give that up.

I saw the doubt on her face even though she didn't voice it.

"And no. Phone sex is not the reason I want to see you every night. I want to see you..." *because I miss you. Fuck, I was a complete hijo de puta.*

"It's okay, Alejandro. I really have to get some sleep."

She didn't want to discuss this further and well, neither did I. Cowards didn't enjoy talking about their feelings, my mother had once said that to me. But I wasn't a coward, I had protested, I was a grown man taking care of the things that were important, family and business.

"Sleep well, *mi amor*."

She paused then. "I have a request."

I waited.

"Stop calling me that."

"What?"

"*Mi amor,*" she whispered.

I hadn't even realized I'd done that. The words had slipped out. Words, that I knew I'd never used before with a woman.

"Okay, baby."

Mierda! This casual affair was already getting out of hand, and we were only talking to each other on the phone. If I saw her face-to-face on the regular there would be hell to pay.

Chapter 12

Maria

I ignored the text that I received from Alejandro in the morning.

Since I'd asked him to stop calling me *his love* in Spanish, he'd shut down. He'd texted politely to let me know he couldn't make our nightly calls most days. The times he did, he'd say he stepped out of a business dinner and apologized for not having time to call later.

He was running again. I had to give this man up. He pulled and pushed, and pulled and pushed, and if I had any self-respect, which I did, I'd ask him to take a hike.

He was supposed to come over today. We'd made plans—but his text this morning said: *Isadora is going to drop Silvano off. I have a meeting in DC that I can't miss. My apologies.*

After making him wait for five hours, I responded to his text with a thumbs-up emoji. If he could be blasé about it, so could I.

Then I gave another thumbs-up emoji to Raya, who invited us all for Isadora and Silvano's welcome dinner at her and Mateo's place.

I'd thought I wouldn't go because of Alejandro. But why should I give up my friends because of this man? If he didn't want me, that was fine.

The minute he felt something more than sex, he went into push-away mode. Did he think I couldn't see how if we spoke for more than an hour, talking about ourselves, he'd send me a message for at least two nights, apologizing for being busy? And then, when he couldn't stand it, he'd call, desperate to see me, wanting to hear me. That was why I felt cheap. That he only wanted me to scratch an itch. Well, the hell with him.

I called Drago and asked if he'd like to join me for dinner. He said he'd pick me up and that I should dress appropriately. This meant he would show up in his BMW S 1000 RR and I should wear pants.

I took a page from Raya's lookbook, who always dressed in jeans, boots, and a biker jacket. I was feeling reckless and abandoned my Victoria Beckham staid style.

Drago whistled when he saw me. My hair was tied back in a ponytail. I wore tight black jeans. Boots that came to my knees. A tank top that was a second skin and a Harley Davidson leather jacket, which was a gift from Drago as a dare for me to expand my sartorial landscape. I had gone all smokey with my makeup. Dark eyes. Fire engine red lipstick. It was a cliché. *Girl gets dumped and shows cleavage.* Well, I was fine being a cliché. It was better than being sad in my house, eating chocolate, drinking red wine, and watching *The*

Notebook.

"I knew that leather jacket would look smoking hot on you."

I grinned. "Appropriate for the BMW?"

"Baby, you're good enough to eat out on the BMW."

"Eww...please."

Drago nodded as he tried to imagine a situation where he and I would get naked and winced. "Yeah, that's never happening again. How come you've become a fucking sister-like person to me? I've seen your tits."

"Mark's seen my tits." I put on the helmet he held out.

"Mark's gay."

"*And* my brother."

The admiration for my new getup continued when I got to Mateo and Raya's place.

"You know my wife has a jacket just like that, and I always want to jump her when she wears it," Mateo teased, hugging me.

"*Va va voom*, baby girl," this from Daisy, who held her large stomach in front of her.

I hugged her and patted her belly. "What name are we going with this week?"

"I'm pretty stuck on Ariel...you know, like the mermaid. But then I think about Ursula. We had the same problem with Jasmine. Too Disney."

Hollywood producer Daisy Delacroix was having a baby with her hot beach bum husband, Judge Forest Knight. They joked that when a Daisy and a Forest got together, they had to make a baby with a name from nature. They'd gone the rounds with Juniper, Cedar, Cypress (!!), and others.

"Where's Forest?" I asked.

She shrugged. "Confirmation hearing prep."

Judge Forest Knight had been nominated for a judgeship in the prestigious Ninth Circuit Court of Appeals, and his senate hearing was in a few weeks.

"All's not well in paradise?" I whispered.

Daisy smiled tightly. "Paradise is fucked up right now. Come on, let's get you in to meet Isadora and Silvano who are charming all of us. If I was any younger, I'd marry that boy."

Silvano hugged me, as did Isadora. My heart melted as I sat next to Alejandro's son during dinner. I loved the father, so it was a no-brainer that I loved the son.

The conversation around the dinner table was boisterous. Dec and Esme couldn't make dinner as they were in Paris with Mireya, their daughter. We sat in Mateo and Raya's new apartment's dining room. They'd bought a larger place, so they had room for both their offices. They'd tried to share, but with all the equipment the two IT nerds had, it hadn't been working for them. Now, they had a four-bedroom apartment with a covered pool patio and ample space for entertaining, which they loved to do.

Raya had invited Gordon Mackinnon, her boss, and CEO of SynthoSoft, for dinner, and he sat next to Isadora. A quiet man, he seemed almost befuddled by Isadora's boisterousness. She talked incessantly about a wedding she was organizing at the Golden Valley Inn, and Gordon, to give him credit, seemed genuinely interested.

Drago was conversing deeply with Daisy about one of her films about a detective. "Usually, the detectives in TV shows and movies are complete wankers...well, except Bosch. But in *Hopedale*, you guys did a great job."

Daisy smirked. "Thanks to my sex tapes, I don't think it'll make the Oscar nominations. Every other award has snubbed us."

Daisy had had a stroke of bad luck, starting with a deep-fake AI video of hers that was released right after she married Forest. The fallout had affected her career, and now it looked like it would take a prime position at Forest's confirmation hearings as well.

Mateo had cooked an excellent meal of chicken mole with rice and a Mexican salad; and Raya was proudly announcing that she was responsible for dessert that she'd picked up at Bottega Louie.

The elegant ambiance of the dinner party enveloped us in a warm glow, the clinking of crystal and hushed conversations forming a delicate symphony. I had not wanted to sit next to Silvano, worried that Alejandro would think I was ingratiating myself to his son. But I threw caution to the winds and was pleased I did so. Silvano possessed a mind that seemed to dance with curiosity and intellect. His eyes sparkled with a unique depth, and it was easy to see that his intellect surpassed his tender age.

I was captivated by Silvano's passion for particle physics—a subject that puzzled even the most seasoned adults. But this young prodigy was excited as he spoke about quarks, leptons, and the universe's fundamental mysteries. His enthusiasm was infectious, and I couldn't help but admire how his voice animated his words.

"I'm really excited about starting the STEM program at UCLA," Silvano began, his gaze earnest. "Particle physics is incredible—how everything is connected at such a fundamental level, shaping the universe."

I smiled at his enthusiasm. "Particle physics is indeed a fascinating field. The way you grasp its complexities is quite remarkable."

He blushed, a hint of shy pride tugging at the corners of his lips. "Thank you, Maria. I've always been drawn to understanding how things work, and particle physics is a puzzle that intrigues me."

As the evening continued, our conversation flowed effortlessly. Silvano's intellect was balanced by an endearing innocence that made him all the more captivating. His insights into the universe were awe-inspiring, yet he never lost touch with a child's curiosity, eager to explore and learn. It was a rare combination that tugged at my heart.

"Silvano, you're destined for remarkable things. Your dedication to your passion and your insightful mind is a gift that will undoubtedly shape your future," I stated.

He met my gaze, a mix of gratitude and determination in his eyes. "I hope so. I want to make a difference, you know? I want to be a scientist who unravels the mysteries of the universe."

After dinner, we spread out; some of us stayed in the house and others went to the patio. Silvano was evidently feeling like a grown-up as Gordon, who loved anyone who could speak science, was happy to discuss Quantum Entanglement and Bell's Theorem with him.

"Imagine a pair of entangled particles; let's call them Particle A and Particle B. They are initially prepared in a state where their spins are entangled, meaning that if you measure the spin of one particle along a certain axis, you instantly know the other particle's spin along the same axis, regardless of the distance between them," Silvano exclaimed. "My task is to design an experiment to test the predictions of Bell's theorem, which suggests that no local hidden variables can explain the correlations between entangled particles.."

Isadora shook her head as she walked with me to the patio. "That kid is just too smart for all of us."

She slid an arm into mine. "So, Maria, how are you doing?"

I stiffened at the straightforward question. "Good."

"Is my brother taking good care of you?"

I stopped walking and turned to look at her. She was all innocence and mirth. "Please, I'm his baby sister. I know *everything* he's doing."

Daisy had her feet up on Raya's lap who was massaging her arches. "Why the fuck am I doing this?" Raya wondered. "This is Forest's job."

"Well, Forest is being a dick about his job, so put some muscle into it, bitch."

Isadora sat down next to Daisy. I purposefully sat across from her, as far as I could, in the outdoor seating area.

Isadora noticed and rolled her eyes. "Maria, stop worrying. I know Alejandro. He probably told you; no one can know. My son is blah blah, and my family is ooh la la."

I couldn't help it, a laugh splintered out of me. "I can't imagine how you and Alejandro are related."

"I haven't had sex in forever," Daisy told all of us. "How's it going with Mr. Stud Muffin, Maria?"

Isadora sighed when I gave Daisy an accusatory look.

"Maria, we all know. I manipulated Raya into spilling the beans. You're lucky I haven't told my mother anything."

"I'm sorry, Maria. She tricked me. Isa, do not tell Paloma," Raya warned. "Now that we all know it's out in the open, how is Mr. I'm-so-Fucking-Afraid-to-Commit - I'd-Rather-Lose-My-Balls-Than-Love-You?"

For all the bravado regarding the outfit and the smokey eye makeup and leather jacket, I felt something punch hard into me. "He's being a perfect jackass, if you must know." I then looked at Isadora apologetically, "I'm so sorry."

"Don't be. My brother is a downright dick. Alejandro can be...well, both he and Aurelio have this weird notion about falling in love, which Mama and I cannot understand. They agree that Papa and Mama have a rocking relationship, yet they seem to think it won't happen to them. And all women except Mama and me are unreliable. Actually, they think I'm pretty unreliable as well. Speaking of Aurelio, I'm dying to meet Caro."

Carolina Vega was counsel for Knight Technology Company, where Mateo was CTO and Dec CEO. We knew her as Vega, but the Santos family knew her as Caro. Apparently, *Caro* and Aurelio met in San Francisco and were in an off-again-on-again relationship. There had been an incident where Caro threw a glass of some drink on Aurelio's face at a bar.

"Vega is in Paris with Dec. They're working on a merger." Raya pulled one of Daisy's toes, and she groaned in relief.

"Maria, I know my brother, and I have noticed that he's antsy as fuck during dinner. Can't wait to hustle Silvano to bed...even better if the bed is in my parents' house. Is he sneaking you into his place?" Isadora asked so casually that I choked on my drink.

"I've only been to Golden Valley once during Mateo

and Raya's reception," I assured her.

"And that's when Maria and Alejandro were K.I.S.S.I.N.G," Daisy said in a sing-song manner.

I flushed. Isadora clapped her hands. "This is delightful. I've been waiting for my brothers to fall in love. I never thought Alejandro would be the first."

"He's not in love with me," I bit out. *I wish!* I waved my glass and caught Drago's attention from across the patio into Raya's living room. He looked at my wine glass and nodded.

"Your detective friend is delish," Isadora complimented. "I'm assuming you both aren't doing the horizontal mambo."

"He's a friend," I said in exasperation.

Isadora shrugged. "No matter. I'm not into him. Raya, is your boss single?"

"He's old," Raya counseled. "And *very* emotionally unavailable. Isa, he's forty-two."

"What can I say, I'm a girl with a daddy complex. I'm all about the age-gap romance, you know." Isadora was a pip and then some. She was like Paloma, petite and gorgeous. A ball of energy. Her honey-colored eyes and dark brown hair complimented her light brown skin. As good-looking as she was, it was her personality that drew people to her. She was wide open, her heart big and strong, ready to accept everyone.

Drago brought out the bottle of red I'd been drinking and filled my glass.

"I'm assuming you've decided to get drunk this Friday night, my darling."

"Yes," I announced. "I want to get drunk and drown my *fucking* sorrows."

Everyone looked at me. I rarely swore. It just wasn't something I was comfortable with. I had no problem with other people using the F word, but I was prim and *fucking* proper. And where had that gotten me? No, *fucking* where.

"I wish I could get drunk," Daisy said enviously.

I downed the glass of wine, and Drago shook his head. "Raya, may I rely on you to ensure she doesn't fall into the pool and drown herself?"

Raya blinked. "I've never seen prim and proper Maria drunk."

"She's a fucking riot when she's pissed. Darling, any chance I can dissuade from—"

I held my glass. "More."

Drago sighed and filled up my glass and left to go back to the men who were now congregated in the living room...the *men*.

Isadora grinned. "Wow. My brother has driven you to drink."

"Oh, *fuck* your brother," I slurred and took another long gulp of wine. "You know what this calls for?"

"No," Raya replied. "What does *this*, whatever it is, call for?"

"A limerick. There was an old man from Golden Valley. Who was like a...dirty pally. When he found a lovely beauty, all he wanted was her booty. Because when she gave him her heart, he went all dilly dally."

Daisy laughed. "This is better than therapy. Thank you, Maria, for drinking."

"Yes, thank you," Isadora replied, amused.

"I have another one," I announced. I stood up and held the bottle of wine I'd emptied like a microphone.

"There was an *ooooollllldd* man called Alejandro. Who had a broken heart and lots of sorrow. When Maria tried to make him whole, he turned into a complete asshole. So, she kicked him in the nuts, so they hung very, very... low."

Daisy and Isadora clapped. "Brava, brava," they cried.

I bowed. "Thank you."

"My mother is going to love you," Isadora mused and helped me sit down. "You want to tell us what happened."

I sniffled and sat down next to Daisy "There was once a girl called Maria; who had a very foolish idea? She fell in love with a complete bum, who threw her some crumbs. When she asked for more, he pretended to snore and broke her heart...guarantee-a."

Daisy put an arm around me. "Oh, sweetie."

"You know we decided we'd see each other when we'd see each other...have some good sex and all that. Then he goes back home, and we have phone sex. Can you believe it? And, Isa, your brother is one hell of a dirty talker."

Isadora sighed. "So many things I can't unhear."

I waved a hand. "And he keeps calling me *mi amor*. So, I tell him please stop saying that. I'm trying to keep my heart in one piece. Next thing I know, he won't have phone sex with me. He was supposed to spend tonight with me; instead, he texts me that he has an important meeting in DC and Isa will drop Silvano off."

"In his defense, he *is* in DC," Isadora offered.

"There was once an old man from DC. He had a very big pee pee—" I broke off when Mateo and Silvano came out to the pool patio. It was one thing to rant about a man to his sister, and quite another to do in front of his son. I was tipsy but not out of my mind.

"Babe, are you ready to go home?" Drago asked.

I nodded and without my asking, my friend came to help steady me. We said our goodnights and Drago held my hand at his waist as he drove, worried I'd fall off his bike. I leaned my head on his back and let the cool air ease the alcohol-laden confusion in my head.

I was drunk and happy by the time we got to my place.

"Well, fuck," Drago cursed as I got off his bike.

"What?" I asked as I took off my helmet and saw why Drago was swearing. Alejandro Santos was sitting on my stoop.

Chapter 13

Alejandro

She had a swagger as she walked to me. I'd never seen Maria like this. Her hair was loose, she wore a leather jacket, tight jeans, and boots that went all the way up.

"I thought you were in DC," she mocked. "Didn't he tell me he was in DC, Drago?"

Drago nodded at Alejandro. "Glad you're here. She can be your problem. Come on, cupcake, let's get you inside the house."

"I'm not your *ducking* cupcake."

"Ducking? What? You have an internal autocorrect filter now?" he demanded.

"*He's* not coming inside my house," she announced and flounced past me.

"What the fuck?" I said.

"She's drunk," Drago confirmed for me. "Piss drunk."

Maria stood in front of her door and looked at the keypad. "Drago, do you remember my pin code?"

He sighed and took her thumb, placed it on a panel. The door clicked open. She grinned. "Damn, I forgot they did the thumbprint thing. *He* can't come in."

I followed them into the house, not sure if I was amused or downright shocked – probably both. The prim and proper Maria was a vision when she was drunk.

She swayed as she walked and bumped into her couch. I grabbed her. She looked at me with narrow eyes. "There once was an old man named Alejandro, who said, fucking is one thing I know. Sheep are just fine, and women divine, but llamas are numero uno!"

Drago burst out laughing.

I was too shocked to laugh. "Did she just call me a llama fucker?"

"She gets creative when she's drunk," Drago replied dryly. "It's a good thing she doesn't do it often. The last time was when Mark and her old man fought two years ago. You must've really fucked up to have her this upset."

"I'm not upset with *him*." She poked me in the chest with a forefinger. "I'm upset with *myself*. Me. Me. Me. Me. Got it?"

"You should get her into the bathroom," Drago suggested.

"She's going to throw up?"

Drago nodded. "Oh, yeah. She cannot handle her liquor."

I put my hands on Maria's shoulder, and she batted them away. "No. I'm not going with you anywhere.

Alejandro was in DC, thinking he had a big pee-pee. But when the time came to whip it out, he got a big pout and ran away from me."

I ignored her protests and lifted her into my arms.

"Drago, don't leave me with him," Maria shouted.

Drago's phone buzzed, and he looked at his screen. "Sorry, darling. I got one dead person on Fig and Thirteenth. Have fun, kids."

I carried her into her sleek bathroom and sat her on the closed toilet. I unzipped her boots as she fought me.

"He said *mi amor, mi amor, mi amor*; until she said no more. Then he ran like a little...bitch, afraid that this was more than an itch, and then came back hoping for some more."

She *was* creative when drunk and fucking delightful.

I took her boots and then her socks off. She removed her jacket and threw it at me. I caught it and hung it on the hook on the bathroom door. She took her tank top off, threw that at me, and then unzipped her jeans. She peeled them off her fucking beautiful body, but as she bent, she moaned; her head was probably swimming.

I helped her out of her pants, and she leaned against me in just a pair of sinful black lacy lingerie. "I hate you."

"I know, baby." I held her, feeling tired of myself.

I'd run away, she was right, and like a bitch, but I couldn't stay away. I'd planned to stay in DC for the night. Instead, I chartered a plane and came to LA. Since I woke up at three in the morning, I'd been on a plane for several hours now to make it back to her.

She put her arms around me. "I will not throw up," she informed me. "But I need to take a shower."

I helped her sit on the closed toilet seat and quickly removed my suit. I turned the shower knob on medium warm because I'd never showered with Maria. I didn't know whether she liked her water warm or super-hot. Well, I'd find out.

She took her underwear off and stepped into the glass-enclosed shower.

"You can't keep running away." She stood under the large shower head as it cascaded over her. She put her head on my chest then, and I heard her whimper. "You're hurting me."

"I know. I'm going to do better."

She looked up at me, the water beating down on both of us. "Are you here for sex? Is that what you want from me? All that you want from me?"

I shook my head. "No, baby. I'm here because I missed you. Because I can't sleep without you."

"Or did you show up thinking this will be better than phone sex?" There was agony in her voice. I remembered she'd said that I made her feel cheap.

"I'm holding you, baby, and it's already better than phone sex. Just being with you is better than…" I trailed off.

"Better than what?" she demanded.

I took a deep breath. "The alternative."

She let the tears loose then, and I hugged her close, aching with her. I preferred her spouting insulting limericks over breaking her heart over an undeserving asshole like me.

I dried her after the shower and got into bed with her. She fell asleep immediately, her head resting on my shoulder, her arm wrapped around my stomach.

My phone lit up with a message. It was Isadora: *Sil is good. Sleeping in his room. I'm going to head back tomorrow. How's Maria?*

Of course, Isa knew about Maria. By this time, it was probably in the news. My sister was gossiping.

Before I could respond, she sent another message: *Don't worry, I haven't told Mama.*

Thank god for small mercies.

Me: *Maria is sleeping. She called me a llama fucker.*

Isadora: *She also mentioned you had a big pee-pee.*

Me: *Kill me now!*

Isadora: *Stop screwing around with her. If you don't want her, walk away. She's hurting.*

Me: *I tried to walk away.*

Isadora: *She's in love with you. Are you in love with her?*

Me: *No.*

Isadora: *Do you even know what it means to fall in love with someone?*

Me: *No.*

Isadora: *Time to learn, Alejandro. P.S. I like her. She's got fire. She's got a big heart. Silvano has a crush on her.*

Me: *Like father, like son.*

Isadora: *Get your head out of your ass, amigo, or you'll lose the girl. Worse, you'll hurt her.*

Me: *Goodnight, baby sister.*

She hated it when I called her *baby sister*. She responded with a middle finger emoji.

Chapter 14

Maria

I was a cheap drunk. It took only three glasses of wine before I turned into anti-Maria, and after the fourth glass, I fell asleep. Luckily, my metabolism didn't indulge in hangovers. Sure, I'd be slower the next day, but I'd have none of the pesky symptoms like headaches, diarrhea, churning stomach, and general dizziness.

I was alone in bed when I woke up, which was a good thing. I was embarrassed. I'd gotten drunk and had allowed Alejandro to wheedle his way back into my bed.

I took a shower and put on my social armor before I went into my living room. I knew he was in the condo. I could feel his presence. I put on my favorite white Frank & Eileen white shirt dress. It always made me feel cool and comfortable. I decided against makeup. He didn't deserve me looking my best.

He was at my dining table, the Los Angeles Times spread, a cup of coffee in his hand. He wore suit pants and an unbuttoned dress shirt with sleeves rolled up.

"Coffee?" He rose when he saw me.

"Get out of my house." I walked past him into the open kitchen and started my coffee machine.

"Baby—"

"No. I told you I wouldn't do this dance with you. You feel something, you run. You feel something else, you come back. I can't be on this rollercoaster with you. I don't want it."

I didn't look at him because if I did, the love I felt would make my words softer. He'd seen Maria, the woman, the one with a heart for a sponge; now he would meet Maria, the CEO of a billion-dollar company, the one who was tough and stood her ground.

I felt him nuzzle my hair, and I stiffened. He moved like a cat. I hadn't even heard him, and he was so close that I could smell him. He put his arms around my waist and pulled me into his embrace. My back against his chest. I could feel his steady heartbeat. He could probably feel mine skitter.

"I'm so sorry, *Duquesa*."

I stood still because I desperately wanted to turn around and snuggle into him. Feel his warmth; bask in it.

"You keep apologizing, Alejandro, but the fact is that you keep making the same mistake over and over again. I'm not interested."

I felt his breath against my neck as he lifted my hair and kissed the skin below my ear. My breath struggled to come out of my lungs.

"You're not being fair."

"I know." He moved his hips so I could feel him against my ass, hard, ready to go. "I know. I'm taking advantage of my advantage, baby, because I am *very* sorry."

We stood like that for a long moment, and then I pushed him away. I took my coffee and walked out to my patio garden, where I usually spent my weekend mornings, reading the paper and working.

He followed me.

I sat on the long wooden sofa, and he sat across from me on a matching wooden armchair, comfortable with blue and white striped cushions.

"My son has a crush on you, according to Isa." He smiled as soon as he mentioned his son, and my heart, traitorous fragile heart, stumbled.

"I like him as well." I took a sip of my coffee.

"May I explain myself? It's not an excuse...but—"

"You don't have to explain yourself. I know what happened. I told you that you keep calling me *mi amor*, and you thought," I changed my voice to sound masculine, "Oh damn, I'm not just thinking with my hard dick anymore." I could see him bite back a smile. "And then you ran."

"I've called no woman *mi amor*, ever. I've been judicious about not using terms of endearment that can be misconstrued. I surprised myself. I didn't even realize...." He stood up and dug his hands in his pockets, his back turned to me as if he was trying to get control over something.

"I don't care for your excuses or explanations because it doesn't change the result. It made me feel like a piece of ass. And I'm okay feeling like a piece of ass, Alejandro, as long as we're both honest. I haven't lied to you about how I feel and I'm not expecting engagement rings and picket fences. But I'm expecting honesty, respect, and kindness. I got avoidance, stiff politeness, and disregard."

A part of me was kicking me hard. *The man is back. Take him before he changes his mind. Stop pushing him away.* It wasn't pride making me take a stand— or maybe it was, but the overriding feeling was one of protecting myself, of treating myself with more respect than he was.

Alejandro turned around to face me. The pain and confusion on his face made me want to go to him and soothe him. *I love you*, I wanted to scream at him; *why can't you love me back?*

"I don't know what it means to be in love. I only know...lust. I know familial love. I understand it well. I won't beat on the Anika drum for you, but it twisted me. I must protect my son. He lost a mother before he even met her, which, to put it bluntly, was not a bad thing. But if he were to lose a woman I bring into his life...that would be me failing as a parent. I desperately don't want to do that."

His honesty undid me. But his lack of faith in me and women in general made me furious.

"I don't want to pay for your dead wife's sins," I bit out. "Let's end this here, Alejandro. You said it yourself, I deserve more, and I do. I need a man who makes me happy, doesn't drive me to be so upset that I'm getting drunk, which I hardly ever do."

I was a tough businesswoman, but then Alejandro was a ruthless businessman. He was in agriculture, for god's sake, which was cutthroat. He came and sat next to me. Took my hand in both of his.

"I can't promise picket fences. But I can promise honesty, respect, and kindness. Next time I waiver—"

"Farmboy, there ain't going to be no next time." I pulled my hand away. *The balls on this man.* He just thought he'd sit here, showing off his abs and sinfully beautiful face and I'd fall over him. Well, hell, Maria Caruso had a big heart, yes, but she wasn't stupid.

"You cut me open," he cried out. "Wide fucking open."

The emotion in his voice shook me.

"I'm a forty-two-year-old man trying to find ways to be alone in my locked bedroom so I can make love with my woman...over the phone for pity's sake. I'm trying to convince my son to stay with his grandparents so I can be free to tell my girl that she makes me so hot that I can hardly keep it in my pants. I'm a grown man for fuck's sake and I'm behaving like a wet-behind-the-ears teenager. I. Have. Never. Felt. This. Way. Even when I was a fucking wet-behind-the-ears teenager." He bellowed the last sentence.

I looked at him, uncertain whether I could hide the sudden spark of joy I felt at his confession or the fear of allowing him back in so he could once again get cold feet and run. I turned away from him and blindly stared at the roses blooming in my garden.

"Maria," he groaned, "Give me the fucking time of day, will you? And forgive me for being lost. I don't know how to handle you. For the first time in my adult life, I don't know how to navigate my life."

I turned to look at him, my eyes bright with tears. "And you think this is easy for me? I'm in love with a man who keeps telling me he can't love me, can't be with me. A man who keeps saying *when* we end this... not *if*. You're so sure there is no future for us. Why should I give you the time of day? I want to get married and have babies. I want...what?"

His eyes had immediately moved to my stomach, and I felt heat rise through me.

He shook his head.

"What? You promised me honesty like two seconds ago."

He sighed. "I just thought of you swollen with my baby and..." He trailed away again and raised his hands in frustration.

"What?" I yelled.

"It aroused me, damn you," he retorted angrily. "My god, woman, you have a temper on you."

"Great, so you're a complete caveman who gets his blood pumping down south because he thinks of impregnating a woman." I kept my tone casual, but he wasn't the only one who was aroused.

"I want to date you," he blurted out. "Can we...date? I don't know what that means. I've had one-night stands for over a decade. But if you teach me, I'll learn."

"You'll learn to date me?"

He nodded.

"It will include taking me out to dinner. Not ignoring me because you felt more than lust for me. It will include you making time for me and not always expecting me to make time for you. I have just as much of an important job as you do."

His lips turned into a smile. "Yes, ma'am."

The way he said it, a laugh escaped me without my

permission. "I don't need to meet your family as...you know, your...whatever..."

"Girlfriend," he supplied. "I believe the correct term is a girlfriend. Though aren't we too old to be called boys and girls?"

He was playful Alejandro now, and I was having a hard time resisting him. "I'm close to my family, well my mother and I'd like for you to meet her. You've met Mark. He asked you to behave yourself because he needs his sleep and not get three-in-the-morning phone calls from his upset sister. You already met Drago."

His eyebrows lifted. "Drago is family?"

"Yes. His parents moved back to Zagreb many years ago, and he has no other family here, except us. My mother is big on bringing people into our family. Esme is like a daughter to them, so now Mireya is like a granddaughter."

"You dated Drago?"

I snorted. "Are you jealous, Alejandro Santos? Of a man I dated when I was sixteen, half a lifetime ago?"

"Yes," he replied immediately, looking sheepish.

"Drago was my first, and I was his first. We lost our virginities—"

Alejandro raised a hand to stop me from talking. "Can we not talk about you being naked with another man?"

"Is that the Alpha Alejandro speaking?" I grinned.

He put a hand on my cheek. "Yes. I feel this insane possessiveness about you. I was in DC yesterday and was getting a drink at a bar as I waited for them to ready the plane to bring me to you. A woman...no need for you to be jealous," he interjected when I frowned, "she came onto me, and she *was* my type."

"What's your type?" I tried to move my face away, but he held my face with both hands.

"Blonde, stacked, available, and looking for a good time. She put her hand on my arm, and I felt like I was cheating on you. Possessiveness works both ways. I feel you belong to me, but I also feel that I belong to you."

My eyes filled with tears. "Don't hurt me again."

He kissed me then, gently, softly, a promise, an apology all combined into one. "Baby, I'd rather cut my arm off than cause you pain. I will try my best not to intentionally hurt you."

I couldn't stop the tears from rolling down my cheeks. He groaned and pulled me onto his lap, holding me close. "No, baby, don't cry."

I gripped him hard not wanting to ever let go. "I love you," I whispered softly, my heart full, wanting to give.

I knew he heard me because his hands on me tightened. He pulled back, his eyes on my lips. "I want you to say it again when I'm inside you." His voice was hoarse. "Will you?"

I gave him a watery smile and nodded.

"Good girl." His lips brushed mine. "But we will not rush it this time."

"What does that mean?" I asked suspiciously. We'd barely started, and he was putting the brakes again?

"That means I want to *date* you and not *just* fuck you. Though I want to very much, all the time. I have to just think about you, and I get hard."

"But you don't want us to have sex?" I was confused.

"Not until I earn it. I never want you to feel cheap. I never want you to feel what we do to and with each other is wrong—less. Every time we're together whether in person or over a phone, it's clean, it's pure... and it's fucking beautiful."

He had me at 'date!' *Damn him.*

Chapter 15

Alejandro

"**Y**ou don't have to stay at a hotel when you're in LA," she told me when I asked her if she'd like to join me for a day in the city so I could get a shower and change of clothes from my hotel.

"Yes, I do," I replied firmly.

This time, I was going to do it right. I was going to woo her as she deserved. Spend time with her. Kiss her. Hold her hand. *Dios mío!* This whole scenario was sounding like something out of a teenage movie Silvano liked to watch with Isa. I was out of my depth. What did grown men do when they *dated* a woman? Besides having sex with them, that is? Did they go to the movies? Fuck, no, I was not doing that no matter what *Dating For Forty Plus Dummies* said. Maybe the museum? Yeah, I loved art, I could do that. What else?

"Do you like ballet?" I asked as she drove us to the

city. As I'd expected, Maria didn't have a fancy car that came with a driver. She drove a Kia EV—a simple car, not a show-off one.

"I'm a patron of the LA Phil," she informed me. "I have box seats if you want to see a performance."

Of course, she did.

"I'd love to." *What could I do with her that wasn't just going to a restaurant? How could I date this woman? I needed help.* I'd ask my brother Aurelio, but he was worse than I was. I at least knew how to speak to people. Aurelio was an introvert. He'd gotten engaged for a hot minute before realizing he didn't want to fuck up the poor girl's life and broke the engagement off, which was the decent thing to do. The problem was he gave little explanation beyond saying, *it's me, it's not you,* and the whole community was up in arms about what a jerk he was. I never understood why he got engaged to Jenn. She was a nice girl, albeit a little boring. She was the daughter of Barnaby Whelan, who owned a large cattle farm. Barnaby had been more excited about Golden Valley and Whelan Farms becoming *related* to one another rather than his daughter marrying Aurelio. My brother was a tough nut to crack. He kept to himself. Wasn't interested in money or business—and was truly in love with the land and farming. He was also no celibate saint. He had an apartment in San Francisco where he went away to *take a break* but according to Isadora, he went to the big city to *sow his wild oats.* Aurelio didn't confirm or deny but the one time I'd been in San Francisco at the same time he'd been there, he'd told me I'd have to find a hotel because he had a guest, and I couldn't crash with him.

Mateo had mentioned that Aurelio had been or

was seeing the counsel of Knight Technologies—but I'd never met the woman and Aurelio didn't talk about the women in his life, period. I didn't blame him, I didn't either, which was probably why our mother and sister felt they needed to play detectives to find out what we were up to in our personal lives.

"Why don't you have a drink at the bar? I'll be back in fifteen minutes tops," I suggested, kissing her on her forehead when we got to the seventy-first floor of the Intercontinental Hotel.

She narrowed her eyes. "I can wait in your room."

"No," I said emphatically and sighed when she gave me an amused look. "You, me, and a bed is a dangerous combination." I lifted the strap of her yellow stress and caressed her shoulder as I traced it. "You've got to stop dressing sexy."

She looked down at her dress. "Baby, if you think this is sexy...wait until I put in some effort."

"I'm an old man from Golden Valley, my heart may stop."

She didn't debate the issue, which was a good thing because I had half a mind to drag her upstairs and spend the afternoon with her in bed. We could take a shower together, my cock suggested.

I called Isadora once I was in my room and took my clothes off.

"Where are you?"

"Driving home," she told me, and I heard the dulcet tones of Etta James in the background. Isa was a lover of jazz, old and new. For a young woman in her early twenties, Isa was an old soul. She loved black-and-white movies and believed music from before the seventies was the only music worth listening to.

"I need your help." She was going to love this. But I was a desperate man. My other choice was my mother who'd start naming her grandkids.

"What can I do for you?"

"What do grownups do when they date?"

There was a long pause. "Are you feeling okay, Alejandro?"

"I don't know what to do when someone dates at my age. Am I supposed to take her to a show, movies, what?"

"What did you do in the past?"

"I took them to bed, Isa."

I opened my suitcase and pulled out fresh clothes.

"I'm assuming you're intending to date Maria. Please tell me you didn't pick up some skank."

I sighed. "Isa," I warned.

"Fine, fine. Well, I've done my research which was talking to Maria's brother Mark whom I met this morning at UCLA when I dropped Sil off. According to him, Maria is not as sensitive as she looks. She's tough when she needs to be. She won't allow you to fuck around on her. Infidelity is a no-no in her book. She likes long walks in vineyards and is a big-time oenophile. She reads like a crazy person—into Nordic Noir. Her favorite author is Jo Nesbø."

"Who the fuck is that?"

"A Scandinavian writer," Isa replied patiently. "She's fond of ballet but *loves* theater and doesn't miss a single play at the Geffen Playhouse. Her favorite play is *Who's Afraid of Virginia Woolf*, and her favorite opera is Bizet's *Carmen*."

"Jesus, Isa. Do you know her favorite color and sex

position as well?"

"Red. I'm assuming doggy style."

I felt a flush. My baby sister wasn't supposed to know about doggy style. I was still pretending she didn't have sex.

I cleared my throat. "Anything else?"

"Yes. She loves, and Mark said *absolutely* loves romantic gestures that don't cost money. So, take her for a picnic, skinny dipping in *my* lake."

"It's not *your* lake. It belongs to Golden Valley." Isa had decided that a lake, which was thirty minutes away from my parents' house, was hers because she'd all but rammed down posts to secure the land as hers.

"If you want my help, Alejandro..."

"Yeah, yeah. I'll take her to Isadora's Lake."

"And this one is important. She's big on family, real and adopted. She'll want you to meet her parents and she'll want you to make a good impression. Her mother is a doll, but I gather that her father is not the easiest guy to deal with. She'll want to meet your family—"

"She's met my family and I'm ready for her to meet them as...what is she to me?"

"How am I supposed to know?" Isa wondered. "That's something you need to figure out. Okay, now I need a cup of coffee, so I'll talk to you later. Be nice to her or Mark said he'll kick your ass. And he's built so I think he can do it."

"Thanks."

Picnic by the lake. Skinny dipping in the lake. Opera. Theater. Musicals? Maybe a trip to New York. We could go to the Met.

As I took a shower, I came up with all the things I'd

do with Maria.

It wasn't until I was walking toward her at the bar, where she was laughing at something the bartender said, that I realized I was once again having a first with Maria. I was, for the first time in my life, planning romantic *dates* with a woman. And that thought didn't make me unhappy—it felt good to have someone to plan something for and with.

Alejandro, she's in your blood, cabrón.

I curbed the sense of panic that came with that thought. If she was in my blood, she could hurt me, she could fucking destroy me. But that knife cut both ways. I could do the same to her.

She turned to see me, and her face broke into a smile. The fucking room lit up. She had her heart in her eyes and the message was clear: *Hijo de puta, handle with care.*

Chapter 16

Maria

"Can you pick Silvano up?" Raya pleaded over the phone. "I'm stuck in traffic and Mateo is in Berlin. Please, please?"

"Of course," I assured her. The Caruso Investment offices were a ten-minute drive from UCLA.

"Is Alejandro with you tonight?" Raya asked.

We had announced nothing, but all our friends accepted without being told that Alejandro and I were *dating*...or whatever it was we were doing. The past five days had been a dream come true. Alejandro had meetings in Los Angeles, and he spent his evenings with Silvano at Raya and Mateo's place, and his nights with me. He'd finally agreed not to stay in the hotel, but he insisted on not sleeping with me—and slept in the guestroom instead. It was like he was doing penance for hurting me by not having sex with me. A part of me minded, another was relieved. I loved having sex with Alejandro, but I wasn't one to make love without my emotions involved. I wasn't promiscuous, but I also wasn't a prude. I'd had a few partners, but they were all people I liked and knew. There were no one-night stands in my sexual repertoire. I was careful. I knew who I was, and I wasn't a woman who could compartmentalize sex as moments of pleasure and nothing else.

"No, he left," I informed her. He had to go home, he'd told me reluctantly, to deal with some issues at work; he'd be back over the weekend to pick up Silvano after his week at UCLA.

Two CEOs dating meant that we consistently could not make our calendars reconcile. Alejandro had wanted to know if I'd see him in San Francisco the week after, but I was going to be in Tokyo for an M&A meeting and couldn't make it. I asked him if he'd be in Sacramento at the end of the month when I had meetings in the capital—but he'd be in New York for an agriculture conference.

Raya texted Silvano about the change in his pickup service and he was waiting for me outside the Physics and Astronomy Building, talking to two people his age. They were having a robust conversation. I got out of the car to wave at him, and he grinned when he saw me.

I was surprised when he gave me a hug. "Hey, Maria, come meet my new friends." He introduced me to Jessica and Paul, who went to school in Orange County and had been selected for the UCLA STEM initiative.

I took Silvano to the Larchmont Bungalow Café in Echo Park when he told me that his favorite food was *breakfast*. The café served breakfast all day long and was a quaint place I went to often. Even at four in the afternoon, the aroma of freshly brewed coffee wafted through the air as we settled into our conversation. I had a latte, while Silvano had a big plate of French toast with strawberries. I regarded Silvano, his eyes gleaming with an unmistakable excitement.

"How has it been so far?" I asked with genuine curiosity.

Silvano's face lit up, his hands animatedly tracing invisible paths in the air. "It's been unbelievable. Professor Jbara has a Nobel Prize in particle physics."

I was captivated by Silvano's enthusiasm and just like I'd fallen in love with his father, I fell in love with him. "I still can't believe you're into particle physics."

"What were you into when you were eleven?" he asked.

I thought about it and smiled. "I had just watched a movie called Contact and was desperate to find proof of alien life. That got me into astronomy. I got a telescope for my twelfth birthday. I wanted to understand the universe."

Silvano nodded, his enthusiasm undiminished. "For me, particle physics is about delving into the very essence of reality, understanding the tiniest particles that make up everything around us."

I couldn't help but smile, charmed by Silvano's passion. "So, what have you learned?"

His words rushed out like a river bursting its banks, the French toast forgotten. "We explored the Standard Model, the fundamental theory that describes all known particles and their interactions. It's like a puzzle where each piece represents a particle, and the way they fit together determines how the universe works."

I sipped my coffee, leaning in further, utterly

intrigued. "Tell me more."

"We talked about quarks, minuscule entities that are never found alone. They're like the social butterflies of the particle world," Silvano explained reverently. "We learned about leptons, which include electrons and carry the charge that powers our world."

I was enchanted, absorbing every word. "And what about the Higgs boson? I remember reading about that...oh many moons ago."

Silvano's eyes lit up even brighter. "Ah, the Higgs boson! It's like the linchpin of the universe. It gives particles mass, allowing them to form matter as we know it. Professor Jbara explained its discovery and the immense effort it took to find it at the Large Hadron Collider."

I was impressed with Silvano's ability to convey complex ideas with such clarity. Just because he had a high IQ didn't mean he had to be a good communicator. "It sounds like you've truly found your calling, Silvano. Your excitement is palpable."

He grinned, his eyes twinkling with gratitude. "This experience has solidified my love for particle physics. I want to contribute to unraveling the mysteries of the universe."

As we chatted further, the café seemed to fade into the background. I listened with rapt attention because Silvano's thirst for knowledge was contagious, leaving me inspired by the boundless curiosity that fueled his passion.

I said as much to Alejandro on the phone when I drove back from Raya's place after dropping Silvano off.

"You could've just sent a car for him," Alejandro said in a way that made my back stiffen. He didn't like that

I'd spent time with his son. Did he think I'd tell Silvano about our relationship?

"You know I don't have a fancy car and driver," I tried for levity. "Raya said Dec and Esme are having a farewell dinner this Saturday."

There was a long silence from Alejandro. I didn't fill the quiet. He had to figure himself out. I was in love with him, but I wasn't his therapist. I knew my boundaries.

"That's nice," I finally heard him say and then he added, "I'm sorry I won't be able to make Sunday dinner with your parents."

Here it was. The wall was coming up again. But loving someone meant being patient with them. Alejandro needed to learn to accept love and not be suspicious about me and my motives.

"That's okay." I'd invited him because he'd be here on a Sunday, but I was fine with him not making it. I wasn't ready for him to meet my father. Retirement had made him grouchy and unyielding...more so than before.

"Ah..."

"Alejandro," I lost my patience, "Stop it. I've met your whole family and I'll meet them again. I'm going to spend time with your son as Esme, Daisy, and Raya do. It means nothing until we tell him it does. Got it?"

Alejandro chuckled. "Aye, aye, ma'am. I was being an ass again?"

I laughed with relief. He was not stubborn anymore, open to learning how to be with me in a relationship.

"They say it takes at least three weeks to break a habit. We're in week one." Again, I deflected. *It's a new relationship, these things take time to settle.* "How was your day?"

"Long. And that's made me testy as well. I'm sitting alone in my backyard, staring at the mountains, drinking my scotch, wishing you were here with me."

My heart warmed.

"What's going on?" I prodded.

"The usual. We have a labor shortage—the immigration policies are fucking with us," he explained. "A shortage of skilled labor means workforce management issues which means inefficiencies in planting, harvesting, and maintaining crops, which means Aurelio is up my ass."

We continued to talk even after I got home. I kept my phone with me as I changed and joined him to watch the stars from my patio garden with a glass of cognac.

"I'm going to have to fire one of my vice presidents," I told Alejandro. "The legal team is looking into it."

"What did they do?"

"Didn't reveal that his wife has personal investments in a biotech company that we're currently working with. If the SEC finds out we have this conflict of interest, it could raise concerns about fairness and transparency, and *would* damage Caruso's reputation and credibility within the industry."

The other men I'd dated were not executives, they came from different professions. This was the first time I could talk to a man I was seeing about issues I faced at work, challenges he'd understand because, as the head of his family business, he faced similar trials.

"I want us to find a weekend in New York," Alejandro told me when we were both in our respective beds.

"I'll ask Ollie to connect with Mercedes and see what

we can make happen."

Ollie was my assistant and Mercedes was his. After unsuccessfully trying to find time for ourselves, we'd decided that it might be easier to let the people who worked for us and were experts at managing our calendars take over.

"I want to spend a whole night with you," he whispered. *"Maria..."*

"I know." It happened every time we spoke. The need for each other soared. "Are you hard?" I breathed, my hands itching to go between my legs to find relief.

"Duquesa, we're not doing that," he said emphatically.

"I—"

"No."

"Is this because I said it made me feel cheap?"

"Maria, don't make this harder than it is, baby." He laughed then. "It couldn't get harder though...pun intended."

"I'm wet, Alejandro."

"Cristo! I want you so much."

"Stay with me this weekend."

"I can't. I have to get Silvano home. He's back to school on Monday," he all but whined. "Baby, we'll make it work. I promise."

"Okay. So...what are you wearing? I'm naked against the sheets," I teased.

He laughed. "You're getting too good at this. *Buenas noches, mi preciosa.* Dream about me."

Chapter 17

Alejandro

I watched her as she talked to Gordon Mackenzie, Raya's boss. Jealousy was an ugly feeling, and I was drowning in it.

I stood in the living room by the open café doors, looking into the pool patio where most of the dinner guests had collected after the meal, including the woman who was an itch I wasn't able to scratch.

Dec came up to me and handed me a beer. "Your son is amazing. I wish he was into tech instead of particle physics. I'd hire him. I can hardly understand the stuff he talks about."

I nodded. "Imagine how I feel! He's smart. I think that's why he gets along so well with Mateo."

Silvano was in a deep conversation with Mateo, who also had an IQ in the 150s or something as high.

Esme Knight was the hostess with the mostest, Raya

had told me and was always looking for an excuse to throw a dinner party. Having not grown up with a big family...or any family really, Esme had adopted a new family. I felt a connection with her because she reminded me so much of Paloma.

Maria's brother Mark was usually a guest at such dinners, but he had the night shift and hadn't been able to make it. Drago was slowly being incorporated into Maria's friend circle since he'd come back from his undercover assignment. It still pissed me off he'd been her first, fucking ridiculous because I could barely remember mine.

"Stop staring at them so hard. Gordon isn't interested in her. He likes her, but she's not...you know his type," Dec informed me dryly.

Had I become that obvious? The inscrutable Alejandro Santos was gawking at his girlfriend like a lovesick fool. Excellent, progress, maldito idiota.

"What's his type?"

"Available, easy, probably the type you used to have," Dec smiled. "The type I used to have."

"Yeah," I agreed. "She's not that."

"Oh, no. Maria is serious. And has the biggest fucking heart. Do you know before Esme took over Safe Harbor, Maria was managing both Caruso and the women's shelter?"

I did not know that. Charitable works were part of the Golden Valley ethos. We didn't have a choice because my mother had raised all of us, including my father, to give back to society—but writing a check was one thing, actually doing the work was quite another.

Esme came up to us then with Mireya in her arms, who was all but ready to leap out into her father's embrace. "Hey, princess." Dec took his daughter and kissed her on a rosy cheek.

The five-month-old gurgled and pulled her father's nose.

"Can you put her to bed?" Esme suggested wearily. "She's too excited with everyone here. If Forest was here, I'd send him in with her." She grinned at me, "She loves him *best*."

"Come on, princess, let's read some stories." Dec took his daughter away, cooing at her. I had cooed plenty at Silvano when he was a baby, and a new hunger gnawed in my belly. Would I never have that again? Did I want it again?

"How is Forest?"

Esme shrugged, a worry creasing her forehead. "A bit too busy with his confirmation hearings and…Daisy is…well, she has her own problems."

"I'm surprised she isn't here today."

"She's tired. You know how it is in the third trimester. She falls asleep at the drop of a hat, she told me. I don't like that she's all alone. Though Hector… that's the Knight family majordomo, he makes sure she's eating. Anyway, your son has charmed us all." Esme deftly changed the topic.

"Silvano has loved being here. He's thirsty for learning. I sometimes wonder if I should've sent him away to one of those schools for the smart kids." I watched as Silvano and Mateo joined Maria and Gordon; they were laughing about something.

I hadn't liked it one bit that Silvano had spent an afternoon with Maria. I didn't want him to get attached. She wasn't permanent.

"You know, I'd asked Mateo once how he managed because he grew up in foster homes. He said that you have to learn both how to challenge your mind and make sure you know how to live in a world populated by morons." Esme slid a hand through my arm and led me to the pool patio. "What he was saying was that life skills are as important as feeding a big brain. I think you've managed to do both with Silvano. Matteo says that he's so well adjusted that it's hard to believe he has a high IQ...but then he talks about particle physics, and you know."

"Yeah, that's why I kept him in Golden Valley. I didn't want him to be one of those intelligent kids with zero social skills," I agreed.

"You know, Alejandro, Maria, and Mark are old friends of mine."

I nodded and waited for the warnings. I didn't know Esme well, but I knew she was loyal and took care of the people around her, just like my mother.

"She's not as strong as she looks. She wants marriage and babies. She's never going to be happy with a *"let's see how this goes"* relationship when she's in love." Esme stopped me at the far end of the pool. She let go of my arm and turned to look at me, her eyes concerned. "You know she's in love with you?"

I took a draw of my beer. "And what does being in love *really* mean?"

"That she wants marriage and babies with you. She wants you to be a lover, champion, best friend, someone who's always on her team no matter what. She wants to share her life with you, the good, the bad, and the very ugly."

"I'm a bad bet for all of that," I raised my hand before

Esme could protest, "I know who I am. I'm not a kid. I'm forty-two and I've made some conscious choices in my life. I didn't end up a single father by default, it's by design. I'm fond of Maria. I care about her. But if the choice came between hurting her and my family, she doesn't stand a chance."

Esme gasped at my directness and then challenged, "But what if she was your family too?"

"But she isn't," I simply said. "She's a woman I'm seeing. When I stop seeing her, she'll go her way and I'll go mine."

Esme slid her hand back. I expected her to be angry or irritated, but she was just like my mother, always drawing more flies with honey. "Dec had said the same thing to me when we got married. You do know we got married because of some stupid company bylaws. And because, thankfully, my sister dumped his fine ass."

I knew. Raya had told us their story. "Maria and I are not Dec and you."

"Of course not," she replied. "But love is still love, Alejandro. When it hits you, I promise you'll know what it means, and you won't seek an explanation."

She led me to stand next to Maria, who turned to me with a bright smile. She was going to hold my hand when I jerked away from her. "My son is here," I hissed under my breath.

What was she pulling? I knew women who had tried to get to me through my son. Get friendly with the kid and reel in the dad, which was why I was protective of Silvano.

I put my arm around Silvano and ruffled his hair. "You ready to go home?"

"Yeah." He leaned into me. "I had a fantastic time,

Papa. Mateo says that the best university for particle physics is MIT. Do you know he has a Ph.D. in cyber security from Harvard?"

"I did know that."

"And Maria is a biotech expert? Man, the people I've met here are so different from Golden Valley. Not a single farmer."

I laughed and tightened my hold on him. "Yeah."

"UCLA is offering a longer program in the summer. I want to apply for that. Do you think I could get in?"

The kid had humility, I had to give him that.

"I have no doubt."

I ignored Maria for the rest of the evening, partly because I knew I upset her by letting her know I wouldn't acknowledge our relationship, even in the slightest way when my son was around. I didn't need to add that complication to his life. And partly because I desperately wanted to claim her in front everyone, including my son. The dichotomy of my feelings was tearing me apart.

I'd never felt this conflicted before, well, not since Anika. That thought sobered me. I knew I couldn't do the pull and push with Maria; it wasn't fair to her, but I couldn't control how I felt. I was emotionally charged, which made me uncomfortable. I didn't want to feel this way. I wanted her—to be with her, fuck her, hold her, talk to her. I didn't want her to get too close to my son and yet, when he spoke warmly about Maria, it filled me with pride, because he was saying I'd chosen well.

We said our goodnights shortly thereafter and Silvano, who was tired after a week of exciting education, was happy to leave for the Intercontinental with me. We'd get on the road in the morning and be home, well in time for Paloma's Sunday night meal that she insisted everyone attended, where she'd grill us on our personal lives. It was a highlight for all of us even though we complained about it.

I texted Maria after I settled into bed: *Goodnight. I'll talk to you tomorrow.*

Her response was immediate: *Sleep well, darling. And give my love to Silvano. Drive safe tomorrow.*

I felt like an asshole. She would not give me a hard time. She was going to be understanding and warm. I couldn't help myself; I called her.

"I thought you'd be angry with me."

I heard her smile. "Why? I wasn't thinking. You were near me, and I wanted to touch you. But Silvano was there and he's a perceptive kid. So, I'm glad one of us was paying attention."

The fist clutching my lungs loosened and I could breathe again. She wasn't trying to get to me through my son. I should've known. This was Maria, ethical to a fault.

We talked for a few minutes and then she kissed me goodnight, making loud smooching sounds on the phone like we were fifteen.

I slept poorly that night. I wasn't sure how my well-planned life had gotten so out of control, but I could pinpoint it all to the moment I laid my eyes on Maria Caruso. I didn't know how to seize control back.

Chapter 18

Maria

I held Kai close to my chest and walked with him as Daisy watched. He came several weeks early but fully cooked and was the cutest baby I'd ever seen.

"I love the new baby smell." I nuzzled Kai, as I put my hand on his head to support him. He was a week old, and I'd already been to see him three times. Daisy and Forest used the time I insisted on being there to catch up on sleep. I had been and still was the same with Mireya and Dec and Esme's favorite babysitter, they joked, when Forest was not around because he was Mireya's favorite.

"Where's Forest?" I asked as Daisy lay back on the couch, looking as stunning as she always did, if a little tired. But her eyes shone so bright that it was impossible to see the weariness.

"I sent him to surf." She yawned. "He's taking paternity leave, but still working on some rulings and he's exhausted. I thought some surf and sand would be good for him."

"How are things with him?"

She beamed, her eyes lighting up like July Fourth fireworks. "Fabulous. I was worried when he pulled his name from the ninth circuit judgeship, but he's so happy and back to being the Forest we know and love that I know he did the right thing. You know, he was so driven to get to the ninth circuit but then I was so driven to win an Oscar. Dreams change and sometimes for the better."

"Don't they just," I whispered. Kai was asleep, and I rocked him gently. "Have you guys decided you're going to live in your place?"

Forest had a jewel of a home in Venice Beach but Daisy's house in Brentwood was bigger, and she'd wanted them to make their family here.

"River is in Nigeria right now but he's coming back and will move into Forest's place. He's moving stateside, leaving the *Times*."

Forest's brother River was a Pulitzer-prize-winning photojournalist who had a special knack for documenting war. He worked in some of the most dangerous places in the world. Considering he was a Knight and had more money than god, this was not about earning a living but doing what he believed would help the world become a better place. I had a tremendous amount of respect for him.

I laid Kai down in his bassinet and covered him with his pink blanket. Daisy had mixed the colors up on purpose, saying that she didn't want her child to be slotted away into a preferred gender box.

"How's it going with Mr. Santos."

I sat down next to Daisy and lay my head on her shoulder. She took my hand in hers.

"I don't know," I said sadly. "One minute he's the man who can fall in love with me and then he's the other, who's wanting to make it clear to me that I shouldn't plan a future. *And* what doesn't help is that we're both so busy. When I'm free, he's traveling, and when he's free, I'm busy. We haven't been able to meet since he was here to pick up Silvano. We talk on the phone."

"Good old phone sex," Daisy remarked.

"Oh no, he won't have sex with me virtually or otherwise. I don't know if it's because as he says, he wants to wait and go slow or if it's his way of pushing me away until he stops wanting me."

The front door opened then, and Forest walked in. He wore his standard board shorts and a T-shirt. He gave me a hug before leaning down and kissing his wife on her mouth. He then walked to the bassinet and smiled at Kai.

"Isn't he the most beautiful baby you've ever seen?" he said in awe.

"Well, it's a good thing he got her looks and her brains," I teased.

"Fuck, yeah." Forest grinned at his wife. "I want him to be exactly like her. Red hair, green eyes, and a big heart."

Damn it, I wanted a man to say these things to me. I wanted a man to feel this way about me.

"Yeah, yeah." Daisy waved a hand, but she was flush with joy. "Forest, how do you feel about a long weekend in Golden Valley?"

I raised an eyebrow and then nodded. I'd received an invitation as well for a weekend party to celebrate Paloma and Arsenio's twenty-fifth wedding anniversary. They were housing their guests at the Golden Valley Inn.

"Are you going?" Forest asked me.

"I don't know. I'll have to see," I evaded. I wanted to go, desperately, but I also didn't want to have Alejandro push me away so his family would not know about us.

"I was thinking of leaving on Thursday and coming back Monday. Paloma is giving us a cottage. She said we deserve a break, and she wants to hang out with grandbabies."

Forest took his wife's hand and kissed it. "Sounds like a plan. You can drive with us, Maria."

"Don't," Daisy warned. "He drives like a grandmother."

"I have a baby in the backseat," Forest protested. "But maybe we can take the Escalade and Hector can drive us and have a weekend away as well."

Hector used to work for Forest's parents but was now retired as a butler/majordomo and was living in Daisy's pool house. He was devoted to *Master* Kai and adored Forest and Daisy. Since Forest's parents were terrible people, it was nice to see Forest with a surrogate parent who loved him.

"Come," Daisy insisted. "We'll make sure Alejandro behaves."

Forest raised an eyebrow. "I heard that you're...ah... do we still call it dating when we're grown-ups?" He ran a hand through his blonde hair.

Forest was a ridiculously good-looking man for a beach bum and was as laid back as they came. The fact that he was a judge surprised most people until you saw him in court, where he was totally professional and no-nonsense.

I smiled. "We had that same discussion. I think he had a problem with the term *boy*friend, since he's not a boy any longer."

"He behaves like one though," Daisy pointed out. "Did I tell you about the limericks that Maria came up with?"

I dropped my face in my hands. "Please, don't."

Forest laughed. "I heard something about Alejandro having a big pee-pee."

I shook my head and rose as Kai was fussing. I picked him up and kissed his nose. "I'm going to give him a quick diaper change and bring him back. I think he's ready for some boob."

"Thanks, Maria." Daisy leaned into her husband. I was so happy that Daisy and Forest had found a way back to one another. Sure, they still fought like a house on fire, but that was who they were, and it worked for them.

Alejandro called as soon as I got back home.

"How was your day?" he asked.

"Long but then I went to play with Kai and now I'm feeling relaxed."

"How is Daisy?"

"Happiest mommy I've ever seen," I told him as I poured a glass of wine for myself. "And Forest looks peaceful. They still argue like they always did but I think they've resolved their issues."

"Did you get Isadora's invitation?"

"Yes."

"Are you coming?"

"Do you want me to?"

"Yes. Please. I haven't seen you in weeks and I'm getting desperate."

I smiled as I settled into the sofa. "I'll drive with Forest and Daisy. That way I get some more time with Kai."

"You're in love with that baby," he joked.

And then we both fell silent. I loved babies. I always had. I wanted my own. Of course, I did. So, the question was, what if I got Alejandro but no babies? Would I still want him? Would that be a fair compromise?

"Alejandro?"

"Yes?"

"I miss you."

His breath was short and his voice hoarse, "Go to bed, Maria and show me how much you miss me."

"Only if you'll come with me."

"I'm stone hard, baby."

That night, we made love again. It wasn't enough— but it bonded us, built the intimacy, without which I'd felt untethered.

"I want you in my bed when you're here," he told me as his breathing finally normalized. "I'll get Silvano to stay with my parents. Will you stay with me?" Through the phone screen, I could see his eyes were blazing with possessiveness.

"Yes." My heart soared. He would not push me away. He was going to hold me close.

"Maria," his voice was strained, and he looked like he

was in agony, "I'm losing myself."

"What do you mean?" I put a finger to the screen as if stroking his cheek.

"I want you all the time and I don't mean just sex. And it scares the hell out of me."

"Don't be scared. I'll never hurt you."

"The other day I asked Esme what it meant to love someone. What does it mean to you?"

He was asking me to be vulnerable in front of him. "It means that I'm with you no matter what. That even if you don't want me, it won't change that I want the best for you, always, and I'll always be in your corner. You'll never have to wonder whose side I'm on. I believe love makes us more."

"The sum of the parts is bigger than the individual parts?"

"Yes."

He smiled at me then. "How's your next week?"

I shook my head sadly. "I'm in Phoenix on Tuesday and Wednesday and then in Memphis on Thursday. I will come back on Friday."

His eyes brightened. "Memphis on Thursday?"

I sat up. "Can you make it?"

"Let me check. Keep your evening free. Where are you staying?"

"Ollie usually puts me in that hotel with the ducks."

"The Peabody," he said, amused. "Okay. I'll ask Mercedes to work with Ollie. We'll go to Beale Street and listen to blues all night."

"And eat the best barbecue in the world."

"It's a date, baby."

I laughed then. "Yes, Alejandro, it's a date."

Chapter 19

Alejandro

I wasn't fighting it any longer, this unbearable hunger for Maria. I accepted it. I was trying to come to terms with it.

"I'll call you tonight," I told Silvano and gave him a hug.

"Are you going to go to Beale Street?" he asked.

My son knew I was a Blues fan. "Yeah, I'll probably do that."

"You travel a lot for work, but do you *see* the place you're ever at? Or do you just see the airport and wherever you're meeting people?" Silvano asked as he walked me to the helicopter pad near Golden Valley Inn. It was easier and faster for me to chopper to San Francisco International and take a chartered flight from there to Memphis.

"I'm usually trying to get home, *mi hijo*."

"I'm eleven...twelve in two months," Silvano began, "It's okay for you to not run back home to me. I have a lot of fun staying with *Abuelo* and *Abuela*. And I always have fun with Isa."

I stopped and turned to look at my son. "What exactly are you saying?"

He grinned. "I'm saying that it's okay for you to have a life, Papa."

"I have a life, *mi hijo*."

Silvano nodded. "You're old enough to know what you want...I just...it's none of my business, anyway."

Sometimes, my son surprised me, sometimes he befuddled me. This was the latter. His IQ didn't mean that he was emotionally also at a higher level than his eleven years—but his IQ meant he could grasp concepts better than most grown-ups; that combined with his curiosity meant that he understood more than most kids his age.

I hugged him tight. "Silvano, I'm making no sacrifices. I'm not making compromises. I love you. I love my family. I love Golden Valley."

"I know you do."

I kissed him on his forehead and walked to the helicopter.

I called Isa when I was on the plane to Memphis. I had about five minutes between Zoom meetings.

"Does Silvano know about Maria?" I asked her.

"I don't know."

"What does that mean?"

"He has said nothing to me. And he usually does. But he's like you sometimes and keeps things close to his chest. I wouldn't be surprised if he has guessed."

"How would he guess that?"

"Because you look at her like, she's your world." Isa surprised me.

"Isa, you're such a romantic."

"Alejandro, you're such a moron."

"Does Mama know?"

"I haven't told her, but I don't know if she knows," Isa explained. "Alejandro, why are you hiding this? She's a wonderful woman. It's not like you're dating a stripper, not that there would be anything wrong with that."

I laughed. "I need time. And...I'm on my way to her. Happy?"

"Yes. I love you, Alejandro."

"I love you too, Button."

It was an old nickname. I'd started calling her that because she was cute as a button when she was a baby. Now, when I felt extra loving, the name slipped out.

By the time I got to Memphis, I was behind. I'd missed a meeting and was late for two—and I still had a couple to go. I hoped that when Maria was back from her meetings, I'd be free as well so we could spend an evening together, undisturbed by our various responsibilities.

I called Mercedes, my assistant, and asked if she'd got everything arranged for my dinner with Maria.

"Yes, Alejandro," she said patiently. "When do I get to meet this Maria? I've struck up a really good rapport with her assistant who, by the way, is in love with her."

"Is he now?" Mercedes was my assistant, and it was hard to hide anything from her, especially regarding my schedule. But she was discreet and had worked for me since she graduated from university nearly a decade ago.

"Fine, I'll mind my own business," she said with a long-suffering sigh. "Have a good evening and if you need me, let me know, boss."

Maria had left me a key to her suite at the reception and I settled in quickly, onto my next meeting and the next. I spread my stuff in the living room of the suite on the coffee table, more comfortable there than the desk. I walked around during my calls—not able to sit still for a long time.

My last meeting was with my brother Aurelio, who hated our weekly meetings—and he'd hate this one even more because we were not meeting at his house but over the phone.

"Where are you?"

"Memphis."

"What's in Memphis?"

I cleared my throat and let it go. "Who."

"Okay, who is in Memphis?"

"Maria Caruso."

"What?"

"Oh, come on, Aurelio. Are you telling me your girlfriend hasn't told you about Maria?"

"I know who Maria is. Are you telling me you're... what are you doing with her?" He paused and then added, "I don't want to know."

"I'm...ah...dating her."

"Dude, I don't want to know. You tell me and then Mama will ask me, and I don't like lying to her. You know that?"

"You have no problem lying to her, your problem is that you get caught."

Aurelio sighed. "Yeah. So you're dating. How's that going for you?"

"How's your on-again, off-again going with that lawyer?"

"I'm also...ah...dating her, which means we're probably on again, but I never know with her. She confuses me. She's *very* different from the women I usually...anyway, why are we talking about this shit like a bunch of girls? Next, you're going to tell me about your feelings," he barked. "Let's talk about work. I hired that training person you wanted me to bring in, and she'll train the hands. I'm hoping this will solve some of the work management issues we've been having."

Maria came in as I finished my call with Aurelio. Her face lit up when she saw me but there were circles around her eyes and she was...well, sad.

I opened my arms, and she threw down her laptop bag on the floor and gave me a hug. *Cinnamon and chocolate.* I groaned and angled my face so I could find her mouth with mine. It had been far too long since I'd tasted her. I hungrily ate her, letting my tongue swirl into her, moving in and out as I would if I were inside her. I was hard almost immediately and the way her hips drummed against mine, she was just as aroused.

"Hey, baby," I whispered, pushing her hair away from her face. She'd tied it up as she always did in a ponytail when she was working but a few strands had escaped. I pulled away her hair tie so I could feel the silk of her hair around my hands.

"I'm so glad you're here." She buried her face in my chest. "It's been such a horrible day."

I felt my dress shirt go damp, and I pulled her face away so I could look at her. She was crying. "Baby, what happened?"

She shook her head and closed her eyes, tears rolling down her cheeks. I kissed her wet face, wanting to soothe her.

"Just hold me," she murmured. "Just let me feel you."

I held her and stroked her back. I found her mouth again and again. I couldn't stop kissing her. I'd missed her so much. More than I had realized, more than I had wanted to admit.

"Let's take a bath," I suggested. "We have..." I looked at my watch, "a couple of hours before we need to be ready."

She raised an eyebrow. "Ready for what?"

I kissed her nose, excited to take her out, give her an evening she'd remember and hopefully dissipate whatever had her so upset. "It's a surprise."

As she undressed, I drew a bath for us. I poured us a glass of champagne each and let her get in first. I joined her in the large bathtub and sat next to her.

"*Salud.*" I clinked my glass against hers. "You want to tell me why you were so upset."

She nodded. "I'm here for meetings with St. Jude Children's Hospital. The Caruso Foundation has some programs running here. I spent the afternoon after the meetings in the wards...and this..." Her eyes watered and she bit her lip as if controlling herself so she could speak, "This boy I used to always see whenever I came, Cole, he didn't make it. I didn't even know. And..."

I took her champagne glass and put hers and mine on the ledge of the tub. I pulled her close. Of course, she'd be upset about something like this. I had wondered if something had happened at work, a failed project, money lost...but it hadn't felt right. Maria didn't care about those things. She cared about people. I'd read the profiles that continually stated how Maria had kickstarted the Caruso Foundation since she became CEO. Javier Caruso, her father, had let the foundation his mother had started languish. His daughter had no such plans. She was making time in her busy schedule to support charitable works. I felt my heart swell with pride. I was with a warm, loving woman who didn't just write a check, she got her hands dirty.

"Will you give me a hint about this surprise?" she asked after she felt better and was back to sipping champagne.

When I shook my head, she chuckled, "What should I wear?"

"Clothes are *not* optional," I remarked unhelpfully. "But what you wear doesn't matter. Show up in pajamas for all I care. Not that you have any."

She slept raw, which I could not do, what with a kid running around in my house. When Silvano was younger, he'd come into my bed in the middle of the night. He didn't do that as often now, though sometimes he'd have a nightmare and sneak under my covers. But tonight, I intended to stay naked and keep her the same. Tonight, I wanted to fill myself with her for the long weeks ahead when we'd probably not be able to see one another.

"Alejandro." She turned to me and nuzzled my throat. "I want you."

I smiled, and my hand squeezed one of her breasts, and then played with the nipple. "I want you too, baby. So much."

She put her glass away and straddled me.

"Maria," I breathed as I felt the heat of her pussy against my erect cock. "I want to—" She took me inside, "fuck." I bucked up into her, slamming inside her. *Fuck!* This felt so right.

I took a nipple in my mouth and suckled hard, biting her. My hands were on her hips, forcing her up and down, controlling the pace. She was whimpering, and I loved to hear the sounds she made.

"You like riding me." My voice was thick, almost unrecognizable.

"Yes." I could barely hear her. Her eyes were closed, and she looked ethereal on top of me.

"Eyes on me," I commanded.

She opened her eyes lazily; they were glazed with pleasure. "Make me come, Alejandro."

Whatever thoughts I had about taking this slow vanished. I swelled inside her.

"Yes, baby. You know I will."

I found her clit with one hand and kept the other tight on her hip. I'd probably leave marks on her, but instead of feeling bad about it, I felt satisfaction at marking my territory. *What the fuck?* She made me feel like a caveman, wanting to thump my chest and roar, "My woman."

"Alejandro," she moaned when I surged inside her at the same time as I bit her nipple and squeezed her clit. The combination was too much, and I felt her spasms, milking the cum out of me.

She lay against me, exhausted and replete and I held her, playing with her nipple, nuzzling one, and then the other with my mouth.

"It's never been like this," she said in awe.

No. It's never been like this for me either. I didn't say the words; I couldn't. These were the things you never said because they led to misunderstandings about the longevity of a relationship.

"I'm memorable, huh?" I teased.

She chuckled. "Well, there was Ivan. He was a physical trainer and well, you know how they are?"

"Yeah, they compensate for their small dicks with muscles." I slapped her ass, and she cried out.

"Ivan, is it? Was he better?"

She looked at me, mischief in her eyes. "He was—" I spanked her again. "Hey, you don't know what I was going to say," she protested.

"I was making sure you wouldn't say something... ah...foolish or untrue."

She kissed me on my lips. I was still inside her, still semi-erect, spent, but if she moved around like this, I could be ready to go again and at my age, it was saying something.

"No one and nothing has ever been like this." She looked me in the eye when she spoke.

"Good." I lifted her, and then, because I couldn't let her go, let her slide back on me. "We need to get ready, *Duquesa*, so I can show your surprise."

The sadness in her eyes was gone, and I felt like a fucking god for giving her pleasure, for making her smile, for making her happy.

Chapter 20

Maria

As the sun began its slow descent beyond the horizon, casting warm hues across the Memphis skyline, I felt a sense of excitement in the air. Alejandro had something special planned for us, and my heart fluttered with anticipation.

For the night, I went all-get-out sexy and wore a daring Saint Laurent mini dress—a classic LBD with a halter and plunging V-neck. The dress had an open back and pleated skirt, giving it a glamorous feminine touch. I paired it with a Dolce & Gabbana bolero that would keep me warm in the cool February Memphian evening.

"Can you walk in these shoes? Or do you want me to carry you?" he admired my Jimmy Choo booties.

"I may drive a boring car, but in what I wear, I go all out. If I couldn't walk in heels, it would be because I broke a leg or something," I chimed.

We walked hand in hand in the direction of the Pyramid, Memphis's iconic structure that stood tall and majestic. Its glass panels caught the fading sunlight, creating a mesmerizing play of reflections. Alejandro's smile was contagious, and with every step, I could sense that this evening was going to be unforgettable.

"The Pyramid?" I asked as he pulled me inside the building.

"You have to have patience, *mi preciosa*." He kissed me lightly on my lips.

We stepped into the elevator, and as the doors closed, my heart raced. Alejandro had never done anything like this before. We hadn't been dating long, but tonight felt different, as though he had something truly enchanting up his sleeve—a way of showing me how much I mean to him. The elevator ride was filled with a mix of nerves and excitement, the anticipation building with each passing floor.

When the doors finally opened, I found myself at the pinnacle of the Pyramid, on the observatory deck that overlooked the entire city. The sight took my breath away, the twinkling lights of Memphis stretched out before us, the Mississippi River shimmering in the moonlight. Soft music played in the background, adding to the romantic ambiance.

I followed Alejandro as he led me to a beautifully set table near the glass walls. Candles flickered, casting a warm glow over the scene—delicate flowers, fine China, and an atmosphere that felt like a dream. My eyes widened in surprise and wonder; I couldn't believe he had arranged all of this.

He pulled out a chair for me, his gaze warm and full of affection. As I took my seat, his fingers brushed against mine, sending a shiver of anticipation down my spine. I watched as he settled into his seat across from me, his eyes never leaving mine. There was a particular vulnerability in his expression, as if he was sharing a piece of his heart with me.

A server approached us, offering menus and a bottle of champagne. As I glanced over the menu, I felt Alejandro's gaze on me, waiting for my reaction. I looked through the glass walls, taking in the breathtaking view and realizing how much thought he had put into this evening. I looked back at him, my heart swelling with emotion.

"I wanted tonight to be special." His voice was a mixture of nervousness and sincerity. "To create a memory that we'll cherish forever."

I couldn't help the smile that spread across my face. "You've already succeeded," I replied, my voice soft but filled with genuine appreciation.

I had asked for Memphis barbecue and got it in spades, gourmet style. As the night unfolded, each course was a delight to the senses, and our conversation flowed effortlessly. We laughed and shared stories, and it felt like time had been suspended just for us. The city lights danced in the background, and I couldn't imagine a more perfect setting.

As the evening drew close, Alejandro stood, extending his hand towards me. "May I have this dance?"

I took his hand, a warm feeling of contentment washing over me. We swayed to the music, the world around us fading as we held each other close. The city lights twinkled around us, a symphony of their own.

I remembered the first time we'd danced, the first

time we had kissed in his mother's garden. Looking into his eyes, I realized how lucky I was to have him in my life. Atop the Pyramid's observatory deck, this moment felt like a fairytale brought to life, a night of enchantment and love that I would forever treasure.

We were quiet when we were driven back to the hotel. We held hands, but the tension between us was at a fever pitch. The evening had been perfect, and we both wanted more. The little interlude in the bathtub had not been enough.

We silently went up the elevator, not letting go of each other's hand.

As soon as we were inside the room, he slammed me against the door. His mouth on mine, hands removing the bolero. He looked at me and took a deep breath. "You're so fucking sexy."

He slipped his hand under my dress, and I gasped when he moved my panties aside to dip his finger inside me.

"Wet. You're wet, baby."

I moaned when he inserted two fingers, and my hips moved of their own accord. "And tight. Do you know you hold me like a vice when I'm inside you? And then when you come, my head feels like it's going to explode."

My lips sought his, and he gave me what I wanted, kissing me with a voraciousness that spoke volumes of his hunger for me.

He unzipped my dress and stepped back when it pooled at my feet. I had worn the sexiest Agent Provocateur underwear I had. A lacy black bra, garter belts, silky hosiery that was so sheer I hardly felt them against my skin, and matching panties.

"*Dios mío*, are you trying to give me a heart attack?"

He seemed mesmerized, and I was glad. I'd worked to make him look at me exactly as he did right now.

"Undress me," he demanded.

I stepped up to him and took his jacket off. He stood there like I was a *houri,* and he was my master. I unbuttoned his shirt, and he helped me by removing his cufflinks, throwing them atop the coffee table without paying attention. My hands went to his belt.

"Kneel," he ordered.

Desire pooled between my legs. I was not a submissive, but there was something about being commanded to service a man like Alejandro, masculine, potent, unabashedly sexual.

I kneeled and unbuckled his belt. I stroked his erection over his pants and heard his indrawn breath.

"You teasing me, baby?"

I looked up at him and bit my lower lip. "Maybe."

"Shoes first, *Duquesa.*"

Any other man would have been told to go to hell. But for him, I bent, and he groaned as he watched me. "You have the sexiest ass in the world. Will you let me take you there?"

I immediately raised my head, fear in my eyes. I'd never done that before.

He smiled gently at me. "I'll never hurt you."

I nodded. Once I removed his shoes and socks, my hands were shaking with anticipation. "Alejandro," I moaned.

"Slowly, baby, so we make this night last. Okay? Now, the pants."

He stepped out of his pants, and his hands tangled in my hair. "Open, Maria."

I opened my mouth, and he slid his erection inside me. "Hold still and let me...just...fuck...." He thrust in and out.

I let him plunder my mouth until tears came down my cheeks as I felt him against the back of my throat. But I wouldn't let him pull away. He may order, but he was mine as much as I was his.

He yanked himself away, gasping. "I'm not coming in your mouth. Not this time."

He carried me to bed and laid me down. Now it was his turn to undress me, and he did so slowly. Starting with my booties, and as he did, he kissed my thighs, right between the hose and my panties. Then he removed my hose, so slowly that it drove me out of my mind.

He took off my bra, and then when I lay in my panties, he watched me, stroking his erection. "I can't believe you're here with me. I've been dreaming of this for days."

I smiled and stretched languidly. "Come inside me, Alejandro."

We'd decided to not use condoms because we were monogamous and clean. And I was on birth control. I knew this had been a big step for him, considering how his wife had gotten pregnant by *accident*.

He took my panties off, touching my legs as he went. And then, when I was completely naked, he went down on me. He licked slowly, smelling, and tasting. "You're delicious; you know that."

"I need to come."

"I know, baby. I know. But I want to keep you here for..." He stroked the rosette between my ass cheeks, and I gasped, almost coming off the bed. "It's okay. Just relax, *mi amor*."

He did it again, dragging my juices from pussy to anus.

When he inserted a finger inside the tight hole, we both moaned. "So tight. You're so tight. You're going to squeeze me so hard. I can barely get a finger in."

Then he licked me again, his fingers opening me up. He was gentle. He knew I'd never done anal before.

I came suddenly, loudly, and he moved up my body to kiss me. I tasted myself, and it was erotic as hell.

He slid inside me and pumped with fervor. "Maria," he bit out my name, "Tell me you love me."

My eyes flew open, and I felt extremely vulnerable, but I couldn't deny him. "I love you, Alejandro."

"Again." He thrust again and again, and then pulled out to probe the opening he'd been opening up for a good part of the night.

"I love you," I whispered.

He had his weight on his forearms, and he was shaking slightly. "Is this okay?"

"Please," I was beyond thought, desperate to find release.

He thrust in slowly, and I'd expected it to hurt, but it didn't. I was aroused and sensitive. When he slid inside completely, I exploded. The pleasure was almost painful.

He moved a hand to my clit, and I cried out. "I can't."

"Yes you can, baby. I know you can." He stroked me gently, and as he increased his pace, his fingers sped up.

We came together, and as we did, I screamed my love for him again. There was something in his eyes, almost akin to a cruel satisfaction like he had me now, which he did. It unsettled me, but soon enough, pleasure took over, and I let the doubts slide away.

Chapter 21

Alejandro

"You're getting married?" I was surprised to hear that the perpetual bachelor, my friend Atlas Callahan, who owned Callahan Vineyard with his siblings, was getting engaged.

"I thought you just started seeing...." I didn't remember *her* name. If I remembered all the names of the women Atlas was monogamously dating, that would include the entire Santa Barbara wine country.

I had a meeting in Santa Barbara, after which I went to the Callahan Vineyard tasting room in the city's Funk Zone district to meet with Atlas. We'd known each other a long time since we were both in similar industries. Winemaking in Santa Barbara was a farming business, and we'd become friends over the years, dealing with similar work-related challenges.

"I'm not marrying Daphne."

We sat at the counter of the beautifully decorated tasting room. Callahan wines were premium, expensive wines that won awards around the world. I enjoyed their Pinot Noir and drank a 2016 vintage as we talked.

"Daphne, is the woman you work with?" I remembered.

He nodded. "Yeah. She's my vice president of marketing, and...*fuck*, I thought we'd get married, eventually. She's great. Smart. Sharp. And she knows the business."

"Okay," I frowned. "*Amigo*, if you like the girl, marry her. I don't understand."

He ran his fingers through his blonde hair. Atlas Callahan was a pretty boy and usually made the cover of Wine Spectator at least once a year because he looked like a fucking GQ model. He ran a successful business with his brother Orion, the winemaker who knew his vine and wine. Their younger sister, Ariel, lived and worked in New York.

"Do you remember Enzo Brooks?"

"Yeah. You bought his wine label out a few years ago."

"He was my father's closest friend, and after my parents died, Enzo stepped in and helped us out. Many people helped us out and thank god for that. Otherwise, Callahan Vineyards would have disappeared. Enzo is dying. He has stage four pancreatic cancer. His time is limited. His daughter, well, he wants me to marry his daughter."

I cleared my throat. "Atlas, you don't have to marry some girl because her daddy helped you out."

"He's worried about her."

"Then give her some money. But marriage? Come on. That's serious. If you don't love this girl, don't marry her."

Atlas nodded. "I don't know what to do. Enzo is insisting."

"Have you met this girl? Do you know her?"

"Yeah, sure. I've known her since she was born. She's a kid. Ten years younger than me. I've never thought of her as a...woman."

"Don't get married, especially to someone you know isn't the right woman. Trust me; you don't need that heartache."

"You speak from experience," Atlas acknowledged.

"Fucking A."

Atlas raised his glass and clinked it against mine. "I hear you're dating again."

"How would you know that?"

"It's a small world, buddy. Mateo Silva is an old friend and one of the people who helped save Callahan Vineyards. He invested in us, gave us an infusion of capital when we needed it most. He came by with his wife for a wine tasting we were doing in West Hollywood. His wife mentioned it."

I shook my head. "My mother probably knows... which is..."

He laughed. "Paloma naming your grandkids yet?"

"She doesn't know about Maria. She's after Aurelio. He's seeing a lawyer from LA. Someone Mateo also knows. It's one incestuous circle we got going here."

I finished my glass of wine and made a cutting gesture when Atlas raised the bottle to pour me some more. "I have to drive."

"Speaking of weddings, are you getting married soon?" Atlas wondered.

I scoffed. "Hell no, *muchacho*. I have Silvano to think about. The way Anika left before he even knew her protected him. I can't have a situation where he gets attached to some woman I'm banging and..." It bothered me that I used that word to talk about what Maria and I did. Her beauty, her elegance...no one *banged* Maria. You made love to her. "Anyway," I continued, "I'm not marrying anyone. Relationships don't last, and I don't need to retest that theory. Once was enough."

We talked a little about business, and then I drove home, wondering about myself. As soon as I was with another man, I'd turned into a typical locker-room-talking alpha male, hadn't I? Maria wasn't just some woman I was *banging*. She was...fuck, I didn't know who she was.

My phone rang as if on cue, and I saw her name flash on my screen. I ignored the call. Since that night in Memphis nearly three weeks ago, thankfully, we'd both been too busy to find a time to meet. Yeah, I was running again. *Alert the fucking media.*

I couldn't get over how great it had felt to have her tell me she loved me when I was inside her. I could almost feel the Neanderthal coming out of me to claim his mate. But I wasn't ready. I met this woman a few months ago. No one made marriage plans until and unless you'd spent a year or two in a relationship. That was normal. And by that time, I'd be what, forty-four, forty-five? I wasn't interested in having more children. I saw men my age with their second wives, starting all over again with babies, and I couldn't imagine myself doing that. As a single father, though I had a lot of help from my family, it hadn't been an easy road to raise Silvano alone. I had no regrets. The kid was awesome, and I felt lucky every day that he was my son. But there was no way I could do it again. Maria wanted children. She wanted it all. I wasn't the man for her.

Aurelio was with Silvano at my place when I got home. Either Silvano would go to my parent's place, or someone would be with him at ours when I was not around. I was lucky to have so many people who loved and cared for my son. Isa usually was the one who spent the most time with Silvano. She worked in the Inn, so he hung out there, doing his homework, trying to convince the chef to teach him how to cook.

But Isa had a big wedding from what I could see in the parking lot as I drove into the estate, which probably meant she'd asked Aurelio to babysit (though we'd never call it that) Silvano.

"Papa." Silvano flew to me and hugged me. Most kids his age didn't want to hug their parents, but not my son. In our family, we hugged a lot. Paloma had taught us that, and we said, "I love you" a lot to one another.

Once, Silvano was on his computer playing a game with friends, and he'd responded to my *I love you* with his own when I'd come to leave a snack for him in his room. As I was leaving, I heard him say to his friends, "What? Don't you love your fathers? Well, that's just sad."

"How was your day, little man?"

Aurelio went into the kitchen and came back with a beer for himself and me. "I fed him. Mama and Papa are away, and Isa asked to stay the *fuck* away from the Inn."

I sighed. "Grilled cheese?"

"It's the one thing I can make," Aurelio admitted proudly.

"And you make it very well, Tío," Silvano agreed.

"Kid's gonna make a fine diplomat; he knows how to butter up all the right people in the right way."

"I'm off to my room, I'm playing Diablo with friends." He gave me a quick peck on the cheek and ran.

I sat down next to Aurelio. "I met Atlas today. And he's getting married to Enzo Brook's daughter."

"I thought he was seeing whatsername who worked with him."

"Yeah. But Enzo is dying and wants Atlas to marry his daughter."

Aurelio shuddered. "*Cristo*. Marrying someone because someone else wants you to is a disaster waiting to happen. You have to *really* want to marry the woman, otherwise...it's going to be a nightmare."

"*You* almost got married to someone you didn't really want."

Aurelio put his feet on my coffee table and leaned back on the couch. "Almost being the operative word. Jenn is a nice girl. But she wanted to become Mrs. Santos more than she wanted to marry me. One day, when I return home from work, she's waiting for me. She's made dinner. Fucking meatloaf and whatever. She tells me she wants to be a good housewife."

I took a draw of my beer.

"I'm like, *honey, you have a job, you're a successful accountant*, and she says she won't work after we get married. What would the point be? She'd keep the house, she says. I say, it doesn't need keeping. I have a cleaning crew that comes once a week. I have Paloma and her elves doing laundry and stocking up my fridge. I mean, what would Jenn do all day? I ask her, and she says she wants to be Mrs. Santos. I broke it off that night. We didn't even eat the meatloaf."

Finally, I got the true story. There were rumors because Aurelio had said nothing to anyone except that he was sorry it didn't work out with Jenn.

"Many people believe you cheated on her," I told him.

"She's been telling that to people. I think it makes her feel better. And if it does, who am I to disabuse anyone of that?"

I raised my bottle and touched it to his. "You think Isa will get married?"

"Of course. Look at her. She loves weddings. She'll probably want a big shindig with half the county in attendance."

I nodded. "Is she seeing anyone?"

Aurelio gave me a piercing look. "Do I look like someone who'd know?"

I shrugged. True, Aurelio lived in his bubble and didn't much care who did what and with whom.

"Why don't *you* want to get married? I know my reasons. I have Silvano."

"I *want* to marry," Aurelio assured me. "I want to marry the right woman. I don't need to fall in love, but I'd like to find someone who gets me, doesn't get in the way, doesn't want drama."

I grinned. "And there's drama with that lawyer from LA?"

He groaned. "Caro is nothing but drama. *Dios mío*, she has a temper on her. It makes the sex hotter than hot, but she also knows how to knee me in the nuts. *And* she won't let me get away with my shit. You know?"

"I know." Maria didn't let me get away with mine either. She didn't fight or argue but laid it out for me. And she was clear about walking away if I didn't get with the program.

"And I like that about her. I like the fire she brings. But she confuses me."

"I think women do that, well, the right women or maybe the wrong women...who the fuck knows," I shrugged. "I'm not confused about Maria. She knows what she wants, and I know I don't want what she wants."

"What does she want?"

"Husband, babies...white picket fence."

"We can paint your fence white, dude."

I laughed and put my feet up on the coffee table. He wore sneakers; I wore dress shoes. He was in a pair of faded jeans; I was in a tailored suit. As different as we were, we were as close as brothers could be.

"I don't want children. I have Silvano."

"And?"

"*And* I don't want to take the risk of getting married again."

Aurelio nodded. "I recently read this study. Silvano sent it to me. They did a median follow-up for eleven years and found that single fathers were more likely to die sooner than partnered fathers and had a mortality risk twice as high as other parents."

That explained why Silvano had been talking to me about living my life and not holding back because of him. "That's bullshit."

"There are quite a few studies that say so. Also,

you'll find this nugget of data interesting. According to research, when dating fails, single fathers, unlike regular men, take rejections extra hard, internalizing that they're flawed as *both* a parent and partner."

"What are you saying?" I demanded.

Aurelio rose and grinned at me. "Getting married and having children could extend your life. Staying single will drive you to an early grave. Therefore, I intend to get married...as soon as I can get past this crazy woman I'm seeing and find an appropriate partner."

"Yeah, I can see you have it all figured out," I muttered sarcastically.

When he said goodnight, I gave him the finger. He was laughing as he left my place.

Chapter 22

Maria

It was a winter wonderland-themed party, and Isadora wanted everyone to dress up to the nines. It was also cold in Golden Valley. Spring was probably on its way, but right now, the temperature was in the low forties, and when the sun was down, there was a distinct bite in the air.

Mark was traveling, visiting a friend in Seattle, and couldn't make the Paloma and Arsenio's anniversary party, which I vociferously complained about.

"I wish you were here," I admonished again as I got ready in my room at the Golden Valley Inn for dinner at the farmhouse.

Isadora had planned a two-day anniversary party for her parents. Most of the seventy-five guests were arriving on Saturday morning—but since I drove with Daisy and co, I'd had to leave work early on a Friday afternoon to get here.

"I'm getting laid tonight, so yeah, I'm glad I'm in Seattle." Mark winked at me as I stopped to stare at him on my phone.

"Who? What? Who?"

"A cardio surgeon I met at a conference in LA. We're...ah...exploring dating."

"But you went there to meet Aiden." A friend who was definitely not gay and had a wife and three kids who looked to Mark as an uncle.

"I can spend time with Aiden and the kids *and* also hook up with...Maria, what are you wearing?"

I stopped in mid-motion as I was zipping up a Khaite beige wool dress. It was long with full sleeves and hugged my skin in a warm embrace. I felt comfortable and attractive in it.

"Why?"

"It's dinner with the family, isn't it?"

"Yes."

"This dress is cleavage city. You should save the seduction for when you and Alejandro are alone."

I groaned and looked at my cleavage. "I like this dress, and it's cold. Is it really too much?"

Mark sighed. "Wear a scarf around your neck, and I'm sure you'll get through the evening without spilling your tits into the salad."

I found a Missoni scarf that matched the dress and modeled it for Mark.

"Just because I'm gay doesn't mean I'm into dressing women," he remarked.

"I'm not women, I'm your sister."

"You look very nice." Mark looked at his watch and

grinned. "Time for me to mosey on."

"What's this cardio's name?"

"Xavier. He's from South Africa but lives and works in Seattle. I'll send you a picture. *Ciao*, sis, have fun."

I picked up my phone and looked at the photo he sent. Dr. Xavier was hot. He had short curly hair. His skin was coffee-dark, and he had obvious muscles under the suit he wore in the photo, which seemed to have been taken at some hospital event. He had a little Blair Underwood going for him. I replied with a thumbs-up emoji.

I put on my brown knee-high Chanel boots that were soft as butter. I left my hair loose because Alejandro liked it like that. My makeup was subtle, I didn't want to overdo it. I looked perfect for a casual dinner at my boyfriend's family home.

I took the stairs down to the lobby. It was not my first time in the inn, and as always, it made me feel like I had entered a realm of refined opulence and comfort. The lobby was the embodiment of understated elegance, with its high ceilings, soft lighting, and tastefully arranged seating areas. A grand chandelier hung from the center, casting a warm glow and accentuating the luxurious materials and textures adorning the space. Plush sofas and armchairs beckoned guests to relax, and a cozy fireplace crackled in the corner, providing a welcoming ambiance.

I still had nearly twenty-five minutes to get to the main house. I didn't want to get there early. As it was, I was anxious to meet Alejandro's family when they knew he and I were seeing each other.

I smiled at the night manager who came up to me.

"Miss Caruso, we have a car waiting for you to drive

you to the main house when you're ready."

I nodded and looked at my watch, feeling sheepish. I was like an eager child, waiting to get to the amusement park. "I'm early. I thought I'll have a drink."

"Of course." He held out his hand, and I walked with him.

"How has your stay been so far?" he asked.

"Very well, thank you. You must be getting ready for the big party tomorrow night."

The night manager grinned. "Isa is a taskmaster and *very* good at ensuring we all do what needs to be done. I have no doubt Arsenio and Paloma will have an anniversary party for the history books."

"Well, it's a twenty-fifth wedding anniversary."

The night manager's face softened. "My wife and I look at them and know that's the kind of marriage we want to have."

We reached the bar, which was a masterpiece of design, blending the rustic charm of California's agricultural heritage with the sophistication expected of a five-star establishment. As I entered the bar, I was immediately enveloped in an atmosphere that transported me to a bygone era. It had a speakeasy feel.

The laughter, clinking glasses, and the soothing notes of live acoustic music filling the air created an unforgettable mood that promised to linger long after the last sip of cocktail was savored.

I looked up at the wooden beams traversing the ceiling, evoking the ambiance of a traditional barn, while reclaimed wood and exposed brick walls contributed to the authentic, lived-in feel. Soft, ambient lighting threw a gentle glow over the space, creating an intimate and inviting setting.

The bar had a variety of seating options, catering to different preferences. High-top wooden tables with wrought-iron accents offered a casual yet refined space where several small groups of people were gathered. Plush leather barstools lined the intricately carved wooden bar counter, and I sat there, leaving a seat empty between me and two men who were having a business meeting as there was a lot of talk about water rights, always a point of discussion in California farmland.

The bartender was a young woman with a bright smile. "Hi, I'm Skyler, the mixologist this evening." She pushed a leather-bound menu toward me.

The menu was handwritten, which was another one of those beautiful touches that made the bar delightful, as did the carefully chosen rustic elements that paid homage to Golden Valley's agricultural heritage. Vintage farm tools decorated the walls. The highlight was a statement piece, which looked like an antique plow head repurposed as a decorative focal point behind the bar.

"We also have an excellent wine list," Skylar offered. "Last page of the menu has the wines by the glass."

I looked through and ordered a Golden Martini, which was described as being a boozy, zesty martini on the wetter side, made with Tanqueray 10, Cucielo Blanco vermouth, Fino sherry, and orange bitters.

I turned to face the wall of windows to watch the sun setting over the Sierra National Forest, casting a warm glow. The snow-capped mountains were much closer here than in Los Angeles and looking at the forest and nature made me realize why Alejandro loved living here. He'd said as much. He didn't mind traveling. He didn't mind staying in hotels in a city. But his home was Golden Valley, where nature was close.

I turned when I heard Skylar putting my drink on the counter. I took a sip and nodded appreciatively. Skylar flushed with pleasure.

Mateo walked into the bar then and grinned at me. We hugged, and he took a seat next to me. "Isn't this a great bar?"

I nodded. "Yeah. I didn't expect it to be this busy?"

"This is a local hangout. And, of course, the guests crowd the place when there's a wedding or a party. According to Isa, the Inn is *very* successful. She's made it into something in just two short years." Mateo was obviously proud of the young woman he thought of as a sister.

Mateo ordered a Macallan scotch, and we cheered. "Where's Raya?"

"She went to the main house as soon as we arrived in the afternoon. We came early. Alejandro's assistant arranged for us to be taken around the property. The Santos are giving us a few acres to build a house."

I put my hand on Mateo's. "That's wonderful."

He nodded, and I think I saw his eyes go moist for the first time since I knew him. "We're so grateful. We want to live here. Build a life here."

"I'm so happy for you."

"Speaking of making a life here, how are things with you and Alejandro?"

I groaned and took a long sip of my drink. "It's complicated."

"How?"

Mateo and I had become friends in the past several months, and I didn't mind him asking the question. It surprised me that I had so easily trusted many of the people Mark and I had met through Esme and her marriage to Dec. Mark had become even closer to Mateo, Forest, and Dec as he was part of the Thursday-night poker group that met at Mateo's place.

"As soon as he feels something, he pulls away. And then he comes back...almost desperate and..." I waved a hand, unable to find the right word.

"Hungry?" Mateo asked.

I nodded.

"I speak from experience because I did the same with Raya. I wanted her *so* much. I was afraid of wanting her, so I pulled away whenever I felt it was getting too serious. But then I didn't know what it meant to fall in love, what it meant to be in love. Once I did, everything changed."

I licked my lips and felt a wave of sorrow. "I don't think he loves me, Mateo. I don't think he's ever going to let himself fall. He's worried about the impact on his son. And I understand that. I do."

"But it doesn't make it hurt less."

"How could I fall in love with a man I barely knew?"

"Love is not about how much you know someone, but how deeply you feel connected to their soul."

"Rumi?"

Mateo laughed. "Yes. It's something Paloma told me once. Speaking of which, I think it's time to go."

Chapter 23

Alejandro

Silvano insisted on sitting next to Maria. I insisted on sitting as far away from her as I could. My mother noticed everything, and I didn't want her to know, not because she'd nag me, but to protect her. She'd be hurt when the relationship ended. She already liked Maria.

I also didn't want Silvano to suspect that Maria and I were together. I didn't want him to get his hopes up, considering he was worried about my life expectancy because I was single.

"Stop looking at her." Isadora elbowed me hard in my stomach.

"Ow." I rubbed my stomach.

"Oh please, there's a better chance my elbow will break before you get hurt."

I put an arm around Isadora and kissed her on her

forehead. "Baby sister, you pack a punch."

"You should tell Mama about her. She's going to suspect the way you both keep eye-fucking each other."

I pulled my arm away and took a swig of wine. *"Dios mío,* Isa. It's disconcerting to hear my baby sister use the f-word."

"You keep calling me fucking baby sister, and see how well I can swear," she threatened.

Maria laughed then, and I couldn't help it. I was mesmerized. She sat by my father at the head of the table, across from my mother. Silvano was next to her. Forest sat next to Paloma, who was holding Kai as he slept. His wife sat next to him. They both touched each other all the time. A stroke here, a caress there. It was almost subconscious.

I watched Mateo and Raya—and they were as close a couple as Arsenio and Paloma were. I had met Mateo for the first time when he came to Golden Valley looking for Raya. I had known then that those two were made for each other. Mateo also had a habit of touching his wife, and holding her if they were standing or sitting. He'd confessed to me that since she'd run away that one time, he needed to keep her close. He worried she'd disappear again. Raya had done nothing to make him feel that way, but the idea of losing her scared the life out of him.

I felt that way about my family. I was protective of them. I loved them and said it often to them. Paloma had made us, as Aurelio mock protested, a *huggy kissy* family. We were all grateful.

Hector sat across from me and in between Raya and Aurelio. I enjoyed getting to know him. He was interesting. He was British with a distinctive career as a medic in the Gulf War. He'd taken over as the house manager for Forest's parents and now was retired. He was now living the *retired* life in Daisy's pool house.

"Miss Daisy works too much," he told me. "And Master Forest is the same. Someone has to take care of them and Master Kai."

His affection for his adopted family was palpable, as was how Forest and Daisy looked up to him, not as someone who used to work for the Forest family but as a surrogate grandfather for their son.

It made sense that the Santos family had become close with the Knights, Mateo, and Raya. We were all people who valued family, blood and otherwise.

"The Beckmans are going to be delayed," Isadora moaned when she saw a message on her phone.

"They're our parent's closest friends. They used to have a farm here, and now they're retired, living in Oregon," I explained for Hector's benefit.

Isadora got up, her fingers typing away at her phone, and our mother glared at her. She looked up from her phone and announced. "Ah…sorry, all, I need to—"

"Where do you think you're going, young lady? And why do you have your phone with you? You know the rules. No phones at the dinner table."

Isador sighed. "Mama—"

I pulled her arm, and she flopped back down on her chair. I held out my hand, and she sulkily gave me her phone.

"I need to prepare things," she protested.

"After dinner." I put her phone next to me.

I watched as Maria rose, laughing about something and then headed to the bathroom. I felt like a teenager, but enough was enough. I gave Maria a five-minute head start.

I picked up Isadora's phone. "I'll just put it away."

"Of course, you will," she said, not letting me even pretend that was why I was leaving the table.

I followed Maria. The guest bathroom was through the hallway. She was walking out of the bathroom when I caught up with her.

"Hi." I took her arm and started to walk her away from the dining room.

"Where are we going?" she asked.

"Keep your voice down, my mother has bat ears." I felt like a kid. No responsibilities, nothing, just the joy of being with the girl I liked.

I took her to the room I grew up in, the one I stayed in even now when I stayed the night, which was rare. It was a large farmhouse with ten-plus bedrooms. So, Mama had enough space to keep our rooms for us as well as have guests over when needed. Usually, she'd place people in the cottages on the property that were part of the Golden Valley Inn.

"What are you doing?" she giggled, and I loved the sound.

I locked the door and watched her walk around the room. "Was this yours?"

I came up to her and pulled her into my arms. "I've missed you." I kissed her hard.

She smiled at me. "I missed you too."

"I wanted to catch up at the Inn with you, but then everyone would know I was there for you and with you. Isa's employees tell her everything."

I kissed her again, and as I did, I found the zipper of

her dress in the back. I slid it down, and the cashmere slid down her body. She wore a lacy gray bra, and I groaned.

"You're so beautiful." I pushed the cups of her bra down so I could taste her nipples.

Her hands went into my hair, and she moaned. "Alejandro, everyone will know...we have to..."

"I need you, baby." I did. Desperately. It had been weeks since Memphis. I lifted her and set her down on my old dresser. I pulled down her panties. I inserted a finger inside her, and we both gasped with pleasure.

"You're so hot for me."

"Come inside." Her hips moved as if trying to swallow my finger whole.

My hands went to my belt, and I had my jeans down my thighs. I didn't bother to take them off all the way, I didn't have the patience to get to my shoes. I drove into her as quickly as I could. Finesse be damned.

"Hush, *mi amor*," I said urgently when she cried out. I pounded in and out of her, unable to control myself. I wanted this woman. She was like a fire in my blood. A warmth in my soul.

"I feel like I'm home when I'm inside you," I muttered as I looked into her eyes.

Her boots dug into my ass. "Alejandro, move."

I smiled then and touched her clit, wet and swollen. I kept my finger there as I moved in and out, watching as her eyes went glassy with pleasure.

"You can't scream when you come, *Duquesa*," I warned her as I felt my orgasm pulse through me, ready to spill into her. I pinched her clit at the same time my semen gushed into her. We came together.

I held her shaking thighs as I continued to twitch inside her, enjoying the last of her orgasm squeeze me.

She licked her lips as she came down to earth. "I like the way you say hello."

Chapter 24

Maria

He snuck into the inn to sleep the night with me that night.

I didn't think he needed to bother with the sneaking-in part. The way we disappeared during dinner and for how long we were gone, no one was under any illusions about the status of our relationship.

He left early in the morning before the staff was around. I couldn't understand his reluctance to be open about the fact that we were seeing each other. But I could see it was a topic he wasn't ready to discuss. So, I pretended to be asleep when he kissed me on my cheek and whispered, "Sleep well, *mi amor*."

He slipped up again and called me *mi amor*. I didn't argue about it. I don't think he even realized he was doing it. The man was in love with me. I was sure of this. But he was also a man hellbent on fighting that love.

A part of me wanted to take a stand, but the other, the one who loved him, just couldn't let pride be my foremost emotion.

I got out of bed early in the morning and put on my running clothes. When I'd checked in, they'd given us maps of running trails in the Golden Valley estate.

I put on my AirPods and cleared my head with a run. I'd run nearly three miles according to the map and ended up in the garden by the main house where Alejandro had kissed me that first time.

It was early, and there was no one around, except Alejandro, who was in the gazebo. I stood away from his line of vision and watched him practicing Ashtanga yoga in the serene garden. He wore sweatpants and a t-shirt, sweat gleamed on his skin despite the cool morning.

I was captivated by the fluidity of his movements and the strength that he released from every pose. The morning sun cast a gentle glow on his form, accentuating the lines of his body as he gracefully transitioned from one *asana* to another.

He began in a grounded Mountain Pose, his bare feet firmly planted on the mat. With a deep inhale, his arms rose overhead, and I could almost feel the energy radiating from his fingertips. As he folded forward into *uttanasana*, his spine stretched gracefully, a testament to his flexibility and dedication to yoga.

He was entirely focused on himself and his movements. It was a pleasure to watch him, and witness the sheer strength that he had cultivated through his practice. He moved elegantly into a new asana where his body hovered inches above the mat in a push-up position, his core engaged and his arms visibly straining against the challenge.

As Alejandro's body curved into Upward-Facing Dog, his chest lifted, and his gaze met the sky. The ease with which he effortlessly moved through the backbend made me lick my lips. His transitions were seamless, his breath steady and rhythmic, creating a mesmerizing dance of movement and stillness.

I walked closer to the gazebo, as he gracefully lifted into a handstand. My heart stopped, and I had to admit, watching him had aroused me. *Wow!* This man was potent.

He finally eased into a *savasana*, the corpse pose. His chest rose and fell with each slow breath, and a sense of calm seemed to envelop him, transforming his energy from fiery strength to serene tranquility.

I waited.

His eyes opened, and he sat up slowly, breathing deeply. He smiled at me. "Good morning. Did you have a nice run?"

"Did you know I was here?"

He nodded. "I sensed you, smelled you. I always know when you're around."

He stood up on his yoga mat and stretched.

"You're very good," I blurted out.

He rolled the yoga mat and closed the Velcro. "I've been doing it for years. After…Anika…there was a lot of turmoil. I worked out a lot then, but it didn't give me peace. Then I discovered *Ashtanga,* and I've never looked back."

"It suits you."

He leaned and brushed his lips against mine—an

intimate, easy gesture. My heart fluttered. "Why does it suit me?"

"Yoga is a delicate balance of effort and surrender. It goes beyond just strength and extends beyond the physical, doesn't it?"

He put an arm around me. "We're both sweaty and we need a shower," he declared.

"Do we?"

"Come to my house," he invited. "Silvano is staying with my parents."

I wanted to go with him, but not like this, not like a teenager sneaking his girlfriend into his home. "How about my bathroom in the Inn? It's a very nice spacious shower."

He looked at me with something flickering in his eyes, a sense of disquiet. "Baby, my mother gets attached and I don't want to hurt her. And I don't want to hurt Silvano."

But hurting me is okay? He'd never lied to me. He'd said that his family came first. I just wished I could be his family, too, as he'd become mine.

"It's not that," I let it go and didn't let him see me conflicted. Nothing good would come of that. "A woman needs her stuff, Alejandro. And my stuff is in my bathroom."

His face cleared. "Well, in that case, go take a shower, and I'll see you for breakfast at the Inn."

He kissed me again before letting me go.

As I walked back to the Inn, I wondered if fate was paying me back for all the times I'd dated men who wanted me more than I wanted them. Every relationship I'd had, I'd ended. It never seemed fair after the point when I knew that the man I was with wanted more than I could give. I was kind and respectful, and most of the time, I could end the relationship with no drama. I always walked away before things got too serious.

Now, the tables were turned. And there would come a time when Alejandro would be kind and respectful, gently leaving me. But it was already too late on my end. It had been from the start. This, when it was over, would hurt a lot.

Don't worry about what is coming, don't borrow trouble from tomorrow. Live in the moment, love him, enjoy him—make memories for a lifetime.

Chapter 25

Alejandro

"You're a grown man," Isadora complained, "Stop behaving like a teenager and just spend the afternoon with her."

"Isa," I began.

She held up her hand. "Everyone knows."

My mother was walking by us at the Golden Valley restaurant, where we'd just had breakfast. "What does everyone know?" she asked.

Isadora shook her head and walked away, annoyed.

"Is she talking about you and Maria?" my mother asked simply, and I sighed. Of course, she knew.

"Yes."

"She's lovely. I think you're lucky she's putting up with your nonsense about pretending you're not dating her."

"Mama, I have Silvano to think about."

"Silvano can handle himself." Her big brown eyes were amused. "I think you're worried about yourself and not him. At least be honest with yourself."

"Mama," I protested.

She shook her head then and held up her hand. "I thought I raised you better than this."

"And what is it I'm doing so wrong?" I demanded.

"It's disrespectful to bring the woman you're with and not introduce her to your family."

Her words were more powerful than a punch to the solar plexus. "Mama, I respect her."

She put a hand on my cheek. Since she was eight inches shorter than my six-three, like Isadora, I bent my head so she could reach me with ease when she went on tiptoe to kiss me on my forehead.

"I know you do, but you're being unfair, *mi hijo*. She's in love with you. If you're not, now is the time to walk away."

"She knows. I've been honest with her."

My mother shrugged. "As Isadora just said, you're a grown man. I can only hope you'll make the right decisions."

I nodded. "I need time to prepare Silvano."

"Okay." She smiled. "But I will not behave as if she's just a guest. Okay?"

I leaned down and kissed her on her cheek "Thanks, Mama."

I went to Maria's room, not caring if the staff found out. My mother knew, which meant everyone knew. I needed to speak to Silvano pronto. But it would have to be after the weekend when I had more time, and *she* wasn't in Golden Valley, taking up space in my heart and home.

I glanced over at Maria when she opened the door and my breath momentarily got caught in my throat. She was a vision of elegance and confidence. Her riding outfit hugged her body in all the right places, and I couldn't help but be captivated by the way it accentuated her natural grace.

The fitted riding jacket, crafted from rich, supple leather, molded to her curves, highlighting the gentle curve of her waist and the delicate slope of her shoulders. The jacket's intricate stitching and tailored seams spoke of attention to detail, a trait that seemed to echo in every facet of Maria's being.

Beneath the jacket, a pristine white riding shirt peeked out, its crisp collar adding a touch of sophistication. The shirt's fabric hinted at the softness beneath its structured exterior, a subtle reminder of the complexity within Maria herself.

Her riding pants, impeccably tailored and snug, emphasized the length of her legs, drawing my gaze downward before gracefully tapering into sleek, flawlessly polished riding boots.

"Wow."

She laughed softly and opened the door wide, letting me step into her room. She picked up her helmet and perched it casually under her arm. The way she held it suggested an air of familiarity with the equestrian world.

"Looks like you ride."

"I am *very* comfortable on a horse," she said cheekily.

I pulled her into my arms. "I've told Isa that you're spending the day with me. My mother approves."

Isadora had planned horse riding as a group for the guests as part of the weekend party. She had planned a lot of things for the day—and I didn't want any part of it because I wanted to spend the day with my girl.

She looked surprised. "Your mother knows?"

"Yes." I pushed some tendrils of hair that escaped her braid away from her face. "She's angry with me, as is Isadora, that I'm not open about us."

Her eyes lowered so I couldn't catch her emotions. But I knew what she was hiding from me. "I'm sorry for hurting you, Maria. That was never my intention."

She kissed me on my mouth. "I know. So, if I'm not riding with the—"

"Oh, you are riding," I interrupted and winked at her, "and not just me. I want to take you somewhere."

As Maria and I set out on our ride through Golden Valley, a sense of excitement coursed through me. The sun's warm embrace cast a golden hue across the cold winter landscape, and I couldn't help but steal glances at her, adorned in riding attire that exuded both elegance and a hint of adventure. The gentle clip-clop of the horses' hooves became a rhythmic backdrop to the beating of my heart, which seemed to quicken in her presence.

We guided our horses along the winding trails, the rustling leaves of the Sierra National Forest whispering secrets as we passed. Maria's laughter filled the air, a symphony that resonated with the beauty of the surroundings. It was as if the world was celebrating our connection, the bond between us growing stronger with every shared moment.

"Where exactly are we going?" She leaned to stroke her horse's neck. I'd given her Luna, my mother's favorite mount, a magnificent creature with a striking chestnut mane, her coat a rich tapestry of deep red and warm brown hues that shimmered in the sunlight. Both her rider and the horse caught the rays of the sun, creating an almost ethereal aura around them.

"To my favorite place in Golden Valley. Whenever I feel lost or upset, I come here."

She rode with ease. "She's a lovely horse." Luna's ears flickered as if she knew Maria was talking about her.

"She's my mother's. Strong and elegant...just like her."

"I never pegged you for a mama's boy," she teased.

"Paloma changed our lives."

We rode again in silence; the rhythmic sound of Luna's hooves against the earth formed a comforting cadence as she carried Maria along the trail. Luna's mane danced in the breeze, and the soft nicker that escaped her lips seemed like a secret shared between them.

"You ride very well for someone who didn't grow up with horses," I commented.

"I was horse mad as a teenager. I had a horse, Blaze. Luna reminds me of her."

"What happened to Blaze?"

"She got old, and now she's living the good life on a farm in Virginia with other horses who give little children rides and spend their last days being horses in the wild."

"We have a horse sanctuary here as well," I told her. "I got Solstice a few years ago after my horse died. He had a respiratory problem. It broke my heart."

"He's a beautiful horse."

I patted Solstice's neck. "He's a good boy."

"He suits you. Both of you are a portrait of raw power and refined elegance."

"I knew he was mine when I looked into his eyes. He has wise eyes. He's an old soul."

The wind tousled Solstice's long mane, which was a waterfall of ebony, adding an air of wildness to his otherwise refined appearance.

As we approached *my* hill, as I thought of it, I glanced at Maria. "Up there," I pointed toward the rising slope. "You're in for a breathtaking view." With a shared sense of anticipation, we guided our horses up the incline.

Reaching the hill's crest, Maria's eyes widened in awe. Spread out before us was a panorama that stretched as far as the eye could see, the whole of Golden Valley, with its farms now quiet in the winter, the vibrant patchwork of fields, and the meandering river that wound through it all. It was a sight that never failed to take my breath away, and I was happy to share it with Maria.

"Wow," she breathed, her voice tinged with wonder.

I dismounted and extended my hand to help her down, our fingers brushed in a fleeting touch that sent a thrill coursing through me as it always did. There was magic between us.

"I thought you might like this," I admitted, unable to tear my gaze away from her awestruck expression.

She turned to me with a radiant smile. "It's incredible. Thank you for bringing me here."

"Come on." I held out my hand, and she took it. "Are you cold?"

"Not at all."

"Hungry?"

"Actually, yes."

I winked at her. I led her to where I had gotten the Inn concierge to set up a picnic for me. I'd chosen a mesa that was ensconced between rocks, so we'd get the sun but not the wind. And the Inn employees had been kind enough to set up an outdoor firepit.

Living in California, we all took fire safety extremely seriously. But it was still too cold for the fire season.

With a flourish, I waved at the picnic, a selection of gourmet treats nestled in a woven basket sat at the corner of a cozy blanket. A few cushions and extra blankets were placed so we could stay warm.

"I can't believe this." Maria put her hands on her cheeks. "I…" she looked at me, tears in her eyes, "this is the nicest thing anyone has ever done for me."

"Isadora suggested that you'd like a picnic." I felt my chest expand with pride and pleasure for making her happy. Had I made up for hurting her inadvertently while I protected my family?

The fire and the sun both kept us warm. I had strict instructions from Isadora to bring Maria and my *ass* back to the Inn by four in the afternoon at the latest so we had time to get ready for the anniversary party that was starting at six and would go on into the wee hours of the morning. My parents loved to dance so the music would keep thumping until the last guest hung up their dancing shoes.

We ate fresh bread with cold cuts and drank a lovely white Chardonnay that I'd picked up at the Callahan Tasting room.

"How did you know this is one of my favorite

Chardonnays?" she asked, bewildered.

"Lucky guess."

After we ate, we lay on the blanket. Her head on my shoulder, my arm around her. We'd kept each other up for most of the night and I knew she was tired, as was I.

"When do we have to go back?" she asked sleepily.

"No rush." I stroked her hair, feeling lethargic myself. "Let's take a nap, *mi amor*. I've set the alarm so we won't be late, or Isadora will hang me by my balls."

She chuckled. "You run scared of all the women in your life?"

"Yes." I kissed her forehead.

"You scared of me?" she asked.

I tightened my hold on her, my eyes closing. "You most of all, *Duquesa*."

"Why?"

"Because you can hurt me."

Chapter 26

Maria

I wore a bronze Versace dress that had a slit that went all the way up my thigh. I had dressed with care—wanting to look like I belonged on the arm of Alejandro Santos.

I walked into the opulent ballroom of the Golden Valley Inn, and I couldn't help but catch my breath in sheer awe. Isadora had transformed the space into an enchanting winter wonderland, a scene right out of a fairytale. Glistening chandeliers hung from the ceiling, casting a soft, warm glow that danced across the room like starlight. The walls were draped in swathes of delicate white fabric, creating an ethereal atmosphere that embraced the winter theme.

Every detail seemed to have been chosen to evoke a sense of magic. Snowflakes adorned the tables, each unique in design, shimmering with a touch of frost.

Ice sculptures of swans and intricate patterns enriched the room, capturing the essence of a winter landscape frozen in time. The air itself felt alive with anticipation, a current of excitement that pulsed beneath the surface.

The scent of gourmet Mexican cuisine wafted through the air, a tantalizing blend of spices and flavors that promised a feast for all the senses. Elaborate dishes were laid out on tables decked with icy blue and silver linens, a stunning contrast against the pure white backdrop. From savory empanadas to delicate *chiles en nogada*, every bite promised a burst of exquisite flavor, a celebration of culture and love.

The music swirled around us, a symphony of melodies that beckoned everyone to the dance floor. The rhythmic beats and infectious melodies of salsa and cumbia filled the room, drawing couples and friends into a whirlwind of movement. Laughter and joy echoed against the ballroom's walls as people twirled and swayed, caught up in the night's magic.

My eyes wandered across the room, and I saw Mateo and Raya talking to Arsenio and Paloma and some other people I didn't know. Daisy and Forest danced while Hector had *Master* Kai in a baby Bjorn on his chest.

I walked up to Dec and Esme, whom I hadn't seen in the afternoon. "I'm so glad you made it." I hugged them both.

"It's been a while." Esme looked absolutely jubilant in a black dress.

"I see Forest and Daisy aren't fighting for a change," Dec remarked as Forest and Daisy left the dance floor and joined us.

"We're married with a child; we don't fight anymore." Daisy hugged me. "You look absolutely delicious, edible. Doesn't she, Forest?"

"Baby, I eat only you; you know that." Her husband grinned. "You look beautiful, Maria."

I flushed at the praise. "I see Hector is dancing with Kai. Speaking of babies, where is Mireya?"

"In our cottage with a nanny," Dec announced and kissed his wife's forehead, which was creased with worry. "The nanny comes with Paloma's stamp of approval. And we're literally a two-minute walk from the cottage."

Esme shook her head. "I'm sorry. I feel like I'm turning into that weird mother who can't leave her baby."

"I think all mothers are those mothers," Daisy remarked. "My kid is actually at this shindig."

As we talked, my eyes wandered across the room and rested on Aurelio, who was talking to his sister. And then I saw them, the two men I was looking for. I excused myself and walked to them, glad I'd dressed with care. Because no one, but no one, should look as good as Alejandro did in a tuxedo.

"Maria." Silvano ran up to me. He was already coming up to my shoulder, and in no time, he'd be taller than me, I thought as I hugged him,

"You look very distinguished," I told him. And he did in a charcoal gray suit and a red tie. He had his father's good looks mixed with his mother's Scandinavian genes. His eyes were gray, and they looked stunning in contrast with his café latte skin.

"Thanks." He held his hand out, "May I have this dance?"

Alejandro put his hand on his son's shoulder. "Are

you making a move on the most beautiful woman in the room, Silvano?"

"I don't care how she looks," Silvano said sincerely, looking up at his father. "She's smart and understands particle physics. Also, she never condescends me." He turned to face me and added, "I appreciate that."

"I'd love to dance with you." I put my hand in Silvano's as he led me away to the dance floor.

Dancing was a joy for me, and I loved to, as the cliché went, dance like nobody's watching. And it was a delight that Silvano had the same attitude.

With *Runaround Sue* blasting away, Silvano and I hit the dance floor like a dynamic duo, ready to shake things up. The beats were like a dance command from the universe. Silvano's energy could give the Energizer Bunny a run for its money. The kid barely reached my shoulder, but he rocked an aura of pure enthusiasm that practically had its own gravitational pull.

We started out with a cheeky side-by-side stance, our feet jamming out like they were having their own party. Those first few beats were like a starter pistol for a dance marathon, and I swear my heart was racing like it was in a 100-meter sprint. Silvano shot me a look that was part determination, part mischief. We were a dance dream team, ready to unleash some serious jive wizardry.

"You know how to jive, kid," I exclaimed.

"I took classes last summer," he explained, and then, *bam!* We exploded into the dance with lightning-fast, syncopated moves. Back and forth, we shuffled like pros. It was like our bodies were having a wild conversation with the music. Silvano's quick feet were a showstopper. Seriously, this kid could've given Fred

Astaire a run for his fancy shoes. Twists, turns, and more twists, we were in full-on jive mode, the crowd probably wondering if we'd swapped our morning coffee for jet fuel.

When the chorus hit, it was like our dance went turbo. I was grinning like a kid in a candy store, and Silvano? Oh man, his grin was a mix of mischief and accomplishment. We were a tag team of experience and youthful zing, grooving like we'd been dancing together forever. Silvano's moves were as tight as a drum, and I couldn't help but be impressed by his dance floor prowess.

The crowd parted, letting us show off and clapped along with the beat. I didn't bother to find Alejandro in the crowd. *Live in the moment, Maria, and this moment* is awesome.

We practically glued ourselves together, our moves weaving in and out like we had some sort of secret dance code. And then, the grand finale, the kicks, and flicks—it was like we'd unlocked the ultimate dance power-up.

The crowd cheered us on, probably hoping some of our dance magic would rub off on them. Silvano's infectious grin was like a dance party invitation, and I was all in. With a twirl that could've made heads spin, we wrapped up the performance just as the song belted its final note.

As the music faded out, we were both huffing and puffing like we'd just finished a dance marathon. We exchanged victorious glances, and Silvano's eyes were practically glowing with pride. I felt a mix of exhaustion and elation, we'd nailed it! That dance was more than just steps; it was a symphony of harmony, fun, and a sprinkle of jive magic.

"Thank you, Silvano. I feel like the luckiest dancer on the planet to have you as a partner." I walked to one of the chairs and collapsed as the crowd clapped.

His face flushed, Silvano searched for his father and gave him a thumbs-up. Alejandro waved as he stood at the bar but didn't come up to us. He looked grim and if I were more like Daisy, I'd have given him the finger.

Silvano and I had busted out moves, shared laughs, and created a memory that would be tough to top. It was more than just dancing, it was a testament to the joyful rhythm of life, and we'd danced to it like nobody was watching—like Alejandro was not watching.

Chapter 27

Alejandro

"Runaround Sue" filled the room, its lively rhythm contrasting with the tangle of feelings within me. Silvano and Maria were dancing, their steps in sync, their connection growing with every move. Silvano's youthful energy and innocence contrasted and were in sync with Maria's vivacious spirit. Seeing them dance together stirred a mix of emotions in me: concern, hesitation, and an overwhelming fear of the unknown.

As I watched them move in tandem, my heart felt heavy with the weight of my unspoken truth. Silvano's trust and his growing bond with Maria were precious, and the thought of revealing my involvement with her seemed like a risk I wasn't sure I was ready to take. The height difference between them seemed trivial compared to the emotional chasm that divided us.

Their steps were a metaphor for the intricate dance

of relationships, one that I had entered hesitantly. Maria's grace and Silvano's exuberance painted a picture of unity and compatibility, an image that both comforted and frightened me. Every twirl, every spin, felt like a reminder of the delicate balance I was trying to maintain.

The chorus brought a surge of energy to their dance. Silvano's trust in Maria was clear in the way he followed her lead, a trust that I held dear and yet felt the urge to protect. My gaze remained fixed on them, my concern growing as they moved closer in perfect harmony.

The kicks and spins in their dance mirrored the uncertainty of my situation. The fear that this newfound connection could shatter at any moment hung heavy in the air, like a storm cloud threatening to release its downpour. I could feel myself torn between the joy of seeing Silvano happy and the fear of exposing him to the complexities of adult relationships.

As the song's final notes played out, I watched them with pride for Silvano's carefree spirit, appreciation for Maria's presence in his life, and a deep-seated apprehension about the consequences of my own actions.

As the music faded, I couldn't shake off the somber realization that I was standing at a crossroads, a juncture where the happiness of my son intersected with the fragility of my heart.

Silvano gave me a thumbs-up, and I waved back, a tight smile on my face.

"You look too serious, *mi hijo*." My father came up to me, holding a glass of champagne for me. "Especially after watching Silvano and your woman set that dance floor on fire."

I took the glass and looked away from Maria and Silvano who were now talking animatedly. "I'm fine, Papa and she isn't my woman. What we have is casual."

He laughed, a big belly laugh. My father had an unmatched zest for life, which I envied. I wish I could be as carefree as him. But our experiences shaped us, mine had made me who I was. I'd always wanted to be as good a father to Silvano as my father had been to us.

"I know all about *that* kind of casual. I had that with Paloma when I met her. It was a cluster fuck. I wanted her, but she was so much younger than me. She lived in Boston, and we lived in Golden Valley. She wanted to save the world, I wanted to make money. *And* I felt guilty that I'd be trapping a woman, bringing her here to raise my sons."

"Paloma and Maria are two *very* different women," I objected. My mother had given up her life to build one with my father and us. Maria had her own life.

"What are you scared of?"

"I'm not scared," I immediately became defensive and then added, "I have a son, Papa," because I felt foolish.

"I know the feeling. I have two."

I sighed. It wouldn't help to ask him to mind his own business, my parents never did. "I don't want Silvano to get hurt. I don't want to get married. I don't want more children. She wants all that. I can't give her any of it."

"Why?" he was perplexed.

I shrugged.

"*Mi hijo*, I'm going to ask you to think about something. Are you afraid Silvano will get hurt or that you will? A woman like that, she'll find someone else.

She's beautiful, smart and one hell of a dancer. She's giving you the time of day, which makes you one lucky *pendejo*." He raised his glass to mine, "Get your head out of your anus, Alejandro, and smell the fucking world. You're spending too much time smelling shit."

I grimaced. "You have a way with words, Papa."

He winked at me as my mother stepped into our line of vision. She looked beautiful in a flowing peach-colored dress. "*And* with women. I am the luckiest *pendejo* in the world, son. The luckiest."

He walked up to his wife and handed off his glass of champagne to a server who was passing by. He swept her off her feet, literally, and took her onto the dance floor. I watched them with a smile because it was hard not to be happy when you saw them together.

Could Maria and I ever have that?

Silvano had moved on to dancing with Isa and Maria was talking to...fucking hell, Lincoln Beckman. He was almost a cousin as his parents and mine were close friends. Linc was a professor of sociology at NYU and had slippery fingers when it came to women. He was divorced, probably because he was screwing around on his wife with someone else's wife. He'd kissed my prom date during the prom. *Son of a bitch!*

Before I knew it, I had my arm around Maria. *She's mine, cabrón.*

"Hey, baby, that was some dancing."

She looked at me with amused eyes like she knew what I was doing. "You know, I'm going to wait for Silvano to grow up and marry him. Cougar style."

"I see you've met Linc."

"Alejandro, how's it going, man?"

I glared at him, and his eyes filled with mischief. It was obvious someone had filled him in on my current love life. "It's good. We're surprised you came all the way from New York."

Linc seemed to have trouble holding a grin back. "Actually, I'm moving to LA for next semester. I'm doing a research project at USC. I was telling Maria here that she and I should hook up."

Maria gave Linc a confused look.

"You hitting on my girl, Linc?"

He rubbed his nose, as if remembering the time we'd fought. He ended up with a broken nose. I with a broken arm. We were fucking even.

"I didn't know she was your girl, Alejandro. I don't see a ring on her finger."

"Walk the fuck away."

"*Alejandro*," Maria protested. "God, Lin, I'm so sorry."

Linc waved like he was a long-suffering acquaintance who had to put up with my rudeness. "Alejandro is just sore that I kissed his prom date... actually, I may have done more..." He laughed when he saw the storm in my eyes. "I'm sorry, man. Your mother asked me to give you a hard time and I couldn't resist. Nice meeting you, Maria and now I'll go find a willing woman who will not cause me to break my now perfect nose."

"What?" Maria asked, confused.

"I broke his nose," I informed her.

"I broke his arm," Linc countered.

"Your nose looks so much better than it ever did. I did you a favor," I remarked.

"I'll see you around, Alejandro. I'm staying at

Whitworth Farms for a few days. Are you up for a game of racquetball sometime this week?"

"Sure. Send me times and dates." I watched him walk away.

"You men are weird. You threatened each other and now you're going to play racquetball?" Maria turned to face me.

"Yes. Now, dance with me. I want to hold you."

Since I had arranged for Silvano to sleep at the main house, I took Maria to my place that night. I wanted to see her in my bed. I wanted to make love with her in my home. I preferred staying at her home with her than at a hotel. And it was the same here. I wanted her scent to stay at home even after she left, to see an errant strand of hair on my pillow after she was gone. For a man who'd spent his adult life making sure no woman ever came too close, this was definitely a reversal.

She seemed unsure as I took her to my home, which was a five-minute drive from the main house. We'd all built homes that suited us.

Aurelio's house had a cabin feel to it. My home was my sanctuary, a minimalist, modern haven kissed by Scandinavian design and blessed with breathtaking views.

With my heart racing and a sheepish grin tugging at the corners of my lips, I turned to Maria; her eyes gleamed with curiosity. "Welcome to my humble abode." I gestured grandly to the open expanse before us.

Her gaze swept across the spacious living room with its clean lines and elegant furnishings. "Alejandro, it's stunning," she breathed.

I took her hand in mine, our fingers intertwining

effortlessly. "I'm glad you think so. But come, there's so much more to see." With a gentle tug, I led her toward the heart of the house—the kitchen. Stainless steel appliances gleamed under the soft glow of pendant lights.

"I didn't know you cooked." Maria admired the setup.

"I've been known to whip up a mean omelet and not much else," I remarked. "Maybe one day I'll prove it to you."

Her laughter tinkled like music. "I'd love to see you in action."

As we strolled through the open-concept layout, my heart swelled with pride. Every inch of the house was a testament to my love for simplicity and nature's beauty. "The kitchen has witnessed many culinary adventures, because both Silvano and I know how to botch a good meal. Over here," I continued, leading her to a cozy reading nook by the window, "is where I lose myself in books on lazy afternoons while Silvano does his homework."

Maria's laughter echoed like a sweet melody, and her fingers danced along the wooden bookshelf. "You're quite the romantic."

I leaned in, my lips brushing her ear as I whispered, "Only when I'm with you." The intimacy of the moment seemed to hang in the air, the warmth of it enveloping us like a cocoon.

As we ascended the sleek staircase, each step seemed to bring us closer not just to the upper level of the house, but to a deeper understanding of each other. The bedrooms, all four of them, were unique in decor yet harmoniously tied to the overarching theme.

And then, the pièce de résistance—the master

bedroom. The walls were covered in muted, calming colors, and a plush bed sat nestled by the window, offering a panoramic view of the forest's embrace.

"This," I murmured, my voice softening with emotion, "is where I dream, where I find solace."

"And this," she declared dramatically, as she walked up to the stand in front of one of the grand windows, "is where you can lose yourself in the beauty of the Sierra National Forest. I'm certain the view during the day must be...spectacular."

"The sunrise will blow your mind. I'm hoping you'll stay the night. I want to...," I trailed off and then told her the truth, "This is the first time I have a woman in my home, my bed."

Maria turned to me, her eyes tender and her smile radiant. "Your home is like you. Beautiful."

Drawing her close, I cupped her cheek with my hand, my thumb brushing against her skin. "And it's even more beautiful with you in it, Maria." Our lips met in a sweet, lingering kiss, a promise of the affection and tenderness that had grown between us.

Chapter 28

Maria

I woke up early. The skies were dark with a hint of gold and amber. We'd kept each other up for a good part of the night. It was our last one together for god knows how long. Our responsibilities seemed to pull us apart.

I watched him in the dim light of the still unrisen sun. He was beautiful. Sharp cheekbones. A mouth that was full and sinful. Eyes when opened, brilliant and blue. His hair which seemed to always have that *I just got a haircut* sincerity was now disheveled.

I slid out of bed, not wanting to disturb him. I picked up his dress shirt and wrapped it around me like a robe.

I walked into Alejandro's living room, surrounded by the floor-to-ceiling windows that framed a breathtaking panorama of the mountains and expanse of the forest. The sun's first tentative rays painted the sky in hues of soft gold and rose, radiating a warm glow over the entire room. The serenity of the scene was a balm to my soul. I could see why Alejandro loved it here.

With a gentle sigh, I prepared a cup of coffee in the espresso machine I'd seen the evening before. The aroma mingled with the tranquility that enveloped the space. As I took a sip, I leaned against the sleek kitchen counter, gazing out at the majestic landscape that lay before me. It was a moment of solitude, a chance to reflect the beauty of nature's artistry.

As the sunlight cast its brilliance on the world outside, my thoughts turned inward. Alejandro had captured my heart with his playful spirit and passionate soul; but he had also stirred a wave of complexities within me. My love for him was undeniably deep and genuine; his feelings toward me seemed to change as the colors of the skies did to welcome the sun.

I took another sip of my coffee, savoring the rich flavor. I understood Alejandro was protective of his family and seemed to care so much about their *apparent* feelings over my *real* ones. He imagined they'd get hurt. He imagined they wouldn't approve. He imagined the relationship would definitely end and hurt his son. It wounded me to glimpse his moments of reticence, his hesitation in fully embracing the possibility of us.

I understood the weight of his responsibilities, the pressures that came with raising a child as a single parent. Silvano was his priority, and I admired Alejandro's dedication to being the best father he could be. But as I stood here, bathed in the soft glow of dawn, a nagging doubt lingered in my heart, could we ever bridge the gap between his role as a father and the man

I yearned to build a future with?

The mountains outside seemed to stand as silent witnesses to my thoughts, their unwavering presence a reminder of the permanence and strength that nature embodied. I wished for a similar steadfastness in our relationship, a promise that we could weather the storms that life inevitably brought.

As the sun continued its ascent, I found solace in the memories we had created together. The laughter, the stolen glances, the shared dreams, which were the threads that wove the fabric of our love story. And as I looked out at the mountains, I realized that as they stood tall and unyielding, so did my feelings for Alejandro.

I was on my second cup of coffee and going through my emails on my phone when I heard him behind me. He wore nothing but a pair of white boxer shorts and a smile.

"Good morning, *Duquesa*," he murmured and grazed his lips with mine before moving to the coffee machine like this was a normal scene— like we did it all the time, every morning.

My heart clenched. This could be our lives, couldn't it? I had thought that coming here, being with him would make it all clear. Seeing him in a home that could become ours, one I could dream about, would bring me comfort, but I felt more lost than ever.

He picked up his cup of coffee and leaned against the counter, facing the big windows. "The sunrise here is truly something, isn't it?"

I nodded, unable to shake off the heaviness that had settled within me. As I took a sip of my coffee, he seemed to sense my conflicted state.

"Maria," he began gently, setting down his cup, "there's something I want to talk to you about. I think it's time to tell Silvano about us."

His words should have been cause for celebration, for affirmation of our relationship. But they sent ripples of unease through me, like a stone thrown into still waters. I placed my cup on the counter and met his gaze, searching for the certainty I had hoped to find.

"Alejandro, I thought I'd be happy to hear that, but..." I hesitated; my thoughts tangled. "I feel like we're rushing into this."

He frowned, his brow furrowing with confusion. "Rushing? Maria, I thought you wanted this. You seemed hurt that I don't want us to be in the open. What am I missing here?" There was a sharpness to his tone. He almost seemed to want me to genuflect in gratitude that he was finally willing to throw me a bone.

My fingers traced the rim of my cup as I struggled to voice my concerns. "Alejandro, it's not about us being in the open. It's about whether we're certain about this step ourselves."

He blinked, clearly taken aback by my response. "Speak for yourself. I am certain."

"Are you?" I took a deep breath, gathering my thoughts. "I want to wait until we're both certain, not just about each other, but about *us*. About our relationship. Silvano is a part of your life, a part of us, and I don't want to introduce confusion or doubt into his world."

His expression shifted, a mixture of understanding and frustration crossing his features. "Maria, if we're seeing each other I'd like him to know so I don't have to sneak around like a fucking teenager. We're in a relationship, I'd like that to be out in the open now. I thought you did as well."

My heart ached with a conflict I hadn't expected. "I know and I'm sorry. I...tell me what you mean when you say you're certain about us? I hate to speak in clichés but what is it you feel for me?"

He hesitated, his gaze flickering as if searching for the right words. "I enjoy being with you. You make me happy. I care about you."

His words felt shallow, leaving me with an emptiness that echoed in the space between us. I had hoped for a deeper affirmation, a more profound connection that would anchor us in the face of challenges.

"I appreciate your honesty." My voice was tinged with a sadness I couldn't hide. "But I think we need more time. I want us to be strong, unshakeable, before we involve Silvano. Let's take a step back."

He looked conflicted, torn between his desire to move forward and my hesitation. "You're suggesting we wait? After you've made it clear to me repeatedly that you want more? What the fuck, Maria?"

I nodded, my heart aching at the disappointment and anger in his eyes. "Let's give ourselves some time. I'm going back to LA. You'll be here in Golden Valley. We can continue to build our connection, to deepen our feelings. And when we're *truly* ready, when we know without a doubt that this is what we want, then we can tell Silvano."

He drank some coffee and set the cup down. "Do you want to end this...whatever it is we have?"

I gasped. "No. That's not what I mean at all."

"Well, that's what it fucking sounds like. But I'm glad

we had this conversation because you're right, the way you feel about me seems to be murky. I agree, I don't want to bring Silvano into this. He's already getting attached to you."

From one moment to another, his tone went from loving to business-like.

"Alejandro," I protested.

He held up his hand. "It's fine, Maria. You're right. We were rushing it."

"Don't turn this around on me. I love you. I've never hidden that from you. I don't know how you feel about me." I stood up, now anger flashing through me, his words knives that slashed and wounded.

"What is it you want? Some platitude about love? Well, fuck that. I don't love you. I love very few people in my life. My parents, my siblings, and my son. I don't have room to love anymore. I care about you. I'd like to… I would have liked to continue to see you."

I took a step back, his words jarring. *I don't love you.* I knew. Of course, I knew but hearing him say it, made my heart bleed.

"Are you saying let's end this?" I asked. How did this conversation go so wrong?

He shrugged "I'm saying let's follow your plan and continue as before. We'll make time for one another when we can and then see what happens. Keep it casual."

My eyes filled with tears. I couldn't help it. "It was never casual for me."

"That's what it sounds like, Maria. I was ready to tell my kid about us—but you got cold feet. And I can't bring that kind of turmoil into his life." He looked at his watch as if dismissing me because of a time constraint, like he would in his office when someone had overstayed their welcome. "I can drop you off at the Inn or get someone to take you there so you can pack up."

I shook my head. "I'll walk."

"It's a good twenty-minute walk, Maria, and your shoes are not made for walking."

I smiled at him because what would be the point of crying? "I always say if you can't walk in shoes for a couple of miles, don't wear them at all. I'll be fine."

He came up to me and kissed my forehead. "Thank you for last night. I'm going to take a shower so I can head to the main house for breakfast with Silvano. I'll see you…ah…when I see you."

Wow! Talk about treating me like some one-night stand he'd picked up at the bar.

I didn't agree with him about telling Silvano and his first reaction was to push me away, no conversation, no discussion. He got hurt, and he didn't bother to see my point of view; he struck back hard.

"Thanks for showing me your home. It's beautiful. You're very lucky to have this." I waved at the picture-postcard-perfect view.

I was not some gauche young woman; I was a grown woman with plenty of experience in being stoic.

I left his home and him, hoping that I could get to my house before I broke down. The distance from Golden Valley to Los Angeles had never seemed longer.

Chapter 29

Alejandro

I was back in Los Angeles. It had been four weeks since my parents' anniversary party. Four weeks since I'd seen or talked to Maria. Four fucking long weeks and now I was back.

Silvano had decided not to take time off during spring break and was going to attend a STEM Camp at UCLA which was being conducted by his now favorite teacher, Professor Jbara, a Nobel Laureate in particle physics. He was once again staying with Mateo and Raya —as I had to leave the following day for meetings in San Francisco. I didn't have to, but I'd asked my assistant to set it up so I wouldn't have time to dawdle in LA. So, I wouldn't want to go see her.

I was still angry with her. I had been ready to give her something I gave no one else, my fucking family and she'd chickened out, asking *what do I mean to you? Dios mío!* This is why I didn't do relationships.

"I'm hoping I can spend some time with Maria," Silvano told me as the driver parked in Mateo's building. We'd taken the Escalade. I needed the room and time to work, and Silvano wanted a nap; both were achieved. We'd left early, around five in the morning, so we could beat traffic and make it here by nine. I had a golf tee time with a state senator at eleven, so the timing was perfect.

I watched Silvano with Mateo and Raya; they were family, I thought happily. I loved them as I did my own siblings. And the way Silvano responded to them made me happy.

"Plans for the weekend?" Raya asked as she poured me a cup of coffee. We sat at their pool patio. Silvano and Mateo were already in deep conversation about the hydroponics Mateo was experimenting with at the far side of the patio.

"I have a golf game with Senator Marchon in a little while; and then I'm going to get to LAX and fly to San Francisco. I have a dinner tomorrow night."

Raya smiled and winked. "Is that what you both are calling it now?"

"Excuse me?"

"Maria is off to San Francisco today. Her friend's restaurant won their first Michelin star so they're celebrating. They have the cutest name for a restaurant, it's called *It's a Fairytale.*" When she saw my blank look, she added, "I assumed since you were going there as well, you were going to be together."

"She didn't tell you?" I asked. But then I hadn't told my family either. I'd just told them I didn't want to talk about Maria and since they knew me, they'd abided by my wishes.

"Tell me what?"

"I think we broke up." I looked at the Los Angeles skyline. I liked downtown, but I preferred where Maria lived. Silver Lake was more accessible, cozier.

"You *think*?" Raya wondered.

"I don't want to talk about it." I used the same tone I did with my family, the one that didn't invite any discussion.

"Well, fuck that," Raya countered. "What happened? She hasn't said a word. We've also not had time to meet up. I know she's been to see Daisy a few times or rather Kai. If she'd said anything to Daisy, I'd have known."

I shrugged. "Nothing happened, Raya. It just ran its course."

"Bullshit. I saw you both at the anniversary party and I saw her with Silvano—"

"Raya," my tone was clipped, "I really don't want to talk about it. It's in the past."

Raya put her hand on mine. "No, it's not. I can see it hurts you to talk about her."

"It irritates me." I smiled tightly and pulled my hand away from under hers. "I should get going otherwise I'll miss tee-time. I'll be back on Thursday evening to pick him up."

I gave Silvano a hug and a kiss and left Mateo and Raya's home before they could ask more questions. I had thought for sure Maria would have told her friends —but she'd done what I had, not discussed the matter. And she was going to be in San Francisco tonight, as I was.

I texted my assistant and asked her to find out where Maria was staying in San Francisco, warning her to be discreet. I didn't want Maria to know. She and Maria's assistant had built a relationship, so I knew Mercedes would get me the information I needed. Knowing her, she'd probably have a hand on her heart, thinking that I was planning to surprise Maria.

"She's staying at the Four Seasons," Mercedes called to let me know. "Should I change your reservation from the IC to there?"

"No."

"Ah...do you want me to cancel your hotel reservation?"

"No."

"Alejandro?"

"Thanks, Mercedes." I hung up on her. Why had I found out where she was staying? Oh, I knew, so I could avoid her. That was it. If Mercedes had said she was staying at the Intercontinental, I'd have come up with ways to not bump into Maria.

By the time I got to San Francisco, it was late afternoon. I had come earlier than I had planned. I wanted to have some time in San Francisco, that's all. Maybe see some friends. Maybe have a drink at the... *fucking* Four Seasons.

I texted Mercedes and asked her to change my reservation. I'd be staying at the Four Seasons as well. She texted back with a thumbs-up emoji.

Mierda! I did not know what I was doing.

I had just gotten to my hotel room when my father called. "Silvano all okay?"

"Yeah," I told him as I unpacked.

"Are you okay?"

"Yeah."

"Alejandro?"

I sighed and sat down on the bed. "I changed my hotel reservation from the Intercontinental to the Four Seasons."

"How is this relevant to your state of mind?"

"Maria is here in the Four Seasons. Raya mentioned she was also in San Francisco. It's like the universe is fucking with me."

I heard my father chuckle. "I still don't know what happened between the two of you. One minute you're dancing with her like she holds your world, and then the other, you tell us to shut the fuck up about her."

I told him what happened on that last morning when I'd seen Maria.

"I'm still so pissed with her. I was giving her something I gave no one. I was ready to tell Silvano about us and then she says, let's wait. What the fuck?"

My father cleared his throat, which usually was a precursor to a long speech. "Son, you're a moron."

"What?"

"You think you're such a hotshot that the minute you give her a little, she'll be all over you like flies on shit? She came to Golden Valley, and you didn't introduce her as your woman. You were hedging your bets. You kept pushing and pulling, and I think she felt that tug of war inside of you. She did what she did to protect Silvano and I for one think feel she deserves better than an *estúpido* like you."

"But Papa—"

"I'm not done, *pendejo*."

"You really should not be calling me names," I said lightly.

"When you behave like you do, what else am I supposed to do? So, you think, ah, *I'm the wronged one.* And you get angry and tell her to get out of your house. You decide it's over. You know what she's thinking?"

"What?"

"That the first time she disagreed with you about something, you kicked her in the teeth. Didn't you kick her in the teeth?"

Yeah, I did. I told her I didn't love her, that I'd never love her.

I had held on to my anger and frustration for weeks, deciding that *she'd* left me. I had not thought of her perspective at all because my father was right, I was a selfish *pendejo.*

"You should've thanked her for being so considerate about Silvano. Instead, what did you do?"

I didn't say anything.

"I asked, what did you do?" my father bellowed.

"I kicked her out of my house."

"And do you know what you have to do now?"

"I don't know, Papa. She's been clear with me she doesn't want to go up and down on this carousel with me. I agree. I can't keep doing this to her."

My father's voice crackled with laughter. "Then stop doing *this* to her. Go live your life, Alejandro. Be with the woman who makes you happy because you've been one miserable little git for the past four weeks since you fucked up with her."

"You know, I'm your son, you should be on my side." I looked at the San Francisco skyline and felt weary. I was tired of myself, of not having her with me, of me not being with her.

"I am on your side."

"You're kicking my ass, Papa."

"But I'm doing it while I'm on your side," my father countered, amused.

Chapter 30

Maria

Keeping busy is how you handle a broken heart. I worked all week like a crazy person. During the weekends, I went away, met friends, and engaged myself so I didn't have to think about Alejandro.

After the first week of the *apparent* breakup, when I couldn't sleep, I asked my doctor for a prescription and went into a drug-induced sleep every night. Drug-induced or not, he haunted me in my nightmares...my dreams...my sleep. Whenever I saw a tall man in a suit, my head turned, and my heart fluttered.

Alfred Tennyson wrote, *"Tis better to have loved and lost than never to have loved at all*, and he could shove it. I'd never been in love before; I knew that now because nothing had ever hurt this much. I felt like a raw open wound. I refused to talk about it with anyone. Daisy had asked. I ignored the question and played with Kai. Drago had wondered where my man from DC with a big pee-pee was (those goddamn limericks!), and I'd asked him to talk about something else.

The only person I had talked about Alejandro to was Mark. He'd come home and hold me as I cried. He'd bought churros, plantain chips, chocolate, and some good bottles of red wine to help me get through the initial pain of loss.

"Why can't you continue as you were?" he asked when I told him the whole sordid tale.

"Because I love him. And he doesn't love me."

Mark nodded. "I know, sweetheart, but that was how it was before, wasn't it?"

"I can't do this anymore," I wailed.

He'd hugged me and let me have at the uncontrollable ugly crying. He'd also stopped asking questions. The matters of the heart, he always said, were fucked up, which was why he'd picked neurosurgery instead of cardio, though he was now officially dating Dr. Xavier, a cardiac surgeon who lived in Seattle.

"Why do you always have these long-distance relationships?" I wondered.

"Because that increases the longevity of the said relationship." *Talk about having an unhealthy approach to matters of the heart.*

No matter what I did, my heart ached.

To continue my theme of self-care to heal, I accepted my friend Storm Andersen's invitation to attend the "We Won a Michelin Star" party at his restaurant, *It's A Fairytale*. I had been one of the first investors in the restaurant, having enjoyed Storm's culinary prowess in another Michelin-star restaurant in Los Angeles where he'd been the sous chef.

Storm had had a hard life. His father had committed suicide, and his mother had lost her mind and ended up in a mental health facility, which meant he'd had to raise his twin younger brothers, Sindri and Stellan, when he'd been just eighteen. Sindri was now a master sommelier, and Stellan managed the restaurant.

I'd met Storm years ago when he had just graduated from the Culinary Institute of America and was a struggling chef in Los Angeles. We'd struck up a friendship, and now, nearly a decade later, I was happy that I'd had a part to play in the success of his dream restaurant.

As I stepped through the elegant doors of *It's A Fairytale*, a rush of expectancy surged. The air was charged with electrifying energy, and I knew tonight would be unlike any dining experience I had ever experienced.

Storm had invited a select group and their plus ones for the party, but I told him I was solo. I would have brought Mark along, but he was on call for the weekend. I hadn't even asked Drago because he was knee-deep in a gang shooting.

I wished Alejandro was with me. I wanted that so much. I shook my head as if the physical act would erase his memory and this feeling of utter devastation that set into me every time I thought about him.

Golden hues bathed the restaurant's interior, casting a warm glow over the intricate details that gilded every corner. Crystal chandeliers hung from the ceiling, their delicate facets refracting the light into a mesmerizing dance of colors. The fusion of French and California influences was evident in the artful arrangement of each table, where delicate flowers and vibrant produce mingled in harmonious unity.

"Maria," Storm called out, and I entered his arms. He hugged me tight. "I'm so happy you're here."

"You won a Michelin," I cried out.

He grinned like a schoolboy, his Scandinavian good looks coming alive as if breaking out of the stone mask he usually liked to wear. "We did, didn't we? Can you believe it?"

"Of course, I can. This is my investment paying off, chef."

"Come on, let me take you to your table. I have put you with some fascinating people you'll love getting to know."

Excitement bubbled within me as I followed the soft, lilting melody of laughter to my seat. I couldn't help but smile as I imagined Storm orchestrating this masterpiece of design and cuisine, his unique touch plain in every carefully chosen detail.

He introduced me to a couple, interior designers, who had helped to make *It's A Fairytale* what it was—a magical place for an unforgettable culinary experience.

As I settled into my seat, a shimmering glass of champagne appeared before me, its effervescence, a toast to new beginnings and the Michelin star that now elevated *It's A Fairytale*. I lifted the glass to my lips, savoring the crisp and delicate notes that danced on my tongue.

I made small talk with Lilah and Bobby Meester who had a storefront on Market Street and specialized in interior design for restaurants and hotels.

Each table was designed for six; ours would have only five guests as I didn't bring a plus one. I didn't *need* a plus one. Soon, two more table mates joined us, Atlas and Orion Callahan, winemakers from Santa Barbara.

"I love your wines," I told them excitedly. "Your 2019 Pinot was...is...magic."

Orion flushed. "Thanks. The weather was perfect, it was a damn good vintage."

After we did the usual getting to know one another chit-chat, Atlas informed me, "We have some common friends."

I raised an eyebrow. "We do?"

"Mateo Silva. He's an investor in Callahan Vineyards."

I beamed as I always did when I thought about Mateo and Raya. "They are dear friends."

"And one of our common friends is joining us at our table tonight."

He didn't say his name, but I felt him. I smelled him. I knew who it was before Atlas even said his name.

"Alejandro Santos," he revealed to my despair. "He told me he was in San Francisco. I asked Storm and you know him, the more the merrier."

He rose then to welcome his friend, and I closed my eyes, my hand clenching against the champagne glass stem hard.

"*Duquesa*, you'll break that glass if you don't loosen your hold on it."

He sat down after shaking hands with everyone and kissing me gently on my cheek. *How dare he come here? How dare he kiss me?*

"What the *fuck* are you doing here?" I whispered.

I saw his eyes narrow. I wasn't someone who swore often—usually, I saved that for when I was drunk and making up limericks.

"I'm here to celebrate *It's A Fairytale's* Michelin star. Isn't that why you're here?"

"I'm an investor. What's your excuse?" I sipped my wine as my stress level climbed. This is when I made stupid decisions like drinking too much and saying things I shouldn't. On the other hand, hadn't I made enough stupid decisions with Alejandro already? What was one more?

I waved to the server.

"I'll have one more," I said to him.

He bowed. "Of course, Miss Caruso."

"Call me Maria," I said in my most flirtatious tone. "Yves, isn't it? You were here the last time I came for dinner."

"Yes, I was."

"Well, I'm glad you're still here." I fluttered my eyelashes, and the server blushed.

"Why are you trying to get that poor man fired?" Alejandro asked.

"Are you talking to me? Why? I don't want to know you. You know what, I'm going to ask Storm to find me —"

"I'm *so sorry.*" He put his hand on my thigh to still me. "Please forgive me. I didn't see it from your point of view. I got hurt, and I lashed out."

"Well, isn't that dandy for you?" My voice rose, and everyone at the table looked at us. I sighed. I was a private person. This was not the kind of thing I did. I was controlled and always effortlessly emotionless.

Alejandro was hell on my equanimity.

"Baby, *please*." His lips were so close to my ears that I could feel him between my legs. I was like a bitch in heat, I thought, annoyed with myself. The minute he was around, I was ready to hump him.

My champagne arrived, and I took a big gulp—the hell with sipping daintily.

"Please, *what*? What do you want?" I insisted.

He took my free hand in his and brought it to his lips. "You. I want you."

My hand holding the champagne glass shook. I set it down, but I didn't look at Alejandro. I couldn't. My heart would break if I did.

Our private conversation was interrupted by the entrance of the first amuse-bouche. It arrived with a flourish, delivered by servers gliding effortlessly across the floor. A plume of dry ice surrounded the shrimp wrapped in ransom leaves, creating an otherworldly mist that heightened the senses and set the stage for the awaited culinary journey.

The server explained what we were eating, and we all nodded appreciatively. Almost immediately, Sindri, Storm's brother, came to our table. I rose and hugged him.

"While you enjoy your amuse-bouche, I wanted to give you a rundown of the wine we're serving and see what would work best for you." Sindri looked like Storm's brother. He was blonde-haired and blue-eyed, but his body was different. He boxed, and you could see it in his body. His shoulders were broad; there were rippling muscles under his tattooed skin. His nose had been broken a few times.

He talked to all of us about the wines that would

pair best with the meal. He flirted with Lilah and had an easy camaraderie with Bobby. He knew Orion well; as a sommelier, he'd probably known one of California's finest winemakers.

Once Sindri left and the courses flowed, so did the conversation at our table. Alejandro and I tacitly held off on our little discussion about what he wanted.

I decided not to be hostile. I put on the mask of polite Maria, the one who had control of all her senses.

It was a grand meal, befitting a Michelin-star restaurant. With each exquisite bite, I savored the flavors that melded together in perfect harmony, a testament to Storm's artistry. The fusion of delicate French techniques with the vibrant produce of California was a revelation, a symphony of taste that left me spellbound.

As the evening progressed, courses dazzled, each more enchanting than the last. The restaurant's design and the masterful use of dry ice lent an air of magic to the proceedings, as if I had stepped into a fairy tale where culinary dreams were woven into reality.

When dessert arrived, a decadent chocolate and milk creation that seemed to glow with its inner light, I felt a surge of pride for my dear friend, Storm.

When he came by our table, I told him as much. "*It's A Fairytale* is your canvas, and each dish is a stroke of your passion and dedication to the craft. It's the most magnificent meal I've ever had."

"I agree," Alejandro added. "*It's A Fairytale* is not just a name, it's a promise fulfilled."

It was so thoughtful of him to have said what he did. I felt my heart melt. I knew how much this meant to Storm; it was written all over his face, a mix of humility and joy.

We joined the chorus of admirers, clinking glasses and raising a toast to *It's A Fairytale's* remarkable achievement.

"I wasn't expecting this...*magical* meal," Alejandro admitted. "Thank you, Atlas, for bringing me alone."

"Bringing you along? You twisted my fucking arm," Atlas grinned and winked at me. "And when I saw you at the table, I realized why."

I flushed. They all knew that Alejandro and I were having a lover's quarrel. It was my fault because I'd reacted poorly to his presence. The shock and surprise of seeing him in San Francisco had robbed me of my usual stoicism.

After we thanked our hosts, Alejandro offered to give me a ride. He had a car waiting. I decided I'd already made enough of a scene and got into his car.

"That was one hell of a meal," he remarked.

We were going to make small talk. *Well, whatever.* As long as he dropped me off and went his way, I could find the time and space to regain my composure.

"It was. I've always believed in Storm. He's an amazing chef, a true artist. But tonight, it felt like he blurred the lines between fairytale and reality, transforming a simple meal into an enchanting journey."

Alejandro nodded. We were sitting in the back of a sedan, the privacy screen in place. The distance from the restaurant to my hotel was short, but it could take some time in the never-ending San Francisco traffic.

"Did you date Storm?"

I looked away from the window where I was

aimlessly watching the city go by and turned to face him. "Oh yeah, I fucked all the brothers and—"

"Don't." He raised a hand.

"Don't what?"

"Swear. You do it when you're angry, when you're frustrated."

"I'm angry and frustrated. You kick me out of your house and say, I'll see you when I see you, and then you show up here? You knew I'd be here, didn't you?"

He nodded. "Raya mentioned and I may have asked Mercedes to investigate discreetly."

"I told you I don't want to play this on-again, off-again game with you."

"Will you let me explain?"

I shrugged. "Go ahead."

"I've never given a woman what I wanted to give you. I wanted to let my son know about you; that is a first for me. I felt like I was giving you something important, and when you turned me down, I felt rejected and insecure and took it out on you."

His honesty surprised me. I wasn't expecting him to admit that he was insecure, unsure of himself. This was a big deal, considering the alpha male nonsense he often pulled.

"I didn't want you to tell Silvano about us, not because of me, Alejandro, it was because I don't think *you're* sure about us. Are you?"

He took both my hands in his and stared at our laced fingers. "No."

I cringed, and saw pure agony move in his eyes. "Baby, I'm so sorry. But I haven't been here before. I'm a forty-two-year-old man who's never been in a relationship with a woman. I know how to be a father, a brother, a son, a friend...but I don't know how to be a lover or a partner. I need you to teach me, help me learn."

My eyes filled with tears at his confession.

"I..." The tears choked me, "I can't keep getting hurt."

He pulled me into his arms then, holding me tight. "I will try my best not to hurt you, but I will make mistakes."

His scent filled my senses, and the rightness of holding him again took over.

"I hurt you as well, didn't I?" I had been wallowing in my grief that I'd missed the point. Alejandro had opened himself to me, and I'd rejected him. Like they say, it takes two to tango.

"No, baby. This was my fault and—"

The car stopped in front of the Four Seasons.

"Where are you staying?" I asked Alejandro.

He smiled. "In the Four Seasons."

"Well, that's a lovely coincidence."

He shrugged. "I'm paying for two hotels tonight, one for my previously booked room at the Intercontinental and now here. I wanted to be in the same hotel as you."

I put a hand on his cheek. "I'm sorry, Alejandro, for hurting you."

"Baby don't say that. You did nothing wrong and—"

I shook my head. "Say, I accept your apology, Maria. You're not the only one who makes mistakes."

He leaned close and brushed his lips against mine. "I need your love, Maria, not your apologies."

My heart did somersaults. "Will you...ah...come to my room?" I asked, suddenly feeling gauche.

"*Duquesa*, I thought you'd never ask."

Chapter 31

Alejandro

"Alejandro, come inside," she moaned as she came back to earth from another high. I kissed her pussy one last time and crawled up her body.

"You taste…like heaven, and after four weeks, I was starving for you," I admitted, kissing her. "How do you taste, baby?"

"Like you," she whimpered because I drove inside her. I'd missed this, *oh absolutely*, but I'd missed *her*. No other woman would do any longer. I only wanted her. The realization made me feel both weak and strong at the same time.

"Spend tomorrow with me." I came all the way out and pumped into her again.

"I have a flight back at ten." She opened her eyes to look at me and smiled. "I'll change it."

"Cancel it," I suggested, slowing my movements inside her. "I'm going to fly back Monday morning. I'll take you with me."

"Fine, whatever. Alejandro, now shut up and make me come."

I laughed and kissed her. "Yes, ma'am."

We'd now slept together enough nights that we'd found our comfort zone. I wasn't a cuddler. Sure, when Silvano was little, nothing beat holding him close. But with women, I wanted...no *needed*, my space.

But with Maria, I spooned her. My cock resting against her ass was a delight—but it was more than that. It was being able to smell her, have her close. I wanted her with me all the time. I admitted that to myself as she snuggled against me, my arms wrapped around her.

"Goodnight, baby," she whispered sleepily.

"*Buenas noches, mi amor.*" This time, the words didn't *just* slip out of me; they were deliberate. *Son of a bitch, I was in love with Maria.* And that was why I felt like my heart was out of my body when she wasn't with me.

I nuzzled her hair with my chin. She was mine, I thought possessively, and that made me hers. I was sure of her, of us. It may have taken nearly losing her to understand myself better, but I had no regrets. Our experiences made us who we are and helped us learn what's inside us.

We slept in as Sunday mornings were for and made love in the shower. It had a certain domesticity; except we were in a hotel suite.

"You just paid for two hotel rooms for one night and stayed in neither room," she teased after breakfast as we strolled hand in hand through the vibrant streets of San Francisco.

I laughed. She made me laugh. She made me happy.

I couldn't help but feel a sense of elation that was impossible to contain. The past few weeks had been a rollercoaster of emotions, but now, at this moment, everything felt right. We were mending the fractures in our connection, and I was determined to make the most of our day together, a day bursting with promise and the thrill of shared experiences.

Our first stop was the MOMA, a haven of art that mirrors the colors and textures of our own journey. As we wandered through the galleries, Maria's eyes sparkled with curiosity and wonder, her enthusiasm infectious. We laughed at the quirky installations, debated the meaning behind abstract paintings, and found ourselves lost in the stories woven by the artists' creations.

"I always thought you look like a Botticelli painting," I told her.

"What?" she was incredulous.

"*The Birth of Venus* and then, at other times, *Minerva*. It's your serenity, unless you're drunk, then you probably are more like François Boucher's *Blonde Odalisque*."

She grinned. "Do you know the model whose name escapes me was fourteen when she modeled for the *Odalisque*? Louis, the fifteenth, was so intrigued by the painting that he summoned her to court, and she became his youngest mistress."

We stopped before Matisse's famous *Femme au chapeau*, Women With a Hat.

"I sometimes feel like that with you."

"Like what?"

She bit her lower lip. "Like someone who belongs in the Parc-aux-Cerfs."

I frowned. "My history is not great, and French is rusty as hell but wasn't that Louis's secret brothel?"

"I'm impressed," she raised her eyebrows appreciatively. "You know your art and your history. What I mean is that I sometimes feel like an houri when I'm with you."

I touched her face gently. "I'm so sorry—"

"No," she cut me off. "No...I don't feel insulted...ah... I made a mess of this. I mean, I feel like someone who is always ready for you. You touch me, and I'm aroused. You're there and—"

"I get hard. The feeling is mutual, *mi amor*. But let's not talk about sex here because I think they'll arrest us if we make love in the MOMA."

We stopped for lunch at a cozy bistro and then ventured into the Presidio, a sanctuary of green that provided a tranquil contrast to the bustling city. The scent of eucalyptus filled the air as we walked along the shaded paths, sharing stories and laughter that flowed effortlessly.

Maria's presence beside me was grounding and exhilarating, a reminder that despite the complexities between us, we could still find joy in each other's company.

"I think this is turning into a perfect day," Maria told me and gazed at the Golden Gate Bridge. "You know what will make it even better?"

"What?"

"How do you feel like bicycling across the Golden

Gate Bridge?"

It turned out to be the highlight of our day. The wind carried our laughter as we pedaled, the sun warming our skin and the breathtaking view of the cityscape stretching out before us. Maria's laughter was like music, a melody that echoed in my heart and banished any lingering doubts. For a moment, it was just us, the bridge, and the promise of an adventure waiting to be embraced.

As the sun dipped towards the horizon, casting hues of gold and pink across the sky, we found ourselves at a cozy restaurant on the pier. The scent of fresh seafood mingled with the salty air, and the ambiance was perfect for our evening meal.

"I love San Francisco," Maria said. "It's one of my favorite cities, well, after Paris."

"You like Paris?"

She nodded. "It's like an open-air museum. Every building, every nuance—the mix of old and new. What is your favorite city?"

I wanted to say wherever you are, but even I knew that sounded a little lovesick. "I must confess that I'm not a city person. But there's something about New York. I love the energy, the un-manicuredness of it."

She held my hand, and I felt like we were old lovers, comfortable with one another, at ease. "What is your perfect vacation?"

"Hiking down the Grand Canyon," I said immediately. "How about you?"

"Safari in Kenya."

"I've never been. I know Silvano would love that. Maybe you can take us since you've already been."

"I'd love to," she said and smiled that secret smile she saved for me, the one that said she loved me.

"Now, I'd like to talk about something you mentioned earlier."

She looked at me seriously. "What?"

"You said something about your *houri* pussy. I'd like to understand that a little better."

She burst out laughing.

Our conversation flowed effortlessly, and I realized I was finally allowing myself to be fully present in this moment with this incredible woman who had captured my heart.

Chapter 32

Maria

It's Murphy's Law that says if your love life straightens out, your professional life goes to hell in a handbasket.

I came back from San Francisco on a high and landed a regulatory crisis on my hands for an acquisition we were supporting for an American company to purchase a Japanese one. I was knee-deep in meetings, *long* meetings because whenever we spoke to our Japanese counterparts, we needed to have a translator—and the time zone didn't help.

"Can you make dinner tonight?" Alejandro asked as he got dressed in the morning in *my* bedroom. He'd come to LA the night before from Golden Valley and was going to take Silvano home the following day.

"I don't know," I confessed. "It's so busy at work."

I watched him as he put on his tie and felt a rush

through me. I was in a relationship. An honest to god, real relationship with a man who I was madly in love with and who I was convinced was in love with me even if he hadn't said the words.

"*Duquesa*, I need you to try. I'd like to have dinner with you and Silvano."

Since I'd never been in a *real relationship* before, I'd never had to juggle my time. In the past, I could always back out dinners or appointments with friends and family with no repercussions.

"Why don't you bring him here and we'll have dinner at home?" I suggested. "If I have time, I can cook, or we can just order in."

Alejandro paused as he saw me watching him. "What are you looking at?"

"You." I waved a hand at him. "You look stunning in a suit."

"I have a meeting with a California Congressman, so a suit is warranted." He stroked my cheek with a finger. "When I'm in Golden Valley, there's a better chance of finding me jeans, even at work, unless we have high-profile visitors."

"Oh, you look very nice in a pair of jeans."

I had had an early meeting that I took from my home office, so I'd already showered and dressed.

"I like you in these dresses." He put his hand on my waist and squeezed.

I wore a dark blue sheath dress that came with a matching suit jacket. I'd paired the outfit with tan pumps and my hair was tied away from my face in a ponytail.

"It's my version of a suit."

"I always want to muss you up when you're standing there so perfectly put together." His mouth brushed mine and then after a few strokes, he dug in. By the time he lifted his head, we were both breathing hard. "And I love to see lipstick smeared across your face."

I touched my face and sighed. "Damn it, I have a meeting in ten minutes."

"Just turn off the video."

"I'll see you later." I hated to leave him. I wanted to join him for breakfast. Read the paper with him.

"Are you sure you don't have time for breakfast? I can make you an omelet."

I looked at my watch and shook my head as I walked to the vanity in my room. I picked up a tissue and removed my lipstick.

"Maria, you have to eat."

"I'm so sorry, Alejandro. This M&A deal is...it's important, and it's a mess. I promise I'll do better."

"We don't have time to discuss this because you have a meeting," Alejandro remarked, "But you're doing fine. We both have a lot of responsibilities. We'll always have busy schedules. Now, go. I'll see you around six."

As I walked brusquely toward my office, I called out over my shoulder, "Text me what Silvano likes to eat."

It was a long day but by the time I dragged my tired self home, I was only an hour and a half late. I'd told Alejandro that he and Silvano should get something to eat and not wait up for me.

I hated that right after Alejandro and I had found some footing, I could not be there when he was in LA. He wanted me to have dinner with his son and I was spending my day talking to lawyers, trying to unsnarl issues.

I heard them laughing when I came in and it warmed my heart. Would life ever be like this? Where they'd always be there, making my home less lonely when I walked in?

They were sitting on my patio, playing chess.

"Hey, guys. I'm so sorry I'm late."

Silvano was first to move. He gave me a hug. "We had dinner at this cool restaurant."

Alejandro rose then and as if he did it all the time, he bent to brush his lips against mine. "Welcome home. Have you eaten?"

My heart stilled and then slowly beat again. He'd told Silvano about us. He'd never kiss me in front of his son if he hadn't. *Oh my god!*

"We got some junk food to stave off hunger while we worked," I replied. "Give me ten minutes to change and then, Silvano, I want to hear everything about your spring break internship."

Alejandro followed me into my bedroom. He closed the door behind him and pulled me into his arms. "I need a proper kiss." He devoured my mouth like his life depended upon it, which was fine by me because I felt exactly the same.

"I missed you today," I whispered. "I missed you so much and I'm so sorry I'm so busy; I wish—"

"Baby, don't," he interrupted me. "You're allowed to have a job. You're allowed to be busy. Trust me, I get busy too—and when I do, you won't see hide nor hair. At least that's what my mother says. So, take your time, change, and come join us."

"You told him about us?" I asked. My chin wobbled

as the pressure of the day and now the change in our relationship overwhelmed me.

He tucked a strand of errant hair behind my ear. "Yes."

"And?" I could feel panic rise. *Silvano seemed fine but...what if...?*

"He said he already knew and congratulated me on my good taste."

"Really?"

He kissed me again. "Yes, really. Now, take some time for yourself."

I nodded and walked toward my closet, taking my shoes off as I did.

"Oh, and Maria," he called out. I turned to look at him. "I want you to know that I'm madly in love with you."

The shoes I was holding dropped on the floor.

I flew back to him and wrapped my arms around him. I peppered his face with kisses, and he laughed, lifting me off my feet.

"You're in love with me?"

"Madly." He nipped at my bottom lip.

"You know this has been such a long and hard day; and now, you made it all better."

"I'll tell you I love you every day if that helps," he offered.

"Yes, Alejandro. That would help."

"I love you, Maria. Very much. Now say it back to me."

I touched his face, madly enamored. "I love you, Alejandro. Very much. *And* I said it first."

"So, you did and thank god you did."

Chapter 33

Alejandro

L ife fell into a pattern. We talked every day on the phone; sometimes when we missed each other too much, we also had phone sex—but it was getting increasingly difficult to make our schedules work so we could spend time with one another.

When I was traveling, she was stuck in LA; and when she was traveling, I couldn't leave Golden Valley. Since that Sunday in San Francisco, six weeks ago, we'd been able to see each other only twice. Once when I came to LA to pick up Silvano and once when she was in Chicago for a meeting at the same time as I was. Each time we'd spent less than twenty-four hours with each other, some of that time was spent sleeping after going at each other in bed like sex-starved maniacs, which we were.

Something had to give if we wanted our relationship to work. But I was in Golden Valley—and I couldn't leave. She was in LA. We both managed our family businesses, so it wasn't a job we could quit.

But this weekend, she was mine—except for Sunday evening when I'd promised to join her at her parents' place for dinner.

Telling Silvano about Maria had made life easier. When I told him I was going to LA for the weekend, he seemed fine with it. My parents approved. My brother high-fived me. Isadora was already planning the wedding.

"Not too fast, Isa," I tried to throttle her brakes. "We barely know each other."

"You've been seeing each other one way or the other for nearly a year."

She was right. It had all begun at Mateo and Raya's wedding reception; and their first anniversary was coming up. A year had passed since I first touched her, recognized her—and realized now, fell in love with her.

What a fool I'd been trying to fight it, trying to protect myself, knowing Maria was being confident in the fact she'd never hurt me. I'd be an ass and fuck things up from time to time, but her gentle soul would forgive me. And I promised myself I'd be more careful. The one thing I'd never do is take this relationship for granted.

Would we get married as Isa wanted us to? That was a bridge too far right now for me. I wasn't even sure if I ever wanted to get married again. The institution led to lawyers and prenuptial agreements—a nightmare when things got sour. In a relationship, it was easy. If things didn't work out, we walked away, no harm, no foul.

Yeah, so I was still pretty sure, deep down that this relationship, as fantastic as it was, would probably not last. Why should it? I looked around me and nearly half my friends were divorced; a quarter were actively working on it by either cheating on their spouses or making a mess of their lives—a small fraction were making it work. A *tiny* fraction.

Most couples I knew tolerated each other.

While I waited for Maria to join me for dinner in the city, she'd said she'd make it on time—though Friday evening traffic could put paid to her plans, I met with one such friend.

Lincoln Beckman and I grew up together, and considering how close our families were, we'd had no choice but to get along and become surrogate cousins. We were both competitive, hence we played racquetball. We were ambitious. However, Linc lied to the women he had sex with, I didn't. He was far more intelligent than me, but I beat him on life hacks. We also looked different, I was Latino, and he was as WASP as they came, blonde hair, blue eyes and skin that burnt to a crisp if he forgot sunscreen, even if he was out in the California sun for five minutes.

I met him close to UCLA where he was going to teach in the summer and was visiting to meet some of his new colleagues. It was also convenient for Maria, who would not have to drive too far in bad traffic. We met at Fellow on Glendon, a restaurant that was in a historic building and served excellent food and cocktails, according to the Michelin guide.

"I'm going to have to kick you out once Maria gets here," I warned Linc as he took a seat next to me at the bar.

"So, you put a ring on that?" he asked.

"Order a fucking drink," I instructed.

"If there's no ring on the finger, she's available," he remarked as he perused the cocktail menu. "Hey..." he looked at the bartender's name tag, "Honey? That's really your name?"

Built like a model, probably working here while she auditioned, *Honey* grinned. "Yeah. It makes it easy for men to not call *me* by the wrong name."

Mierda! We just got here, and someone was already hitting on him.

He smiled back, all white teeth. "Now that is a pleasant side advantage," and then he took an eyeful of her tits.

"Her eyes up there, *pendejo*." I gave him a playful slap at the back of his head as my father would if he were around.

"*Honey*, ignore my father here and make me a Los Angeles sour."

Honey flicked her blonde hair. "Sure, handsome. You want that vegan?"

"Fuck no."

She made the drink while I sipped my Macallan. "It's nice that you're moving back. How do your parents feel about it?"

"They'd rather I moved to Oregon...but seriously, I'm a tenured professor at NYU, there's no fucking way I'm leaving. LA is...well, a little bit of fun and research."

"LA is fun," I agreed. "Don't you miss the Central Valley?"

He shrugged. "Sometimes." Honey placed his drink on a napkin, which I noticed had her phone number on it. She'd inserted a heart instead of the O in her name. *Dios mío! Not much had changed since high school.*

"I miss the quiet. But I don't miss the lack of opportunities. I would never run Beckman Ranch; my parents knew that. My sister was going to get married to that asshole she hooked up with in high school and they would not leave the farm to Brick." His disgust for his brother-in-law was apparent and I couldn't blame him. Brick was a complete prick.

"How is Lacey?"

"Mother of two kids and miserable as fuck. My nephews are adorable, and I try to see them at least once a month. Because Brick is too busy climbing the corporate ladder to take his kids camping or show up for them."

Another marriage that was a shit show!

"Is he still cheating on her?" I remembered how when they were dating in high school, Brick's zipper was greased to slide at the slightest provocation.

"Probably. She says he's promised...but you know what? Once a cheater, always a cheater. I'm one and I can tell you that there is no woman out there who's going to make me stop thinking about new pussy."

He looked at the napkin and, with a smile, tucked it into his suit jacket's inside pocket.

"New pussy? How old are you?" I commented.

"I'm new in LA. I have to build that black book. You were never that guy though, were you? You were always loyal. Always monogamous. And then there was Anika and man, she was a headcase."

The problem or benefit of talking to someone who had known most of your life meant he knew everything about your past and felt free to comment.

"I try not to think about her."

"Not surprised." He took a sip of his drink. "I hope she gives head as well as she makes a drink."

"*Cristo*, you're an asshole, Linc. One would think studying sociology would make you a decent human being."

Linc laughed. "Dude, she gave me her phone number so I can fuck her brains out, not because she was hoping I'd respect her in the morning. Now, I *will* respect her in the morning, but I'll also fuck her brains out the night before, and maybe in the morning as well."

I sighed. "I thought once you became an erudite professor, you'd be more discerning about where you put your pecker."

Linc laughed. "I am *damn* discerning, Alejandro. Look at her," he tilted his head toward *Honey*, who was serving another patron at the bar, "She looks fine."

"She's alright."

"You say that because you're in love. I'm not in love."

There was something sad in his tone, as if he wished he were the kind of man who could fall in love. I could tell him I'd felt the same way until Maria walked into my life, but he wouldn't believe me; I wouldn't have believed him if it were the other way around. These were things you had to experience to believe.

"Speaking of being in love," I breathed as *she* came into the restaurant. Her dark hair curled glossily around her shoulders. She'd painted her lips red, and it looked damn good with the little black dress she wore that hugged her in all the right places.

Wrong places since Linc was enjoying watching her.

"Stop ogling my girl." I punched him good-naturedly on the shoulder and rose to meet Maria.

She beamed as she came up to me. She always was so happy to see me that it made me feel like I was ten fucking feet tall. I kissed her. "Hey, baby. You look beautiful."

"And you look...very delicious." I wasn't wearing a suit, I didn't have any meetings, and I'd left Golden Valley in my home uniform of jeans and a dress shirt.

"Hey, Maria, leave that asshole and come here to a real man," Linc called out.

She laughed. "Hi, Linc. Are you joining us for dinner?"

"No, he's going to go away as soon as they take us to our table," I assured her.

Linc gave her a hug and made a face at me. "She smells like fucking cinnamon."

"Stop sniffing my girl."

"You look great, Maria, and my friend here is smitten. It's good to see him happy after all these years," Linc said seriously. He brushed his lips on her cheek. "Thank you for taking such good care of him."

Maria was surprised by the change in tone, I wasn't. Linc was a lot of things, but he took friendships seriously. And sure, he kissed my prom date, but she hit on him first. They always did. He was the Golden Boy of Golden Valley while I was the dark thunderstorm. The girls who liked bad boys came to me—the girls who didn't know he was the bad boy looking like a pretty boy ended up with him and a broken heart.

"Thanks for meeting me, Alejandro." Linc and I shook hands. "Oh, and I told Honey, you'll pick up the tab."

"Why me?" I demanded.

"I'm a lowly professor. You own the biggest fucking farm in California. I'll see you around, Maria."

"You know he's quite charming," Maria said to me, and I growled at her. "No, really. He's not my type though."

"And who's your type?" I waved to the hostess to let her know we were ready for our table.

"You," she said without hesitation. "You are *exactly* my type."

Yeah, love made the world go around, I thought, and she was making mine spin in the best way possible.

Chapter 34

Maria

I was nervous about taking Alejandro home, not because I worried about the impression he'd make on my parents, but more about the impression my father would make on him. My mother was fabulous, and she'd love Alejandro, I just knew it.

My father, on the other hand, wasn't happy with anything right now. He felt he was forced to retire, which was true. The board had not been happy with him and had been extremely supportive of my taking over as CEO. Although I was a Caruso, the board could very well have chosen someone else to run the company; that they had blessed me was a clear sign to my father that I was better than him and that drove him nuts with jealousy. Yeah, he was *that* kind of parent.

He was unhappy that Mark had not wanted to have anything to do with finance. My father's family was from San Sebastian and patriarchy was nailed into his soul. He had always wanted Mark, his son, to take over the family business after him. When he didn't, it increased the split between them that first came into existence when Mark announced at fifteen that he was gay. My father thought he should give it time— Mark told him he didn't need time; he knew his own sexuality.

My mother was an artist, a painter and spent vast swathes of time in her studio. She was *very successful*. It hadn't mattered to my father when he'd been the CEO of an investment bank but now, it pissed him off. He had been offered opportunities to consult and mentor startups, but he had turned those down. He was going to work on his golf handicap, which he did regularly and he ran the business with the same determination, all numbers, and no heart. His handicap was doing no better than Caruso Investments had under his leadership.

"What's bothering you?" Alejandro asked as I drove us to my parents' house in Beverly Hills.

I stopped at a red light and turned to look at him. "My father is...well, not very nice. I don't think there is any other way of saying it. He was tolerable when he was working, but now he's...out *there*. My mother knows how to manage him. They love each other, you'll see there is doubt there but, I wouldn't be able to if my husband ever did and said the things my father does."

Alejandro put a hand on mine, on the steering wheel. "He will not scare me off."

"It's just, your family is open, wonderful, warm, and loving and my mother is all that. But Daddy is a special kind of person. Most of the time I don't even like him, which is hard for me because it hurts my mother. Mark and I tolerate him. She's emotional. She's an artist."

Alejandro sat back. "Yes, I know. I looked your family up, Maria. And you have a painting of hers in your dining room."

I smiled as I did when I thought of my mother. "Judith Caruso is one hell of a painter, isn't she? You know, neither Mark nor I have an artistic bone in our bodies and she's fine with it. But my father gets his knickers in a bunch because Mark didn't want to go into finance."

I took a deep breath. I was getting worked up, and we were ten minutes away.

"I should've taken a Valium or Xanax or something," I mutter.

"Hey, baby," Alejandro tried to calm me. "I'm not interested in your father. I'm into you. I don't care about him. Okay?"

I nodded but wondered how it was all going to turn out. *Would Alejandro run for the hills? I should've asked Drago to come along as a buffer.* He'd known my father for so long that he knew how to handle him. Drago couldn't stand my father but tolerated him as we did because he absolutely adored my mother and would do anything for her.

I stood at the threshold of my childhood home, my heart racing. I swiveled my head to release the tension in my shoulders.

"You look like you're getting ready for battle." Alejandro stood behind me and put his hands on my shoulder, gently massaging me.

I leaned into him.

"I love you, *Duquesa*," he murmured close to my ear. His breath washed over me and despite the stress, I felt arousal.

"I know what you're doing."

He let his hands fall from my shoulder to my hips so he could pull me against him. "You make me so hard, baby."

"Alejandro, not here."

"Absolutely here." He turned me around, so I was facing him and kissed me, long and deep.

We heard someone clear their throat and I all but pushed Alejandro to turn around. He held me and smiled. "Hey, Mark."

"My mother is cool, dude but if you debauch my sister on their front patio, my father is likely to swing his golf club at you."

I hugged Mark. "How's he?" I asked.

"Did you know I could make three hundred percent more money if I had your job instead of what I'm doing right now?"

"No shit," I muttered.

We walked in and the aroma of a delicious meal filled the air. My parents had a cook, a *bona fide* chef. They'd always had someone to cook because my father couldn't cook if his life depended upon it, and also, *women do the cooking* according to him. My mother spent so much time immersed in her art that she forgot to eat most of the time.

My father was sitting in his favorite chair in the living room, his back to the entryway. He did that on purpose so he could decide if he wanted to turn around and address you or insult you by ignoring you.

My mother came down the stairs right as we stepped into the living room and all but ran to me. My mother and Mark shared features—and were both blondes. My father and I had similar eyes and hair.

"Maria, it's been so long." She hugged me tight. She was the same height as me, nearly 5'10". We were a tall family. Daddy was as tall as Mark, nearly six two.

"Alejandro, it's lovely to meet you." My mother was a big hugger, but Alejandro was used to it because his family hugged a lot as well. "I've heard so much about you from Maria, but also Raya and Esme." She took his arm and walked him to the living room and then turned around in a mock whisper and said, "And he's hot. Good work."

"Great, my mother is hitting on my boyfriend."

Mark put his arm around me. "Don't worry, your father will cut him and everyone else to size. I wish he'd find something constructive to do with his life instead of sitting around and golfing. Mama won't let him interfere with her art, so he just stews in his juices until she gives him the time of day."

My father didn't rise from his chair and didn't extend his hand when he was introduced to Alejandro, until my mother snapped, "Don't be rude, Javi."

He reluctantly rose and did as his wife asked. If Alejandro was perturbed by his behavior, he didn't show it. We sat down in the living room, Alejandro next to me on a couch. My father was in his chair. My mother and Mark on another couch across from us. It was like Daddy was presiding over us as the monarch of the family.

"Mark, darling, can you make us some drinks?" my mother requested.

Lucky bastard, I thought, and he winked at me, indicating that he was happy to leave the unpleasantness that had settled into the living room.

"I'll have scotch. Macallan if you have it," Alejandro told Mark.

"Champagne for you, sis?"

"Ah...actually, I'll have scotch as well." I needed the fortification. My father was like a dark cloud, and I wished that he'd let my mother rub off on him because he could use some of her sunshine.

"I'll have a dirty martini, Mark, you know how I like it." My mother seemed absolutely unflustered by my father pouting like a child. I looked at Alejandro beside me, his easy smile calmed my nerves.

"I've heard lovely things about Golden Valley. I was thinking maybe I could spend some time there and paint."

Alejandro was all smiles. "Absolutely. I can set up a studio for you. We have plenty of space."

"Really?" My mother hadn't expected the warm welcome. Alejandro was certainly laying it on thick, offering to build a studio for my mother.

"It's nothing. We have lots of barns and cottages. My mother would love to meet you."

"This is your stepmother, right?" my father piped in.

"Yes, she's my mother," Alejandro maintained.

"She raised you?"

Alejandro shrugged. "I was fifteen when my father met her."

"How old is your son?"

Oh crap! I knew where he was taking this conversation. I was about to say something, but Alejandro put a hand on my thigh, an intimate gesture meant to soothe me but also to show my father I was his now.

"Eleven."

"Raya and Esme are in love with your son," my mother chimed. "I've seen photos. What a handsome young man. And I hear that he's very smart. I'm sure he and Mateo are getting along."

"Yes, I think they have a common understanding of the challenges people with high IQs face." Alejandro thanked Mark when he handed him his drink, as did I.

I tried not to chug the whiskey down.

"Are you hoping that Maria will become your son's mother?" my father asked, deliberately, loudly.

"*Javi*," my mother protested, "What they do when they're together and build a family is their business. Ignore my husband, Alejandro."

"It is *our* business. She's my daughter," my father was adamant, "and I think she deserves better than taking care of some woman's leftover ch—"

"Stop, Daddy." I stood up. "Enough. Don't you dare say anything about Silvano? I love that kid."

Alejandro had stiffened, and I wished he hadn't had to hear what my father was about to say.

"Alejandro, I apologize on behalf of my husband." My mother rose and looked angrily at my father. "What's going on with you?"

My father shrugged. "You don't need to apologize for me. I have a right to—"

"Nothing," my mother interrupted him. "And if you continue to behave like this, you'll find that your kids will not tolerate you even for me. Now get your head out of your ass before we get to the dinner table."

Alejandro's eyes danced with amusement. My mother never admonished my father in front of people, not even us, that she was doing it now was a big departure.

My father seemed torn between walking out, yelling at my mother, blaming me for his mood and taking a shot at Alejandro. Thankfully, he did none of those things because the chef announced that dinner was ready.

"I'm so sorry, Alejandro," I whispered as we settled into our seats at the dining table.

"Don't be. You are not responsible for your father's behavior."

He said the right things, but I could feel his stiffness. As the evening progressed and my father focused on the steak, we dissipated some of the tension with Mark telling stories about being a resident.

"Why did you choose neuro?" Alejandro asked Mark.

He straightened. Mark always liked to tell a story. "Well, I was thinking cardio, but I changed my mind. This was probably in my first year of medical school. We had the task to identify and label different structures on a human cadaver. I had a partner and she and I were both overwhelmed, overeager, and exhausted. We wanted to do a good job." He raised his glass and cheered.

"And then what happened?" my mother asked. "I've never heard this one before."

"He changes the story each time," I informed Alejandro.

"The confusion started when we came across a complex network of blood vessels around the heart,"

Mark began. "We were supposed to identify the coronary arteries and veins, a task that proved to be quite the challenge. Feeling a bit like bumbling detectives, we began sticking labels on what we hoped were the correct vessels. Let's say we had the most labels sticking out of our cadaver...and we mixed up pulmonary and coronary arteries. Since then, I decided neurons probably would be less complicated."

"Yeah, like I'd let you anywhere near my brain," I teased.

My father sat sulkily and then, as if he'd waited long enough, he asked Alejandro. "Where are you from?"

"Excuse me?"

"Where are you from? My family is from San Sebastian."

"Two generations ago," I interrupted.

"Oaxaca," Alejandro said. "We still have family there. Paloma, my mother is from Boston, I think second or third-generation, part Spanish and part Italian or some other mix. We're all probably mutts."

"We're European."

I stood up. I'd had enough. "You need to stop speaking now, Daddy."

"What? I can't make conversation."

"Not racist conversation." Mark stood up as well. "I have an early shift tomorrow, so I'll leave with you."

My mother looked hurt. "Maria..."

I shook my head. "It's one thing when he does it to us but he's doing it to the man I brought home. And that's not okay."

"Drama queens all of you," my father stated.

"Daddy, I'm leaving and not coming back until as

Mama asked you to do, you pull your head out of your ass and stop behaving like a misogynistic racist."

So much for wanting a quiet Sunday evening, I thought as I yanked Alejandro's arm to drag him out of my parents' house.

Chapter 35

Alejandro

S he was embarrassed.

I honestly didn't give a shit about her father. I also didn't like her mother, regardless of what Maria said. She was probably a lovely person, but she both emasculated her husband and made her kids suffer through her husband's verbal abuse in the name of Sunday family dinner. There had to come a time when everyone agreed that this was toxic and walked away from it. I knew familial complications were challenging. I was lucky. My family loved each other, supported each other, and didn't tear each other down, but I knew other families where this was rote.

She didn't speak on the way home and I let her be silent. I knew instinctively what she needed to do was to gather her thoughts.

Once we got to her place, I poured both of us a glass

of wine and joined her on her patio with the twinkling lights.

She had tears in her eyes, and it hurt me that she hurt. "Baby, no. Don't cry."

She took the glass of wine from me and set it on the side table next to the wooden outdoor couch she was seated on. I joined her, and she immediately buried her face into my chest. The sobs were almost silent, coming from deep within her.

I stroked her back, holding her, wanting to make the pain inside her go away. There wasn't much I could do. This was something she and her brother had been dealing with all their lives. Their mother had kept the family together, but I wondered at what cost.

I rocked her gently and after a while, the sobs stopped and her breathing normalized. She pulled away and looked at me with puffy eyes.

"You're not a pretty crier," I teased.

She gave me a watery smile. "I know. Oh, no, there's mascara all over your shirt."

"It'll wash." I took her hand in mine. "You want to tell me what that crying jag was all about?"

She sniffled, her eyes downcast. "I wanted you to like them. I like your parents so much and I wanted you to like mine—and I know you didn't."

I put a finger under her chin to lift her face so she would look at me. "I love you. Does anything else matter more than that?"

"Family is important to you and me. I love my brother. Mark and I are close, almost like survivors of Daddy. My mother...I know she enables my father's bad behavior but today she stood up to him in front of you, which shocked us and him, I think." She touched my lips, tracing them with a finger. "Mama wanted you to like us, all of us, because she's heard so much about your family from Raya and Esme."

I kissed her finger. "You are not to blame for your father. He's a grown man, and he's making his own choices. Just because I'm lucky to have the parents I do doesn't mean I'm going to judge you for not being as fortunate."

"He was really awful, wasn't he?"

I didn't respond. It was one thing to complain about your own parents, quite another to have someone else do it. I didn't like the man. He had behaved like a pompous racist, and he'd gone after my kid. But Maria had verbally kneed him in the *cojones*. She'd protected my son, and that was what had made my pulse hammer, knowing that I was loving the right woman.

"Is this the first time you walked out of dinner?" I asked even though I knew the answer.

She nodded. "Usually, Mark and I...well, we don't want to hurt our mother. She's really wonderful, if a little flaky. But she's an artist, her mind wanders. It's who she is. But she's kind and loving. She embraced Esme who has worse parents than mine. I mean, her father is in jail and her mother is in denial."

I didn't say that I thought her mother was a manipulator. She took advantage of how she treated people to make them tolerate her husband. I couldn't say whether she did it knowingly, or it was a habit from years of living with a man who had not learned his social skills—either way, the result was the same. Her children felt guilty for not loving their father.

I kissed her on her forehead. "You're a wonderful,

fabulous, loving woman and I feel very fortunate that you love me. I feel proud that you love me. I feel relieved that you love my son so much that you stood up to your father even though you knew it would hurt your mother."

Her eyes glistened with tears but also joy. "I love you. And I love him. And...my heart is full, Alejandro. So full and..."

She hugged me then tight, and I felt the rightness of it.

We went to bed after and made love with a sense of euphoria. I'd never made love with a woman I was in love with, and all the songs were right, I realized—it *was* magical. There was a peace to the lovemaking, a poignancy to the passion that made the sex hotter and the love brighter.

Afterward, we lay in her bed, her thigh across mine, my semi-hard erection nestled against her, my cum leaking slowly out of her—which was enough to make my semi go to full alert.

I stroked her back as our breathing evened out. *Would it always be like this?* I wondered. *Would it always be new, every time?*

"Do you have to go into work every day? Can you work remotely?" I asked her.

She tipped her head up, her chin resting against my chest. "I can work remotely. Why?"

"If we set up an office at my place in Golden Valley, could you work from there?"

It was a big decision, I knew that. But I was having trouble juggling my family, my work, and Maria. Something had to give. I couldn't work remotely. I ran a fucking farm, and I had to be at the farm when I was not traveling for meetings with distributors, regulators, agriculture agencies, and lawmakers. I didn't enjoy spending my weekends away from Golden Valley because that was the time I spent with my son, quality time, not time where my head was in my job. Now, I was conflicted, wanting Maria and him.

Now that Silvano knew and my family accepted, it would be easier for Maria to come and stay with me.

"I'll still be traveling...and will need to come here when we have certain meetings," she speculated.

"Just a few days here and there," I emphasized. I wasn't asking her to move in with me. *Or was I?* No. I wasn't ready for that.

She understood and nodded. "I can do that."

"I can send a car for you, or you can fly. Whatever is easy? I don't like being away on the weekends from Silvano. If you could come to Golden Valley, it would mean I don't have to miss either of you." *That sounded right, didn't it?* And not too much like my life is more important than yours, so you need to hang out with my family and me in bumfuck Golden Valley.

"Sounds lovely." She rolled away from me and laid on her back, her eyes closed. "You could also bring Silvano here. I can set up a room for him."

I had thought about that but that seemed...a bit too intimate, too close to *let's live together and get married.*

"We can work that out," I evaded.

"I bought this house so there would be room for children," she mused.

I stiffened. I didn't want more children. I was done. No more diapers for me until Silvano had kids, and that was a long way away.

I pretended I'd fallen asleep instead of opening a whole new can of worms with Maria. The relationship was still in its infancy. We misunderstood each other more often than the other way around. I didn't want to start a new drama, so I let it go and decided that we'd discuss it if she explicitly brought it up, until then we'd continue as we were, two people dating, not planning some grand future with fucking babies and that whole nine yards.

Chapter 36

Maria

Days turned into weeks and weeks into months—
and before I knew it, summer was here. Of
course, in LA, the weather was always nice, but
summer was special because everyone at my office
worked from home at least three days a week. This
meant that I could be in Golden Valley from Thursday to
Monday.

Since Alejandro had asked me to stay with him
and work from his house, I'd been able to go there
during most weekends. But during the week with work
consistently at a high pitch, finding time between air
travel, airports, meetings, and work for us to meet had
been challenging. We talked every day, but with our
busy schedules, sometimes it was hard to find the time
to have a proper conversation. We looked forward to
the weekends when we'd be together; the other days, we

missed each other.

"I don't know what to do, this long-distance thing is killing me," I confessed to Raya when I was invited to a girl's night one summer evening at Joey DTLA with Daisy, Esme, and Vega.

I didn't know Vega well, having met her only a few times. I knew, though, that her full name was Carolina Vega. She went by Vega with the Knight Tech crowd, and by Carol in the Santos household, where there was much speculation about her relationship with Aurelio. She was a complete knockout. Her dark hair was tied up in a chignon, and she had the body of a supermodel crossed with a fighter because those muscles that showed in her sleeveless dress did not come for free. Her elegant persona and magnolia-smooth accent were potent, and I could see why Aurelio was attracted to her. She was a striking woman who was noticed as soon as she entered a room.

"If he wants pussy, then he needs to travel. If you're looking for dick, you travel. It's a fair equation," Vega offered, holding up her glass of red wine as a toast.

Esme had once told me that Vega intimidated her, but she also loved the woman who was an intelligent lawyer. She started her career as a public defender in Dallas and had risen to the role of Assistant District Attorney before leaving the state and moving to California, where she was now the Knight Tech legal counsel.

"What if we both want each other?" I countered.

"No such thing," Vega informed me. "There's always one party in a relationship who is more eager... depending upon time and place. Am I right, ladies?"

Daisy shrugged. "I think Forest has an erection all

the time. So, yeah, he's more needy regarding sex."

"And you help him out," Raya teased.

"I'm just trying to be a good wife." Daisy laughed, and it was infectious. Her laugh was big and loud, coming from deep within her. She was a woman who didn't disguise her feelings; she was as authentic as they came.

"How about you, Raya?" I asked.

Raya twisted her mouth as she thought about it. "I don't know, Vega; I think we want each other the same amount."

"Oh, please. I know Mateo, and he's the one who is ready to crawl over broken glass for you."

"That's true," Esme agreed. "So, does Aurelio want you more or..."

Vega took a sip of her wine. "He shows up when he wants me and when I want him, I demand he shows up. I don't want to complicate matters by going to his place. He lives with his parents."

"Not *with*," I protested, "just close by. Actually, from what I hear, he's closer to the mountains and at least a 30-minute drive to the main house, and when it snows, it's sometimes days before they see him."

"He probably likes that," Vega muttered. "The man is an introvert."

"Are you seeing each other exclusively?" Raya wanted to know. "I hear tidbits, and then there was the time when you threw a drink in his face."

Vega sighed. "He aggravated me. He never said we were exclusive, so, *maybe* I pretended to see other people, and he lost it. It ended with me throwing a glass of shitty Chardonnay at him."

"So, you are now exclusive?" Daisy asked.

"I think so. Can we stop being clichés who talk about men and talk about something else? Daisy, how was Cannes? I saw *Hopedale* was a big hit."

Yep, she *was* intimidating. It would be interesting to see her with Aurelio, who was quiet and easygoing.

Daisy was flushed with pleasure. "It was a dream. And Kai was fabulous. You know how much Forest hates the limelight, so I took Kai with me for one of the red carpets."

"Those photos hit the media hard." Raya held up a hand for a high five, and Daisy reciprocated.

The photos of Daisy in a designer Gucci dress designed for her with a baby carrier were a huge hit. Many social media sites hailed them as the best-dressed couple at Cannes.

"I know you said no men, Vega, but I need to ask Maria something." Daisy held up a hand to keep Vega quiet. "Is Drago seeing anyone? I have a couple of single friends."

Vega threw her hands up in the air. "Do you think when men get together, they talk about women?"

"Yeah," I laughed. "I think they do. Drago is not seeing anyone. But he'll resist you every step of the way if you try to set him up."

"Do you know Drago?" Raya asked Vega.

"I've met him," she said tightly.

"Please tell me you didn't sleep with him. Or you did, which is fine," I smirked.

She shook her head. "No. I didn't sleep with him. It was...ah... an official thing."

We all turned to look at her, and she drank some

wine. "What?"

"Is something going on?" Esme put a hand on Vega's shoulder. "Is it the company? My father?"

"Drago is in homicide now, so it can't be your father, Esme." I was concerned because Vega, who revealed little, had shuttered further.

"I...I don't want to talk about it."

"Yeah, we don't care about what you want," Raya snapped. "What the fuck, Vega?"

"Fine," she relented. "Someone I put in prison in Texas is here, and Dallas PD informed me about it, so I wanted to check in with LAPD. That's all. Drago was the detective who they asked me to speak with."

"What cases did you try in Dallas?" Daisy asked, and when Vega didn't answer, she added, "I can ask Forest to look it up. It'll take him minutes to invade your privacy."

"He has no jurisdiction in Dallas," Vega quipped and waved to the server. "Can we all have one more round of the same, please?"

"Wanna bet?" Daisy was not giving up.

"I prosecuted lots of people. Murders, rapists... crimes against persons. It was complex and challenging, so I left all that to come here and be a corporate shill. Can we let this go? I'd rather talk about men and their penises. Speaking of which, how big *is* Alejandro's dick?"

I burst out laughing. "I haven't measured it."

"It's big," Daisy confirmed. She'd had a one-night stand with Alejandro many years ago.

"Last question, and we can move to measuring erections. Are you safe?" Raya asked.

"Of course, I'm safe. I can take care of myself," Vega

retorted.

We all looked at each other with concern for Vega.

"If you need anything," Esme used her schoolmarm tone.

Vega patted Esme's hand. "I will."

Daisy clapped then. "Okay. I want to know about summer plans. You were all very kind to give Forest and me a fabulous honeymoon in Santorini, and we were thinking of renting a big place in Greece where we could all spend a week this summer."

Esme's eyes brightened. "Oh, that would be so much fun."

"I'm in," Raya agreed immediately.

"What about Mateo?" Daisy asked.

Raya took a sip of her drink and shrugged. "That would be a question for him. I don't believe couples should spend all their vacations together. I sometimes need my space, and I take the Ducati and take off. Mateo is fine with it."

"That's because he can track your whereabouts," Daisy countered.

"True. But I don't have the heart to give him a hard time. He's so petrified I'll get up and leave again. I hope he'll calm his titties soon because it drives me nuts."

Raya had left Mateo and all her friends, disappeared for several weeks, and found refuge in Golden Valley. It had been a difficult time for both of them—but now I could see that they were closer than ever.

"Why don't all of you look at your calendars, and I'll get my assistant to reach out so we can plan this?" Daisy suggested and then looked at me pointedly, "And now let's get back to Maria's predicament about work-life balance and long-distance fucking."

Everyone had outrageous suggestions, but in the end, one thing was clear, if I wanted to have my cake and eat it too, I needed to become more flexible about my job and start delegating more, so I have more time for a life outside of work. As a young CEO still trying to prove herself, I feared taking that chance. I needed more time, I thought.

"Talk to Alejandro," Esme suggested. "Tell him you're conflicted about how to make this work."

I worried my lower lip and finally admitted, "I feel like if I say anything, he's going to get upset like he did last time and run."

Vega narrowed her eyes. "You can't be afraid in a relationship. Either he loves you and is open to discussing issues with you, or he can go fuck himself."

I chuckled. "I know. But it's still fragile, this new relationship of ours. There are still so many things up in the air. He just told Silvano about me. I don't want conflict."

"Talking to him isn't conflict; it's finding a solution together. It's what you do when you have a partner, Maria," Esme said.

I took a sip of my drink and nodded. I felt like a coward, walking around eggshells with Alejandro, scared he'd do a runner as soon as something went amiss. "I'll think about it," I soothed, changing the topic to Esme's daughter Mireya. We checked out her photos and cooed about how cute she looked, especially in the pictures where she was with Kai.

That only made me more contemplative. I didn't even know if Alejandro wanted more children. I wanted to be a mother, no question about it. But what if he said he'd had enough and Silvano was all he needed?

As great as this relationship was, it also drove me up the wall with how difficult it was to navigate. Something had to give and soon.

Chapter 37

Alejandro

I liked seeing her in my house. She had commandeered my office and I loved that she had. I wanted her to be comfortable in Golden Valley and my home.

I'd never seen Maria in her CEO persona and it was a kick to watch her in business mode. She worked hard. She worked a lot. But she was also much younger than me. I'd been CEO for nearly a decade now and I remembered how it had been when I'd first taken over from my father. Maria had been CEO for two years at most; and she was so young. No wonder she was running around like a chicken without a head.

I said as much when we sat down for dinner when she came in harried from the home office.

"Papa, that's patronizing," my son contended.

I blinked. "No, I'm just saying—"

Silvano shook his head, which silenced me. "She's working hard. Just like you did when you took over from Abuelo. You shouldn't make what she's doing trivial because you're past that."

Maria grinned, raising her glass of wine. "Thank you, Silvano."

I felt chastised and rightfully so. "You know they say parenting is a learning experience—and I'm learning. You're right, Sil, I was being patronizing. I'm sorry, Maria."

She shrugged and patted my hand. "I think you were trying to tell me to slow down and you're right. I should delegate more. Teaching me from your experiences is not patronizing. I'm happy to learn from you."

"*And* she's a diplomat," Silvano mused.

Sometimes it was hard to remember that he was eleven, well nearly twelve in a week.

I'd asked him what he wanted for his birthday. A long time ago, we'd stopped giving presents for birthdays and Christmas—and instead, shared experiences together. We usually took some time off and traveled between Christmas and New Year as a family. Last year, we went to the Maldives and the year before, to Finnish Lapland. The experiences we shared as a family were varied and we remembered those more than any gift wrapped under a tree. For birthdays, we requested an experience. When I turned eighteen, I'd asked to drive a Ferrari; and when Aurelio turned eighteen, he'd asked to get a tattoo. Now at thirty-four, he had a tattooed sleeve; apparently, you couldn't get just one.

For Silvano's twelfth birthday, he'd asked to visit CERN in Switzerland to tour a particle accelerator, which we would do in a month's time in early July when he was on summer break. On the day, he was going to go to UCLA to work in Professor Jabra's and learn to use a virtual particle physics simulator to conduct experiments, which would give him a hands-on feel for what happens inside particle accelerators and detectors. When I was twelve, I asked to go see a soccer game.

After dinner, which I cooked, Maria and Silvano cleaned up. I watched as I drank my wine, sitting at the kitchen counter. They had become friends. Silvano was a smart kid—not just about particle physics but about people. He was open and engaging, but he didn't seek them out as he did Maria. From the start, he enjoyed her company more than that of others who were not family. It had caused me some heartburn, wondering what would happen when Maria and I broke up but as the days passed, I started to believe that maybe this relationship would be for a longer term (*please don't ask me how long*). I was grateful that they got along so well. No matter how much I loved a woman, if she and my son had a problem, I'd always choose my son.

After cleaning up, Silvano told us that Isadora and his grandparents had arranged a horror movie night in their theater room.

"We're going to watch *The Exorcist* and *The Conjuring*...and after that, you know, Isa is going to want to sleep in my room," he said masterfully.

"Or rather, you'll want to sleep in her room," I guessed more accurately.

"You know me, nothing scares me," Silvano grinned.

While Silvano packed up for a horror night at the main house, I put my arms around Maria. "Why don't you get yourself naked and into the bathtub while I drop him off."

She linked her hands around my neck. "Okay. Will you join me?"

"Yes." I kissed her softly. "I've missed you, *Duquesa*."

We nearly dived apart when we heard Silvano coming down the stairs. We'd not yet become comfortable with PDA in front of my son. He knew we slept in the same room, and we touched each other here and there, but we'd maintained decorum around him. It was a habit and maybe I wasn't yet ready to show him how much I loved Maria. I think it was because all his life Silvano knew he was the most important person to me and now with Maria joining our twosome, I didn't want him to wonder if he was in second place.

"You know you're going to be scared for weeks, so why are you watching horror movies again?" I asked as we drove the quick ten minutes to my parents' place.

"Because it scares me so good," he said with a laugh. "And it's fun. Isa hides her face in her hands for about fifty percent of the movie. Abuelita leaves after the first gory scene and Abuelo and I hold hands during the *really* scary parts."

"Hey, how do you feel with Maria here? I know she's been here for weekends, but now she's here from Friday to Monday."

Silvano seemed to think about it. "I like her, Papa. I like how you're with her. You seem happy...not that you weren't happy before but a different happy. I don't know how to explain it. And she's smart. I enjoy talking to her. She doesn't dismiss me like some people do and she isn't putting on an act of being interested in me because she's interested in you, which some people do."

"What if she lived with us?" I broached.

"Like if you two got married?"

I let out a breath. "Let's not go all the way to the M word. Let's say we live together. The three of us."

"Would we live here or her place in LA?"

"Here, of course." That was a no brainer.

"I don't mind but I think she will."

"Why do you say that?" I parked outside the main house and waited for him to answer.

"There's nothing to do here, Papa. I mean, we grew up here and we like it but for a city person won't this place be too boring? You know Beto, my friend at school?" I nodded. "Beto's father was seeing this woman from Fresno, and she said she wouldn't move down here in the middle of nowhere and Fresno is like forty minutes if you drive within speed limit. Faster if you don't, which *you* don't. LA is bigger than Fresno. Have you asked her?"

"I wanted to check with you first."

Silvano shrugged. "I'd ask her. If it makes you happy, we can live in LA. I'll miss Isa and Abuela and Abuelo... but we'd visit, right?"

"I can't live in LA, Sil. The noise and crowds would drive me mad."

He gave me a quick hug and opened the car door. As he was stepping out with his backpack, he turned and said, "Maybe we should continue the way we are. She's here for part of the time and we go see her once in a while. Abuelo said that all relationships require compromise."

Fucking smart kid. I was sure he didn't get that from Anika...and probably not me. Maybe Paloma, which made no sense since she wasn't related to us in blood. But if we weren't an example of the fact that blood was bullshit and real relationships were about the heart then I didn't know who was.

Chapter 38

Maria

I rarely took the evening off. When I was at home, I worked unless I was going out, which was not more than once a week. I worked a lot. I'd never felt guilty about it until I met Alejandro. Now, I felt like I needed to make time for him and Silvano. I worried that if I didn't, he'd leave me. There seemed to be a constant fear inside me that I'd lose him if I made the slightest mistake. Probably a sign that this was not the healthiest of relationships.

I lay in Alejandro's massive bathtub and let the warm water do its thing. I was exhausted, I realized.

"Hey, baby."

I opened my eyes as a naked and very aroused Alejandro slid into the bathtub. He lay across from me, his feet tangling with mine in the huge bathtub.

"Hey."

"You look supremely relaxed."

"I am. This bathtub is heaven."

"*You* have a bathtub."

"It doesn't have you in it." I crawled in the water and straddled him. He held his hands on my hips, balancing me atop him. "Alejandro."

"Yes, baby." He moved me so I felt him between my legs.

I moved my hips so I could stroke my clit over his silky erection. Velvet over steel.

"Are you wet, *mi amor*?" His voice was harsh, which happened when he was aroused.

"Yes," I whimpered.

He stilled my movements and lifted me, and then slowly slid into me. I gasped when he was fully inside.

I tried to move, but he stilled me. "No."

"But—"

"No," he said firmly. He brought one hand between my legs and found my clit. He stroked me, not letting me ride him until I was frustrated, sobbing with a need to release.

"I know, baby," he whispered.

Would sex with him ever become monotonous? Pedestrian? I couldn't imagine a time when I'd be so used to him I wouldn't feel the way I did whenever he was around. My heart, body, and mind were involved— attracted—impaled by him.

He pinched me, oh, so gently and I came hard. I fell apart, not able to recognize the cries coming from deep inside me.

He pulled me off him and dripping wet, came out of the bathtub. He held out his hand, and I followed, my legs feeling like jelly. He pushed me against a wall and pulled my hips out.

"Hands on the wall, *Duquesa*," he commanded.

And then just like that, he was inside me, hammering hard. It had never been like this, I thought as the world collapsed around me. But it was never the same with him, was it? His hands were punishing against my hips and then they moved and grabbed my breasts, rolling my nipples between fingers until I hurt. Pleasure and pain dissolved within each other.

He came as I did, this time it was softer but just as potent. I felt so weak that he had to carry me to bed. I lay in bed, drowsy. I felt even lazier when he cleaned me with a warm towel.

I was nearly asleep when he pulled me against him, my head on his shoulder, one thigh over his, between his legs.

"Alejandro?" I called out.

I felt his hands stroke my back. "Yes, *mi amor*."

"Never leave me."

I felt him kiss my head and then I fell asleep. It wasn't until the next day I realized he hadn't responded to my plea of never leaving him. Our relationship was still as tenuous as ever and my heart was still, very much, in danger of being ripped apart.

We both pretended the next day that we were doing just fine—but a stress had entered our relationship.

I asked Mark about it as I drove home from Golden Valley.

"Relationships have a resolution...people live together, make plans to get married...but you guys have been together for more than a year and you constantly feel you're at the beginning of the relationship."

Mark may not be a psychologist, but he had the insights. And he never ever hid the truth as he saw it from me.

"I keep thinking we're doing well and then I realize we're not. He said he loves me and told his son about me and yet, I feel that there is a lack of commitment from his side. Am I being a drama queen?" I leaned back in my seat and navigated the Sunday evening traffic on I-5.

"Don't denigrate your feelings," Mark urged. "You're a beautiful, loving, and wonderful woman. You're *not* and have never been a drama queen. You don't need to justify your feelings."

"I constantly feel on the edge with him," I admitted. "I keep worrying it will end."

"Talk to him about it," Mark suggested.

"I'm scared and yes, I know that is a sign that this relationship is not as solid as either of us think it is or wish it would be."

"What does he need to do to make you feel secure?" Mark asked.

I knew the answer to that, but I hadn't even voiced it inside my heart because I didn't think it was possible. But this was Mark, and he knew the right questions to ask to make me unravel. "I want him to propose to me."

"And you don't think he will?" I heard sounds around Mark. He was in the ER this evening and was taking my call because I was a selfish sister.

"Go work, Mark. I'm so sorry. You're saving lives and here I am—"

"Stop *denigrating* yourself," he repeated. "If I can't talk to you, I'll let you know."

"I don't think he'll ever ask me to marry him. I keep waiting to ask him to move in with him, but he keeps it as me *visiting* them."

"Can you move in with them?"

"I can make it work. Be in LA for a few days and Golden Valley the others…but he doesn't ask. And I keep thinking today is the day he's going to pull the rug from under my feet."

Mark sighed. "Maria, you need to tell him how you feel or end this."

"I don't want to end this," I protested in panic.

"Maria," his voice was cool, and he used the tone he did all our lives when he wanted me to do what I knew was right, even if I didn't want to.

"I love him. And he says he loves me."

"Then you should be able to talk to him."

I sighed and ignored the finger a driver gave me as I recklessly passed them.

"You're no help," I snapped.

"I think you know what you need to do, and you need to find your balls to do it. And speaking of balls, we have a situation in the ER that I need to go handle."

"It's got something to do with balls?"

"Close. I think we have a Viagra overdose situation."

Chapter 39

Alejandro

We celebrate birthdays in the Santos family. We have good food, cake, and a party. For Silvano's twelfth birthday, he had two parties, one with his friends and one with the family and close family friends.

Raya and Mateo had called from two different locations, and we'd talk to them on a group video call. Raya was in Johannesburg, and Mateo was in London.

Maria had come early in the morning. This time, she'd had a car and river so she could work on her drive over. I had suggested shortening the journey by taking a helicopter, but she'd turned it down, preferring to drive. I knew it hadn't been easy for her to make the time, considering it was smack in the middle of her workweek.

Even though it was a tradition not to have presents

for a birthday, Maria had asked me if it was okay to get Silvano something.

"I know he's going to love it," she said when we talked on the phone, which was our nightly ritual.

"Of course. It's just in the family that we don't do presents. So, you're most welcome. Why? Did you find something great?"

She assured me it was and Silvano's response to the present proved it.

"Oh my god," Silvano screamed when he unwrapped the present, a book, and looked at the first page. "It says, *Dear Silvano, welcome to the club from one physicist to another. Alain Aspect.* It's Alain Aspect. He wrote this book, and he signed it for me."

Isadora elbowed me. "Who's Alain Aspect?"

"I'm guessing a physicist."

Silvano explained excitedly. "He won the Nobel Prize for quantum mechanics in 2022 for experiments he did with his partners in entanglement."

"What's entanglement?" my father asked.

"It's a phenomenon when two particles behave as one and affect each other, even though they can be at a vast distance from one another, maybe on opposite sides of the planet or the solar system."

We all looked confused.

Silvano waved a hand. "Never mind. Just know this is super cool. Maria, how did you do it?"

"A friend of a friend of a friend knows Professor Aspect and did me a favor." She ruffled his hair, and I felt a weight lift off of me.

"She's great with him," Isadora whispered.

"Yeah."

"You're going to marry her?"

"I'm thinking about it. Geography will be a problem."

"When love is right, everything can work," Isadora said longingly.

Aurelio approached us while watching the interaction between Maria and Silvano. "You need to put a ring on that finger and close that deal down."

"That's what I said." Isadora slipped an arm through Aurelio's.

The three of us stood at the doorway between the living room and dining room, having just finished cleaning up after dinner, while Maria, my son, and my parents were in the living room.

"Oh, and before I forget, Alejandro, you must be here for tomorrow's meeting. The USDA is sending a rep over, and you know I get hives whenever the government is hanging around."

"I can't. I'm taking Silvano to LA. He has that thing on Friday at UCLA."

We both looked at Isadora, who raised both hands, shaking her head. "I can't. I have the Crazy Woman & Hot Guy wedding this weekend."

"You mean the Patterson party?" Aurelio asked. "He's not a hot guy."

"He's hot," Isadora confirmed, "And so pussy whipped, it's painful to see. And she's nuts, wants pink roses, and then changes her mind and says she wants red...like you can do that two days before a wedding. Sorry, Alejandro."

"Why don't you let Maria take him?" Aurelio suggested. "She works close to UCLA, and they get along well."

How do I tell them I was uncomfortable leaving my kid with her without sounding like an ass? He'd be safe, but I didn't want her to get the wrong impression that she was suddenly responsible for him because we were dating. He was my kid, and I didn't want to burden Maria.

"She's swamped," I objected.

"Ask her," Isadora recommended. "I think she'd love to have him all to herself. Maybe they'll listen to some jive and do some jive."

"That was some dancing, wasn't it?" Aurelio mentioned.

I strolled toward Maria and sat beside her, my shoulder touching hers. I took her hand in mine as I watched Silvano explain to my befuddled parents why quantum mechanics was such a big deal.

"Thanks. That was very thoughtful of you. He'll treasure that book forever."

"I was worried I wouldn't get it on time, but a friend who teaches at the Sorbonne did some magic."

Purposefully, I slid an arm around her, and she immediately leaned into me. I had kept my distance from her when others were around, but now, with everything out in the open, I didn't resist my impulse to touch her, which I seemed to want to do all the time.

"I can't come with you tomorrow because the USDA is doing a drop-in. Could you take Silvano with you, and I'll come down on Friday?"

"I'd love to. Thank you for asking me. I'll take good care of him."

"I know you will, *Duquesa*. I don't want to inconvenience you."

She banged her head gently against my shoulder. "Silvano is never an inconvenience. I'm honored that you'll let me have him all to myself."

"You are a treasure, Maria." I brushed my lips against hers. She flushed, aware of what bringing our relationship into the open meant. To give my family credit, no one acted like an asshole with whistles and catcalls, which they could do and would have done, but didn't so as to not embarrass Maria.

I thought I could get used to this as the family sat around drinking our after-dinner coffee, and Silvano ate more cookies than he probably should. There was a sense of peace for the first time, and I owed it all to the woman sitting next to me.

My mother smiled at me as if saying, *good work, son.* My father's approval was explicit when he thanked Maria for coming over by saying, "At least now Alejandro will be in a better mood." Silvano was smitten and had been for a while. Isadora was ready to plan the wedding and dropped enough hints that I wondered if I should find my way to Tiffany's in LA and look at rings. Aurelio hugged Maria, which for him, said it all: *Welcome to the family.*

That night, we made love in leisure because we had all the time in the world. She was a vision as she rode me, her hands cupping her breasts and her eyes closed in reverie.

After she fell asleep, her head resting against my shoulder, I decided that I'd go to Tiffany's and look for a ring. It was time. I was ready to get married again—to Maria. With that happy thought, I let sleep claim me.

Chapter 40

Maria

Silvano had the best time playing with the virtual particle simulator. After I picked him up from UCLA, we went to Broken Spanish, a Mexican restaurant. We ordered a feast of tamales, caracoles and pollo prensado.

Being alone with Silvano made me feel even more connected with Alejandro, like we were in a real relationship. He trusted me with his son. The only people he trusted his son with were family. *Was I now family?* I wondered.

When I'd asked him if I could give Silvano a birthday present, he'd said it almost nonchalantly, *"Of course. It's just in the family that we don't do presents. So, you're most welcome."*

That hurt. I'd covered it up, but if this continued, it would be death by a thousand cuts. Finally, the relationship with such promise would end. But my brother was right; I had to talk to Alejandro, be open with him about my vulnerabilities and insecurities. I didn't think Alejandro wanted to discuss my concerns about our relationship. He never asked how we were doing, if this was working.

I did, and he said, "You're the first woman I've taken home since Silvano was born." For him, that said everything, but I needed more. I wanted a commitment. I was thirty-two years old; I wanted to have a family and children, and, as terrible as it sounded, if Alejandro wasn't interested in *all that*, I was better off not wasting more than this one year on him.

"Papa would love this food. You should bring him here next time he's here to see you," Silvano recommended.

"I'll do that." I was in love with this kid, I thought, and his father. I wasn't wasting my time with them but living my life. And even if Alejandro didn't commit, where would I go? What other man would appeal to me after this was over?

"Maria, I need to talk to you about something. But before I do, I need a promise."

I was about to say I couldn't promise something without knowing what it was and then realized I wanted to. I'd keep my word with this kid. That's what parents did. Well, at least some parents did.

"What do you need me to promise?"

"That you won't tell Papa."

Oh....well...now that's complicated!

He looked at me with such sincere eyes that I agreed, "Unless it hurts you, I promise not to tell him anything."

Silvano smiled. "Thank you. I'm thrilled that you and my father are together. You both feel right. You make each other happy."

"I know he makes me happy, and I'm glad you think I make him happy."

He pushed his plate away and sat up straight. "Papa never talks about my mother."

Oh no!

"I have seen some photos of her but that's all. I know she died in a car accident when I was a baby, and it's not like I miss her or anything, but...I do."

He paused and looked around aimlessly at the other patrons in the restaurant. I waited. He had something on his mind.

"I heard some people talk about her."

I took a sip of my margarita and said nothing.

"They said that my mother committed suicide."

I gasped. "Oh, Silvano."

He nodded. "I need to know what happened. I don't know her, and I want to know who she was. I've tried to ask Papa, but he shuts down, and...you know how he is? He won't allow a conversation to happen if it's too confrontational. He's not mean; he just won't talk about it."

That was precisely how I felt when I tried to talk to Alejandro about our relationship. He would steer the conversation away from the topic. He did it so deftly that I'd let myself be manipulated. It was one thing doing this with me, I was a grown-up, but Silvano was a child, albeit a smart and sensitive one. I felt angry at Alejandro. He needed to deal with his past, so he could help Silvano deal with his.

I cleared my throat. "I know nothing about your mother, Silvano. I just know her name, and that's about all." It was a white lie, but I didn't think he needed to know that his mother hadn't wanted him.

"You have a friend who's a detective."

"Drago, yes."

"Can he help me find out what happened to my mother?" he asked. "I just want to know about the car accident. I've tried to tell myself that it doesn't matter, but I can't stop thinking about it. I've looked online and found her obituary but nothing else. That's how I found photos of her. She was beautiful."

Well, this was tricky and way out of my league. I didn't know what the right thing to do here was.

"And you're sure you don't want to talk to your father about this?" *Damn it, Alejandro, you're driving this kid nuts with your avoidance behavior.*

"Yeah," he said firmly. "I thought about it a lot before I came to you. I don't want him to get hurt; he will if he finds out I want to know about her. He's a great father, and I don't want him to think that he's not enough. He is. But I just want to know about my mother too. Is that wrong?"

"No, Silvano. It's pretty natural. Let's think about it a little and get back to it. Okay?"

He nodded. "Do you think we can order dessert?"

"Yes," I laughed.

After we got home, Silvano entered the bedroom I'd set up for him to play on his computer and talk to his friends. I'd been thinking about Silvano's request all evening, wondering what the right thing to do was. Unable to help myself, I called the one person I knew who could guide me.

"Maria, I'm so glad you called. How is Silvano? And how are you?" Paloma peppered me with quick questions.

"Silvano is good…and…I need your help."

There was a pause, and then Paloma spoke, "I think it's perfectly okay for a woman to propose to a man."

I grinned. God, she was persistent about Alejandro and me getting married.

"It's about Silvano."

Her tone went from playful to serious in an instant. "Okay."

I told her what Silvano wanted me to do for me and asked her the question that was burning through my gut. "I feel like I need to tell Alejandro, but Silvano asked me to promise I wouldn't. I don't know what the right thing to do here is."

Paloma was quiet momentarily and then, to my surprise, said, "You keep your promises to children, Maria. If you don't want to reach out to your detective friend, that's your decision, but you don't betray Silvano's trust."

"And won't that piss off Alejandro?"

"Alejandro is a big boy; his emotions and feelings are not your concern. He needs to handle himself. Silvano is a child, and it's his feelings that you need to be careful with."

Paloma made things seem crystal clear when, just a minute ago, everything was so muddy. "What do you think I should do about his request that I reach out to Drago?"

"Let me ask you something. What do you think is the

right thing to do here?"

I took a deep breath. "A child wants to know about their parents, it's the most natural thing. He's worried she killed herself because she had him. He didn't say it, but I could hear it. Knowing it was a car accident will put his mind to rest."

"Then you know what you need to do."

Chapter 41

Maria

Drago came over the following morning as his shift didn't start until later. I canceled my morning meetings and made breakfast for Silvano and Drago.

After my conversation with Paloma, I called Drago and explained what I needed. He'd been remarkably supportive.

"I'll find out what happened. I will not give him the case file, no matter how smart he is, he does not need to see that. But I will relate the facts to him. Kids want the truth."

"I don't know how to talk to him about this," I confessed.

"Don't worry, I worked vice; I have a lot of practice talking to kids about things they never should have the need to know about. "

After waking up, I'd told Silvano that Drago would join us, and he could talk to him about his mother. I felt comfortable now that I'd spoken with Paloma. I knew I was doing the right thing.

"I looked up your mother's case," Drago began as we ate pancakes with maple syrup, strawberries, and whipped cream. Quite the contrast between our innocuous food choices and conversation.

Silvano's eyes were wide. "Thank you."

Drago nodded. "You're welcome. Your mother was driving a Porsche Carrera GT. It was a brand-new car; according to the file, nothing was wrong with it. So, they ruled out mechanical failure. Your mother's blood alcohol level was not high, and her tox screen was clean. This means she was not under the influence. Unfortunately, we can't say the same for the truck driver who hit your mother. He was high on both alcohol and some other chemicals. He lost control of his truck on Highway 99 in Madera County and slammed into your mother's car. She died on impact, and the truck driver died a few days later because of internal bleeding."

Silvano took a deep breath as if processing what Drago had told him. "And you're sure she didn't...you know...kill herself?"

"Yes, I'm sure. I went through the case file and also called the detective who worked the case in Madera County. He assured me this was vehicular homicide because the truck driver was impaired. I know it doesn't change the fact that you lost your mother. I see so many of these cases—and families sometimes want there to be a reason to explain the death because it's so meaningless, but accidents happen."

Drago was sympathetic and put a hand on Silvano's arm. "I'm sorry for your loss, son."

Silvano looked at Drago in surprise, his eyes filled with tears. I gave Silvano a hug while he sat on the chair. "Oh, baby, don't cry. I'm so sorry."

He shook his head. "It's not that... it's just that no one has ever said they're sorry my mother is dead. It's almost like everyone has forgotten her and expects me to do the same. But I lost my mother, and when Drago said he was sorry for my loss, I realized that not having a mother is a loss. I have lots of people in my life, but I don't have her."

Drago pulled an envelope from his blazer pocket and put it in front of Silvano. "The case file had some of her photos. This was routine information gathering. Her parents gave these to the detective, and he sent them to me. Maria said you wanted to see her, so I printed them out for you."

Silvano grabbed the envelope and pulled out the photos. I watched from over his shoulder.

Anika Madsen was a beautiful woman. She'd been thirty years old when she died. Two years younger than I was.

There were three photos. One was of her on a beach in a sundress and a hat, her golden hair curling around her shoulders. She was laughing, her eyes wide with amusement. If I had to guess, she'd probably been in her early to mid-twenties then. In another photo, she wore a wedding dress with an empire waist. She looked stunning with flowers in her hair and a love for life in her eyes.

My heart clenched. I didn't know that Alejandro had had a proper wedding with Anika. Of course, he had.

I wasn't exactly jealous, but I felt a pang of green that she'd had something I so desperately wanted.

She was in riding gear in the last photo, standing by a horse. It looked like the Golden Valley stables where I'd recently been with Alejandro. *Had he taken her riding to his favorite place as he had done with me?*

Silvano put the photos back in the envelope. "Can I keep them?"

"Of course. I got them for you."

"Thank you so much." Silvano held out his hand, and Drago shook it. He turned to look at me. "Thank you, Maria. This was important for me. Thank you for taking it seriously and not brushing it aside because I'm a kid."

I ruffled his hair. He had so little of that woman in the photos. He was all Alejandro. "I'll always take you seriously, Silvano. How do you feel now that you know what happened?"

He shrugged. "Weird. I've wanted to know about her for so long, and now that I do, I don't know how to feel. I feel like I betrayed my father...I also feel that...I wish I'd met her. She's so pretty, isn't she?"

I nodded, tears clogging my throat.

"Silvano." Drago put a hand on his shoulder. "Don't dwell on the past. You don't live there. You live now. And also, don't bring a past you know very little about into your present."

Silvano, who was wiser than most kids his age, nodded somberly. "I'll try but...I wish she was here now. I wonder what that would be like."

It would have been hell, I wanted to tell him—but it would hurt him more to know that his mother hadn't wanted him over the fact that she wasn't there with him right now.

Chapter 42

Alejandro

Maria was in a video conference in her home office when I came to her place. She'd given me thumbprint access to her house. The modern version of giving the key.

I was exhausted after some long days battling it out with the USDA. But as things stood, Golden Valley would continue to sell produce across the United States. I had taken the helicopter, too tired to drive the distance. I intended to go back the same way with Silvano the following day. Maria could join us. Maybe I should propose to her in my home...soon to be our home.

The little blue box with the big rock I bought this afternoon was secure in my backpack beside my computer. I went straight to Tiffany's in Beverly Hills after I landed in LA. I'd bought jewelry before for my mother and sister, so it wasn't my first time in Tiffany. However, this was the first time I bought anything for a woman who wasn't family.

In the past year and especially the past few months, Maria had seamlessly become a part of my world. This woman not only had my heart but also won over my family and son.

The door's soft jingle echoed through the air as I entered Tiffany, greeted by an overwhelmingly elegant atmosphere. I wanted to find a ring that reflected Maria's sophisticated taste without being over the top. A sales associate whose name tag said they were Clifton welcomed me with a friendly smile, and I got straight to the point.

"I'm here to find an engagement ring," I confessed, my voice steady despite the moment's significance.

Clifton's genuine enthusiasm was unmistakable. "Congratulations! We have a collection that I'm sure you'll appreciate. What kind of style are you thinking of?"

How the fuck did I know?

"Honestly, I don't know. I know she likes to wear pearls, and she has jewelry from here and Chanel, the usual." My hands immediately went into my jeans pockets in a defensive gesture.

Clifton smiled. I was not the first clueless man to walk into their life at the store. "Why don't you tell me a little about her?"

"She's...ah...a capable businesswoman. She's beautiful. She's about five, eight- or -nine and dresses professionally. You know, skirt suits and dresses with jackets, that sort of thing. She's practical...but likes designer stuff."

She's magic in bed, and I get hard just thinking about her. But Clifton didn't need to know that.

"I think we have something for you."

No shit, Sherlock. This is Tiffany & Co.

They took me to a display of rings. Diamonds in various cuts and sizes glittered before me, but I knew this choice had to be about more than just sparkle. It had to symbolize the commitment I was ready to make, the future we would build together. And it needed to suit her, be evidence that I knew her. *Did I know her? Shouldn't I know what kind of ring she'd like? Was I rushing into this?*

Carefully considering each option, I felt a flicker of excitement and dread with every glance.

But when you know, you know, they say, and I knew. There it was—a solitaire diamond on a platinum band. The design was classic, yet it had a unique flair that felt right for Maria. It was a ring that exuded confidence and timelessness.

I asked Clifton to take it out for a closer look, and as the ring caught the light, I could picture it on Maria's finger. It suited her.

Turning to the sales associate with a nod, I said, "This is it." And then wondered if I should spend more time looking for the right ring? How much time did people usually take? *Fuck.*

"It's a great pick," Clifton remarked, but he probably said that to everyone.

"Give me a minute." I held up my hand and called Isa.

"What?" she barked.

"I need help."

"Alejandro, I'm in the middle of—"

"I picked a ring for Maria, and I need to make—"

She screeched. "Oh, Alejandro. Of course." She turned video on, and I could see she was in the ballroom at the Inn, where they were setting up for a wedding.

I zoomed the phone onto the case of rings and then on the one I'd chosen that was on a small silver ring holder.

"You picked that?"

"Yeah. Why?"

"I...you have such crap taste in jewelry that I'm impressed."

"I don't have crap taste in jewelry. You love the stuff I buy you."

"Because you're my brother," Isa retorted. "You buy such old-fashioned stuff. I give it to Mama; it suits her better. But this...this is Maria. I love it. It's simple and elegant. Just like her."

"It took me two minutes to find it," I explained nervously, "Is that a good thing, or am I rushing it?"

Isa smiled. "When you know, you know. And it's not the ring, Alejandro, it's the wedding, which I can't wait to plan, and—" She turned around with her phone and cried out, "Not there. Come on, guys, I said specifically that goes out in the garden. Alejandro, I have to go."

She hung up on me, and I looked at Clifton, who was smiling.

"I've had some people walk in, spend hours, and leave without a ring. Sometimes, someone walks in, and they know, like you do," they comforted.

"Okay. Let's do it." I pulled out a credit card.

Cradling the ring box in my hand, I felt a mixture of anticipation and nerves. This step wasn't just about fulfilling expectations and sealing a promise as accurately as the diamond in that box. With the ring secured, I thanked Clifton. I stepped back into the California sunlight, the weight of the ring a reminder of the commitment I was about to make.

"Silvano," I called out once I was in the living room.

My son stuck his head out of his room at the end of the hallway. "Hey."

I went into the room he was staying in and was not surprised that it had been set up for him. Maria had made sure there was a King-size bed, a desk with a large monitor for gaming, and an ambiance right for a boy of twelve with a bookshelf, a place to hang a backpack, and an armchair with a wide arm to hold a laptop. The room had a large window with blue drapes that let light pass through, so the room was bright.

I hugged Silvano from the back because he was deep into a game. I kissed him on his hair and sat down on the bed so I could watch him.

He had his headphones on as he played, and I knew he was talking to his friends. "No, no, no. Yes! Did you see how I did that?"

He was comfortable here, I thought. Once I proposed to Maria, we'd have to discuss where to live and her schedule. I couldn't leave Golden Valley. Maria would have to figure out how to work remotely. We could make it work with a few days for her here and the rest in my place. We both traveled for work and had to find the right balance, so we weren't always alone with Silvano. I wanted the three of us to be a family.

I walked to the bookshelf and browsed the books,

thinking about how and where to ask Maria to marry me. *Should we have the children's conversation now or later? Now, obviously. She needed to know that this marriage would mean one child for both of us. Would she become a mother like Paloma had to Aurelio and me?* I could see that happen.

I picked up a white envelope on the shelf, and two photos slid out. I froze as I pulled the last photo out. My hands shook. What the fuck were Anika's pictures doing in—.

Silvano turned then, and his face fell when he saw what I was holding. "Guys, I have to go." He took off his headphones and rose.

"What...how...do you have these?"

"Ah...Papa, don't be angry."

"I'm not angry. I'm confused."

"Drago got them for me."

Drago? The detective who was Maria's first lover? That Drago?

"I don't understand."

Silvano took a deep breath. "I heard someone say that my mother committed suicide. This was months ago, and it's been...well, it's been on my mind."

"She didn't commit suicide, and I don't want you to worry about these things, Silvano."

"I know you don't. But I do, anyway. I wanted to talk to you about her, but every time I tried, you shut me out."

My heckles rose. "That's bullshit. I've been open and transparent with you, always."

He took a step back and I reigned in my temper.

"Papa, I wanted to know and didn't think I could talk

to you."

"So, you talked to Drago?"

He bit his lips and then stood straighter. "I talked to Maria. I asked her to help me. She talked to her detective friend. He told me that my mother died in an accident. He told me what happened. And he gave me these photos. Do you know we have no photos of her? I want to know who she was?"

I could barely control the rage I felt. *What the fuck did Maria think she was doing? How dare she expose my son to this?*

"There's nothing to know. She was your mother and died when you were a baby."

"No one talks about her. Why did you both get married?"

So much for being honest and transparent. "We... ah...were dating, and she got pregnant."

"So, you got married because of me?"

That was the truth, so I nodded. "We didn't know each other well, but once she was pregnant, there was no way I would not be a father."

He folded his arms at his chest then. "I want to know about her."

I hated that we were having this conversation. I had shielded him for years, and I would continue to do so. He didn't need to know Anika left both of us for a couple of million dollars. I was a meal ticket, and so was Silvano.

"Like I said, I didn't know her well and—"

"Are her parents alive? I'd like to meet them."

My heart thudded against my chest. I had told Anika's parents that there was no world in which they'd know Silvano. Their daughter had walked away, and they should as well. They'd tried in the early days of Silvano's life and then had given up. They died a few years later.

"Why?" *Hadn't we given him enough love and affection? What had we done that he wished for this other family?*

"I just want to know about her," he explained. "Please, Papa."

I nodded. "They're dead, Silvano. But...we can talk about her if you want."

I softened my stance and walked up to him. I hugged him close, and I calmed myself when his arms went around my waist. Silvano was a boy. He was curious. Maria should've been more circumspect. She should've immediately contacted me, so I could've managed the situation. Instead, she'd exposed him to his mother. There was no way I'd allow this woman back into my life. She'd interfered in my relationship with my son, which was the end of the line as far as I was concerned.

"I love you, Papa."

"I love you too, Silvano."

Silvano looked up at me. "Are you angry with me?"

"Of course not," I replied sincerely. No, I was angry with Maria.

"Thanks, Papa."

There was no way I would spend the night here, but I didn't want Silvano to feel like he'd caused a rift between Maria and me. He was fond of her, but he'd get over it. Just as I would.

"How do you feel about spending the night with Mateo and Raya?" I asked.

I knew he'd think I wanted to be alone with Maria, which was true. The conversation I needed to have with her didn't need an audience, especially my son.

I texted Mateo and told him my car would drive Silvano to their place. He and Raya looked forward to spending time with him since they'd missed his birthday.

But unfortunately, Isadora had already sent out the bat signal because I got a message from Mateo: *Congratulations, by the way.*

I didn't reply to that. I'd talk to my family after I spoke with Maria. They'd agree with me because they wanted to protect Silvano as much as I did. Sure, they'd be disappointed as I was, but we'd all get over it. Protecting Silvano was more important than a good lay.

Chapter 43

Maria

Alejandro was on my patio when I came out of my endlessly long meeting. He stood, looking away from the door, his hands in his pockets.

"Hey." I ran to him, wrapped my arms around him, and rested my cheek against his back. "I missed you."

He put his hands on mine and moved me away as he turned to face me. He stepped back when I tried to walk into his embrace.

"Did you see Silvano?" I asked.

"I sent him to Mateo's place. You and I need to talk."

He looked so serious that I felt the first frisson of fear climb up my spine. "Okay."

"How dare you interfere in my relationship with my son?" His tone was repressed anger, ready to burst out of its containment.

"What?" I was puzzled with his barely controlled

rage. His nostrils flared, and he reminded me of an angry bull.

"When my son asked you about his mother, why didn't you contact me?"

Well, it was going to come out sometime. But I had not expected him to be *this* angry.

"Ah...Alejandro, I promised him I wouldn't tell you. How did you find out?"

"*He* told me."

I swallowed. Silvano had no subterfuge, and I knew he would not have willingly told his father about his desire to learn more about his mother, so I wondered how Alejandro got it out of him.

"I saw the photos of his mother, and he told me what you did."

"He said he didn't want you to know. He didn't want you hurt."

"So, you crossed lines and talked to him about something you have no fucking business doing? And you get your fucking boyfriend involved? Who the fuck do you think you are?" His voice had been steadily rising, and he all but screamed that last question out.

A part of me wanted to run and hide, but the other, the one that had found her balls, which Mark had asked me to see, would do no such thing.

"Keep your voice down," I said coolly. "You don't get to talk to me like this. No one does. Your son asked me for help. He wouldn't have had to if you weren't so adamant about avoiding difficult conversations."

He looked at me with disgust that everything inside me recoiled, and my heart broke.

"Don't tell me how to be a parent," he scoffed. "Don't

tell me what it means to have a close family because you know nothing about that. Between your manipulative mother and vindictive father, it's no wonder you think this is how relationships work."

"Alejandro," I protested. His words were bordering on cruelty.

"How dare you, Maria? I trusted you, damn it. I—"

"You can always trust me, Alejandro." His son was everything to him, and I was compassionate about his feelings. I wanted to bring down the temperature of our conversation.

"Trust you?" He bellowed. "I think that ship has sailed. What is it you were trying to do? Become so close to Silvano that he'd convince me to stay with you?"

Compassion be damned. "Don't flatter yourself."

"You think you're the first woman who's tried to get to me through my son?"

"Alejandro, I was helping your son. He asked me for a promise, and I kept it. You're a grown man, and you should be able to manage your feelings; Silvano is a child, and I felt it was my duty to—"

"You're not his fucking mother," he interrupted me. His hands were out of his jeans and were rolled into tight fists.

"I know."

"You are no one to him. Got it?"

I felt sadness claiming me, replacing all the fight. I felt empty. Whenever I had thought about breaking up with Alejandro, my throat tightened with emotion. But then, I hadn't known that sometimes the heart was so broken that there was no room for anything but the broken pieces, not even tears.

"Got it." I planted a plastic smile on my face. "I think you should leave now."

Alejandro looked surprised at me. He'd probably thought I'd beg and plead, try to make it right, allow him to unload all the anger and loathing for me inside him. As Paloma had said, he was a grown-up and had to manage his emotions; I was not responsible for him.

He stood rooted where he was, so I left my patio, my garden haven, and went into my bedroom. I locked the door behind me so he couldn't follow. I sat on the bed, my hands steady. I hurt so much, but I'd always known it would end. I'd always know he'd leave. And if he left me because I'd taken care of Silvano, so be it. I had no regrets.

I wanted desperately to cry and release the tightness in my chest, but nothing was inside me. I'd been waiting for this to happen, and now that it had, it felt like an expected explosion, something I had been preparing for.

He always had a foot out the door, didn't he? Mark had been right; I should've talked to him as soon as I had doubts. Maybe then I wouldn't be this affected, broken, or destroyed. I had seen this happen in books and movies and always thought those women were weak and vapid. *Karma was a bitch! I* was now one of those women.

I lay on my bed after a while and watched the ceiling as the room darkened. I'd never see the sunset in Golden Valley again, I thought, or the sunrise. I'd never make love with Alejandro again. I'd never walk hand-in-hand with Silvano. That was the more considerable hurt, losing him along with Alejandro.

I could hear my phone ring, but it was far away,

somewhere in my office. I ignored it.

Then there was a knock on my bedroom door. *Alejandro?*

"Maria?" It was Raya. I turned to look at the clock; it was ten at night. It had been five hours since I'd left Alejandro on my patio.

I rose tentatively and opened the door. "Hi," I said wanly. "How did you get in?" The door locked on its own when someone stepped, and Raya didn't have thumbprint access.

"I let her in," Mark said from behind her.

I walked to the living room and gasped at the number of people in my house. "What are you all doing here?"

"I brought ice cream. I know it's a cliché, but it works," Daisy announced. She had little Kai at her breast.

"My go-to is Chinese food." Raya pointed to the Chinese food cartons.

Mark held up two bottles of Châteauneuf-du-Pape, my favorite wine. Esme came to me and hugged me. "How are you?"

"How did you all know?" I asked, resting against Esme.

"Alejandro came to pick up Silvano and..." Raya hesitated, "Well, we all knew he wanted to be alone with you. We thought it was because he was going to propose. Then he comes over and says he ended it with you."

Propose?

"Apparently, he bought a ring at Tiffany today." Mark brought out wine glasses from my glass cabinet. He opened a bottle of wine and poured it into several glasses.

"Come on." Daisy patted the space next to her. "Tell us the whole sordid story."

They were all here because they knew I'd be upset. The front door opened then, and I gave out a choked laugh when I saw Drago walk in with a box of chocolates from Edelweiss, my favorite chocolate shop.

So, I told them the whole sordid story.

"You did the absolute right thing," Drago was first to vocalize his support since he was part of the *scheme,* so to speak. "You promised the kid, *and* you checked with his grandmother before proceeding. Did you tell that asshole that?"

I shook my head.

"She didn't want to mess up Alejandro's relationship with his mother," Mark explained.

"I see the benefits of shielding children, considering my childhood." Raya sat down next to me and put her booted feet up on my coffee table. "But Silvano wanted to know more about his mother, which he has a right to. And he felt he couldn't ask anyone in his family. Alejandro must consider why that is, not blame you."

"He's going to come back hat in hand." Daisy held Kai onto her shoulder and stroked his back to burp him. "What will you do then?"

I hadn't thought about that. The way Alejandro had looked when he talked to me, there was such ugliness in his tone and the way he said, *you're nothing to him*; I couldn't imagine that man coming back.

"She'll turn him away. Right, Maria?" Drago narrowed his eyes.

"No pressure, Drago," Esme admonished. "Whatever you decide to do, we're on your side, Maria. No judgment. Okay?"

I looked at Mark, who knew me best, and he nodded sadly. He understood. I loved Alejandro, but we couldn't return to where we were. The problem was not just what happened a few hours ago; it was how he made me feel like I couldn't speak to him about what mattered. He shut down, and when I said or did something he didn't like, he punished me by walking away.

He'd done that when I'd voiced my concerns about telling Silvano that first time. And it was not personal because this was Alejandro. He did the same with his family too. But they were family and tolerated it; they knew he loved them and would die for them if need be. I was an outsider, and I needed the reassurance of communication.

"First, I don't think he's going to come back...and if he did, he probably would need to crawl back, and second, even if that happened, I can't go back to how it was. It was too stressful for me. I felt like I had to walk around eggshells with him," I spoke from my head; and then added from my heart, "It's going to hurt a hell of a lot because I love the man and his family and son. And I don't know how long it will take to recover."

"Let's get this recovery party started then." Daisy handed Kai to Raya, who immediately cuddled him, nuzzling his soft cheek. "Drago, let's get that greasy Chinese food out and about. What's your favorite breakup movie?"

I shrugged. "This is my first breakup."

Drago snorted. "I thought you were broken up when we broke up."

"Neither of us was broken up. You were having sex with whatsername cheerleader in the locker room, literally banging her against the wall two days after we broke up."

Drago grinned. "True."

"I think *Mamma Mia!*" Esme declared.

"Let's go old school, *He's Just Not That Into You*," Daisy countered.

Mark added his two cents. "*Call Me By Your Name*."

Drago offered me greasy spring rolls. "I usually go to a strip club."

We all made a face.

"To bust it up," he added. "I used to be a vice cop."

"Right. That's like saying you read Playboy for the articles," I proclaimed.

Everyone nodded, but it was Raya who won the round. "*Magic Mike*."

"XXL," Daisy quipped.

We stayed up most of the night, eating bad food, drinking good wine, and watching hot men with steaming bodies.

I hugged Mark when I dragged my tired ass to bed at three in the morning. The others went home, but Mark and Drago stayed.

"I'll clean up," Drago offered. "You get some sleep. And before you make any sounds, Mark and I are staying the night."

I raised an eyebrow. "Together?"

Mark nodded appreciatively. "I have a thing for that cop vibe."

"Mark, if I swung that way even by a little, you'd be the one I'd go for."

I laughed and let Mark lead me to my bedroom. He tucked me in like a child and kissed me on my forehead. "I'm here."

"Thank you. I feel numb inside."

Mark stroked my cheek with a hand. "Yeah, it's like taking painkillers when you have a wound; at some point, you stop taking them, and it hurts like a motherfucker."

"He was going to propose, Mark."

"And you would've said yes...but this part of your relationship, this inability to talk about issues, would still be a problem that needed to be dealt with."

"Just because I'm not Silvano's biological mother doesn't mean I'm an imbecile."

Mark sat down next to me. "Alejandro has a temper, and when he's cornered, he rides out on that anger. This is not on you. It's on him."

"I feel like I'm at a crossroads and need to make some changes. I've for so long made room for others and maybe not had enough boundaries, and now I feel like this is an opportunity to do better."

Mark listened as I planned my thoughts.

"I've decided to not do Sunday dinners with the parents."

"Excellent. Then I don't have to go."

"Were you going because I was?"

"Yeah." Mark kissed my cheek. "I didn't want you to deal with them on your own."

"And I'm going to tell Mama that if Daddy doesn't behave, he doesn't get to spend time with me. She can't keep dragging us into his toxicity because we love her."

"I love Mama," Mark mused, "But she can be

manipulative."

That's what Alejandro had said. Then it felt like an insult; now I knew he was right...about my mother, not how I handled Silvano. But guilt gnawed at me. Maybe I should've reached out to Alejandro before I talked to Drago. Maybe I...

Woulda, Coulda, Shoulda!

Chapter 44

Alejandro

"**T**his is a surprise." Not! I said when my parents, brother, and sister showed up the morning after Maria and I broke up.

Isadora pushed me and walked past me. "Silvano?"

"Is this an intervention?" I went for levity. When you had an angry family around you, humor is all you're left with.

"You bet your sweet ass it is," my mother announced as she stormed past me.

I looked at Aurelio for support, but he shook his head at me, his sentiment clear, *Buddy, you fucked up, and I don't even know where to start with you.*

Silvano's eyes were red when he came downstairs from his room.

"Hey, what's wrong?" I immediately went to him.

"What's wrong is that you broke up with Maria,

and he feels it's his fault," Isadora lashed out, hugging Silvano to her. "How could you?"

"You don't know what she did. And I don't want Silvano to listen to this conversation. I—"

"I think it's time that Silvano listened to some conversations, and you had them," my mother interjected so forcefully and calmly that we all fell silent. My mother was always cheerful, and when she wasn't, it was clearly because someone fucked up, and there would be hell to pay.

"I'd like to know how you all already know."

"Because Silvano overheard you talking to Raya and Matteo, and then he told me, and I called Raya and Matteo and then connected with ground zero." Isadora kept her arm around Silvano and led him to sit on a sofa.

"So, you all know what happened?"

My mother held up a hand. "Do you remember when I first moved here? Your father and I were dating, but I rented a Golden Valley cottage while working for the county."

I remembered well, and a smile splayed on my face. "Yes." It had been such an exciting time in our lives to have Paloma in it with her kindness and generosity, easy hugs, and confessions of love. She'd taught us so much.

"You came to the cottage one evening. You were sixteen?"

I nodded, waiting for her to explain what this was about. And then realization struck me. "Oh, come on, Mama. You're drawing a false equivalency. I dented Papa's car, and Maria got a detective to tell my son how his mother died."

"I thought you were the one who dented my car," my father raised an eyebrow.

Paloma shrugged. "I never told him it was you."

"It *was* you, wasn't it, Paloma?" My father looked at my mother in bewilderment. "You told me it was you and had it fixed before I could find out."

"I asked her to do it," I remembered. It was my father's brand new truck, and at sixteen, I was scared shitless that I'd dented it.

"You know why I never told him?" My mother asked.

I nodded. I knew. I knew it then. I'd gone to her and asked her to promise that she wouldn't tell my father. It was a small thing, and she'd kept my secret. Something inside me awakened—probably the realization that I was an idiot.

"And that's what I did, Papa. I told Maria that I didn't want you to know," Silvano claimed.

"And you know what she did after Silvano asked her?" My mother looked me in the eye.

I nodded. "She contacted her detective friend and—"

"No," my mother shook her head. "She called me. She asked me what she should do because she was conflicted. I told her to do what was right because Silvano was worried, and we'd created an atmosphere where he didn't think he could ask us about Anika."

Silvano looked uncomfortable. "*Abuela*, that's not—"

"It's okay, Silvano. I absolutely understand. We knew Alejandro didn't want to talk about her, so we didn't as well and didn't contemplate that you would be curious."

I stood up and shoved my hands in the pockets of my sweatpants.

"I'm sorry, Silvano," I murmured. "Your *Abuela* is

right." I looked at my family then and sighed. "I make it difficult to talk about things I don't want to discuss, don't I?"

They all made assenting sounds. Silvano came to me and hugged me. "I love you, Papa."

I hugged him back. "I love you too, Silvano, and I'm so fucking sorry. I...we can talk about your mother or anything else you want. I will not change overnight, but I will try my best."

Silvano stepped away and joined the rest of my family—it was them against me or them supporting me; the perspective was hazy.

"Then I want to talk about Maria," Silvano announced.

I took a deep breath. "Okay."

"What's there to talk about?" my father grumbled. "He's in love with her, and he bought a ring—"

"It's beautiful," Isadora interjected.

"He should ask her to marry him," my father finished.

"She's going to knee him in the nuts rather than say yes," Aurelio spoke for the first time. "You hurt her, *amigo*; she's not going to just turn around and say, *hey, great, you pulled your head out of your ass, now we can walk hand-in-hand into the sunset.*"

You mean nothing to him. That's the last thing I had said to her.

Oh, yeah, Maria would not let me back. I'd hurt her, oh god, so much. I had seen it on her face, but when she accused me of being a bad parent, I felt cornered and lashed out. She was correct; whenever she doubted our relationship, I'd cut her off, silenced her, and avoided the whole thing.

"Do you love her, Alejandro?" my mother asked.

"Yes, Mama. I love her."

"Do you remember when I broke up with your father and was packing up to go back to Boston?"

"*Cristo!* That was unpleasant." My father put a hand on my mother's shoulder as if worried she'd go away again.

Aurelio leaned back on the chair and laughed. "Papa sent me first to go talk to you."

"And then he sent me," I added.

"And then he came with flowers and apologies," my mother remembered fondly.

"And this ring." My father picked up my mother's hand and kissed her ring.

"I can go talk to her," Silvano offered. "Tell her you've taken your head out of your ass."

"Language," every adult in the room cried out.

After that, everyone discussed bringing me back into Maria's good graces. Matteo and Raya were included on the phone. Esme and Dec joined the conversation, and ultimately, Forest and Daisy added their two cents with Hector commenting in his prim British accent.

That evening, we had dinner at the main house with the same bustle and discussion as always. After dinner, I asked my mother if she'd join me for a walk.

It was a lovely summer evening, and Golden Valley was as beautiful as ever, if a bit brown. The evenings here were always pleasant; the river flowing through the valley lowered the temperature.

"Did you ever feel that Aurelio and I were a burden?" I asked her as we walked on the path that led to Golden

Valley Inn from the main house.

"No," she replied honestly. "I worried you wouldn't like me, and then there was no way Arsenio, and I could survive. I worried I wouldn't know how to contribute to your lives because you were grown up. Aurelio was ten, so he was still...a boy, but you'd become a man."

"I think we loved you because of what you did for Papa. We'd never seen him happier."

"And we see that in you when Maria is around," my mother informed me. "Silvano can see she makes you happy—that you make her happy. Why are you so reluctant to get married?"

"I don't know...I always felt no woman could love Silvano as much as I did." I raised my hand before my mother could mention the obvious, "And, yes, I know that with you, we became a family, and I know it isn't about blood ties. I just didn't want to bring an Anika-type woman into his life. I felt like I dodged a bullet with that one, and it makes me feel tremendously guilty that I felt relieved that she was dead."

Paloma nodded understandingly. "And that's why you don't want to discuss her with Silvano."

"That and...I didn't know what to say about her except that I barely knew her. But I know Maria and...I hurt her, Mama."

My mother slid her hand into mine. "I know."

"She may never forgive me."

"I know."

"Well, that shows confidence in my abilities to win her back," I said sullenly.

My mother laughed softly. "Maria is a strong woman. She is a giving and loving woman, but you've been pushing and pulling. I think she already thought she'd had enough. I noticed how you said to her without noticing that it was okay for her to bring Silvano a birthday present; it's just family that doesn't. Do you remember saying that?"

I closed my eyes and stopped walking. I had said that. I hadn't meant it that way...but I had meant it precisely that way. She brought a fantastic present for my son, and I'd told her she wasn't family, and then I'd told her to her face that she meant nothing to my son or me.

"You don't think she'll forgive me."

"I think she's going to worry that you'll revert to the man who pushes her away every time she gets close."

"I can't change right away...but I want to. I don't want to hurt her, Mama. I love her."

"I know, *mi hijo*. And we'll do everything we can to help you convince her to give you another chance."

"And then there's another thing. I don't want more children."

"Arsenio said the same thing," my mother said gently. "Do you regret Isadora?"

"She's the glue that holds us together, as you do."

"Why would yours and Maria's baby be any different? Ask yourself why you don't want children and then talk to her. You can discuss the matter with her like a grown-up and see where you end up."

Chapter 45

Maria

"I don't feel like a party, Raya." I also didn't want to go for Raya and Matteo's anniversary party because the Santoses would be there. It hurt too much. It had been a week since Alejandro had walked away and the only reason I was able to get out of bed was because I knew if I didn't, Caruso Investments would fall apart during yet another crisis.

I had little going on in my personal life, so my professional life better be an amazing success.

"Maria, please."

"I…Raya…"

"Alejandro won't be there," she assured me.

"Fine. Just send me an email with the details," I snapped and then took a deep breath. The calm and elegant Maria Caruso had turned into a downright bitch in the last week.

Raya didn't seem to mind and replied with, "See you soon, *beyatch*."

I was on a call with Japan in the evening when my doorbell rang. I walked with my headphones to the door and the security screen showed me that my mother was on the other side, a Chanel bag on her arm and a Hermes shopping bag in her hand.

I opened the door and put myself on mute when she walked in a flurry of energy.

"I'm on a call. Why don't you pour yourself a glass of wine and I'll finish this and be with you in ten minutes."

My mother waved a hand after she dropped her bags on my couch. "Take your time, darling."

I knew she'd come. I'd called her and simply said I would not be coming for Sunday dinner any longer. She cajoled and protested but I'd been steadfast. So, it was only a matter of time before she brought her case to me in person, along with my favorite designer brand for scarves.

She was in my living room with a glass of wine, perusing the latest Vogue when I finished my call. I took my time, got myself a glass of wine and joined her in an armchair across from her.

She put the magazine away and sat up. She looked like a French woman at rest, as she always did. Slim cigarette pants, a shirt, a scarf around her neck and flats. Her hair was tied up into a ponytail. She looked a little like Audrey Hepburn with her flawless skin and angelic face.

"I want to talk to you about Sunday dinner."

I took a sip of my wine and indicated with a shake of my head that she should continue.

"I know it didn't go well when...ah...what's his name, darling?"

She did this when she wanted to look befuddled. Now, I wondered if this was all an act. I hated how I felt this way, but it was becoming increasingly clear that she wanted us to be a family, but she also didn't want to manage her husband.

"Does it matter?"

"Of course, it does, darling."

"It didn't go well. That is a fact. Daddy was a complete asshole."

"Language, Maria," my mother was offended, and I waved a dismissive hand at her.

"Come on, Mama, he was."

She pursed her lips and nodded. "I know. But we're family. If you won't come for dinner, then Mark won't and...it hurts me to see my family broken."

"Mama, you know what happens during Sunday dinner. Daddy spends a good part of the time going after Mark for choosing medicine over finance. Then he tells me all the things he thinks I'm doing wrong at Caruso Investments. And then for dessert, he tells us how he's intensely unhappy with us as children."

"You exaggerate." She drank some wine.

"No, I don't. And we eat and you flit in and out, asking Daddy to be nice in that playful way of yours. He doesn't listen. You get your dinner where you can pretend we're a close-knit family and essentially what you do is give Daddy an opportunity to vent his frustrations."

"Maria, you never speak to me like this." My mother was shaken up. And she was right. I never did. I was agreeable Maria, who wanted to make everyone happy. "Is this the influence of Alejandro?"

"I thought you didn't remember his name," I bit out.

My mother took a deep breath and then, as if following some internal meditation, the smile was back on her face. *I did the same thing, didn't I? Good god, I was just like her, pretending everything was okay because I was afraid of confrontation.*

"Maria, I don't ask for much. But I need you to come for Sunday dinner if you're not traveling or otherwise busy. It's important to me."

I raised my wine glass at her. "My mental health is more important to me."

"You make it sound like dinner is torture."

"It is. Can't you see it? I've tried to talk to him, but he behaves like Mark, and I are the problem. And now you're doing the same thing. I will not be gaslighted."

"Maria," my mother admonished. "We are a close-knit family and sometimes we say harsh words to each other, that doesn't mean—"

"A close family supports one another. You and Daddy don't support us. We take care of each other, we always have. Mark and I would love to come for Sunday dinner if Daddy will behave himself. And since I don't see that happening, the alternative is that you and Mark come for dinner at my place. I'll be happy to host."

My mother rose on unsteady legs. She rubbed her hand on her thighs. "I...I'm disappointed in you, Maria."

"Okay."

My mother picked up the Hermes bag and handed it to me. "I got you a present."

"Thanks, Mama." I set my glass aside and took the

bag. I pulled out the orange box and opened it. The scarf was beautiful, blue with red poppies. I wrapped it around my neck and gave my mother a peck on the cheek. "It's beautiful."

Her eyes filled with tears. "Maria, I can't lose my children."

"You're not losing your children, Mama. We're just not going to normalize toxic behavior any longer. Would you like to come to my place for dinner this Sunday night?"

"I can't without Daddy."

"That's a choice, Mama and I don't judge you for it."

She looked sad as she left my house. A part of me, the old Maria, wanted to run to her and make up. But the new Maria, the one I'd become in the past few months because I'd found love and now because I'd lost that love —that Maria would not let anyone ride roughshod over her any longer.

It felt good to have had this conversation with my mother. I wished I could've had a conversation with Alejandro so I could get some closure. I missed his family. I'd received texts from Isadora, Aurelio, and Paloma, all insisting that I was family regardless of what happened with Alejandro. I couldn't reply to any of them. I replied to the one from Silvano where he said he was sorry for what had happened. I'd tried to assure him he was a dear boy and nothing he could ever do could make me angry with him and he had nothing to be sorry about.

The one person I had not heard from was Alejandro.

He'd bought a ring, Raya had said. *How could he have changed his mind?* I kept waiting for him to come back, hat in hand as Daisy had said, though I was absolutely certain I'd send him on his way with a stern, "Thank you but no thank you."

The fact was that I missed him. I missed seeing his face. I missed listening to him. I missed discussing work with him where he'd tell me how to deal with a challenge. I missed how he always said I was a damn good CEO. I missed how he held me and made love with me.

I'd never fall in love like that again. How could I? This was a once in a lifetime thing, wasn't it?

I slept restlessly and woke up with a headache. It was the day of Raya's wedding anniversary party and I'd made an appointment to get my hair done, but I really didn't feel like going. I'd just do it myself; I decided and canceled the appointment on the salon app while I drank my coffee and popped a couple of painkillers.

The doorbell rang at ten in the morning.

It was Silvano.

I opened the door immediately, joy searing through me. *Was Alejandro with him?*

He was alone, but I wasn't disappointed, not when I had his son with me. I hugged him and we sat on the patio as we did when he'd been here.

"How are you?" he asked.

"I'm good." *Yeah, not good at all.*

"Maria, I'm here to apologize for my father's behavior." He sounded so formal that I broke into a smile.

"That's not for you to do," I told him firmly. "You have nothing to be sorry about."

"You see, Maria, we're family and when someone scre...messes up, then we all need to make amends. Do you think you could forgive my father?"

My heart constricted. *If he asked me himself, maybe. Damn it, Alejandro!*

"Does your father know you're here?"

He shrugged but didn't reply. It was obvious Alejandro didn't know Silvano was here. "Would you like something to eat or drink?"

"I had breakfast."

"What are you doing in LA? Are you here for Raya and Matteo's party."

He nodded but didn't look me in the eye. I felt confused but before I could probe it further, my doorbell rang again. This time, it was Paloma and Isadora. They had flowers with them and champagne.

As always, there was a flurry of activity and we all sat on the patio, drinking mimosas, except for Silvano who was relegated to orange juice, though he had asked nicely for champagne. I was reminded of when I first saw Alejandro a year ago at Raya's wedding reception. Silvano had had the same conversation with his father then, insisting that he was old enough for a splash of bubbly.

"Do you have a dress for tonight?" Isadora asked.

"I'll find something from my closet."

"Oh, no, no," Paloma insisted. "You know what they say? When you have a broken heart, retail therapy is the best."

What happened next was like a weird dream. Nova Cárdenas of *the* Cárdenas Atelier was in my house with dresses for all of us. Cárdenas was one of the most exclusive names in bridal fashion. Only the best of the best got a tour of their atelier and a chance to wear one of Valerie Cárdenas' creations on their big day or any day.

Nova and Isadora knew each other well as they'd gone to Stanford together.

"She dresses brides, I help them have the wedding of their dreams in Golden Valley Inn." Isadora and Nova stood arm in arm. They were the opposite of each other in looks. While Isadora had Latina looks and dark hair, Nova was blonde and fair-skinned.

"This is when I take my leave, ladies." Silvano bowed expertly. A car was waiting to take him to Matteo and Raya's house where he had a designated room and a computer to play on.

I ended up with a cream-colored satin slip dress that had a plunging neckline and a crisscross back. It hung on my shoulders on spaghetti straps and had an A-line silhouette. Paloma went for a navy blue dress, while Isadora wore a beige confection of tulle that made her look like a fairy princess.

It was fun. There was nothing like dressing up with women, laughing, and drinking champagne to take your mind off a broken heart.

They refused to leave me—and insisted that we were all going to drive together to Raya and Matteo's place where the party was being held.

"Gordon Mackenzie will be there," Isadora murmured as she looked at herself in a handheld mirror in the sedan that drove us.

"Don't you think he's a little old for you?" I wondered.

"He's as old as Alejandro. And does it really matter?"

Paloma frowned. "Is this Raya's boss?"

"Hmm." Isadora shut the mirror and slipped it into her bag. "He's gorgeous. I have a thing for him."

"The poor man," Paloma lamented, "Does he know you're interested in him?"

"Maybe...but he's doing the whole, you're a young girl thing."

"You are a young girl," I interjected. "Paloma, he's *really* old."

She shrugged. "Isa is a smart girl. It's none of my business who she's doing what with as long as she's safe. Will you be safe?"

"With a man who won't touch me with a ten-foot pole? Yeah, I think so," she muttered.

I'd never be able to have such a conversation with my mother. It was a different relationship, a more formal one. My mother had accepted my friends into her life, and she truly cared for them. Esme loved my mother and so did Drago, but I didn't have this easy camaraderie with her. When I was twenty-four, if I'd suggested I had a thing for a man in his forties, she'd have died with shock.

"Why don't you go up and we'll join you. I need to look through my suitcase in the back," Isadora suggested.

I was dropped off at the front of Matteo and Raya's building while the sedan drove into the parking garage. I went inside and told the concierge who I was there to see, and he sent me straight up to the penthouse.

I fiddled with my platinum necklace with small diamonds. I had absolutely loved spending time with Paloma and Isadora; but it also made me sad because I'd hoped we'd become family. It seemed that they were going to be my friends even though Alejandro and I had broken up.

I stepped out of the elevator into the living room, expecting lots of people but there was no one there. A path was made with candles and *Make You Feel My Love* by Adele was playing. It was the song that Alejandro and I had danced to that first time.

I followed the candle pathway that took me out to the pool patio where...there was only one man, Alejandro. He wore a suit and looked...well, he looked like the man of my dreams. He came to me and picked up a white rose from a vase on the way.

"May I have this dance?" he asked, handing me the rose.

The patio was lit up with romantic lights. And the mood of the place, the fact that my heart was sore with longing for him, made me do what I'd promised myself I wouldn't. I took the rose and went into his arms.

We danced in harmony and once the song ended, we stood, my hands around his neck and his on my waist.

"I love you, Maria," he started with the big guns.

"Alejandro—"

"Please, baby, let me finish. I'm so sorry for being a complete moron. You were right, I'd created a situation where Silvano didn't feel comfortable speaking to me about Anika. I also never let you voice any of your concerns. The one time you did, I asked you to leave. I will not become a different person overnight, but I want to be a better man. Will you help me? I promise I will try my best to never ever again avoid a difficult conversation."

I licked my lips and turned away from him. He let me go. I put a hand on the side of my forehead, which had started to throb again.

I turned around to face him. "Alejandro, you've said similar words before and...we seem to end up here. I can't do that anymore."

He didn't look upset, he looked like a man who'd expected something like this. "What can I do to convince you I love you? That I want to do better?"

Chapter 46

Alejandro

"**I** don't know, Alejandro," she said with such pain in her voice that I wanted to bring her back to me so I could comfort her. She looked so beautiful when she walked onto the patio that my heart ached.

"I've been afraid of getting hurt. Instead of facing that fact, I've been pushing you away. I made up excuses that I was protecting Silvano but now I can admit that I'm the one who's afraid. But knowing you, I know that you'll never hurt me."

Her eyes filled with tears. "But you hurt me. And now all you have are apologies and…I can't live like this. I can't constantly worry that you'll leave me. I can't…I just can't. I'm sorry."

Tears were flowing down her face, and I wiped them. "Give me a last chance, *Duquesa*. I won't let you down."

"But...you have in the past."

"I'm wiser now. Smarter now. I'm..." The hell with it. I dropped to my knees, both of them. "I'm begging you, *mi amor*."

She gasped. "Don't do that."

"Do what?"

"You don't have to do that. Go on your knees. Please. This is not what I meant."

She didn't think I'd do it. She thought I'd be too proud to go on my knees and beg for her. A minute ago, I had been, but that had been a minute where I didn't have her with me, and life had been empty, the future dark.

"Stand up, Alejandro," she admonished. "Please."

"No. Forgive me. I am begging you for forgiveness."

She sighed. "You're serious."

"Like a fucking heart attack."

"And what about the rest? Where do we live? How do we...you know, all that?" She waved a hand in the air.

I smiled at her. God, I loved this woman with everything inside me. "We'll figure it out. We're fortunate to have the resources to live in two homes. As long as we have love, we can work it all out."

"I want babies," she whispered.

"And I want them with you." I'd thought about what my mother had said, and it wasn't that I didn't want more children, I wanted to not have to go through what I did with Anika. "I want to see you get pregnant. I want to see you nurse our baby. I want to see Silvano with our child. I had that with Isa, and it's one of my life-defining experiences."

"Now stand up," she requested.

I pulled out the box from Tiffany and opened it.

"Marry me, Maria."

She gasped. I took the ring out, letting the box drop to the ground and slipped it on her finger.

"I haven't said yes yet." She laughed as she looked at the ring closely.

"Well then?" I asked. "My knees are hurting, baby. I'm an old man."

"Stand up, Alejandro Santos and I'll give you my answer."

I stood up, and she looked at the ring again. "It's stunning. It's perfect. And, yes, I'll marry you."

"Thank the fuck god." I pulled her into my arms and kissed her. It felt like it had been years since I'd touched her, kissed her, held her.

She moaned softly, and I had the presence of mind to not let my hands wander inappropriately over her body. After all, my family was waiting in the wings.

The patio was filled with our friends and family— people who loved and cared for us.

Raya and Matteo's wedding anniversary became our engagement party. During dinner, there were a few short speeches. Mine, I believe, was the most profound.

I stood up, cleared my throat, and winked at Silvano who had helped me. "As many of you know, Maria and I've had a tumultuous love story."

"Mostly because you were a jackass." My father held his drink up and everyone said, *salud.*

"One of the epic moments was when I was a *jackass* and drove Maria to drink, and she started to spout limericks. *Mi amor,* I am not drunk but this one is for you."

I paused dramatically and with as much of an Irish

accent as I could muster, I recited, *"There was a stupid man named Alejandro, couldn't see past his sorrow. He was lucky when Maria came into his life; luckier still when she agreed to become his wife. Now he is known as the wise man, Alejandro."*

"When the fuck did you become wise?" Aurelio wanted to know.

Maria laughed and licked her lips in the way that wanted me to take her away somewhere so I could fuck her until I couldn't see straight. She stood up. She planted a kiss on my cheek and tugged at my arm so I would sit down.

"I'm not drunk so this has a U rating." She smiled and her eyes shone with tears of joy. *"Maria was the luckiest girl in the world. She fell in love with a man and her heart twirled. The love grew and grew and grew; and when she met his family, she knew; she loved not just the man but his son, his brother, his sister, mother and father, and her love was returned a hundred fold."*

The laughter and love in the room matched the giddiness in my heart. I was one lucky *pendejo,* as my father would say.

We danced that night away, in love and feeling connected and close. "I need to get you away from here and into bed," I whispered as we danced to Etta James's *At Last.*

"I can't believe you planned this."

"My family helped."

She leaned into my arms, and I looked over her head at my brother dancing with an elegant woman.

"Is that his Caro?" I asked.

Maria turned to see who Aurelio was with and then

nodded. "Yep."

"Poor Aurelio, Mama is going to be his case now."

"Now that your case has been solved?" she teased.

I looked down at her and kissed her gently. "Maria Caruso, the love of my life, I'm so grateful that you found me and kept me. I was lost without you and didn't even know."

"Thank you, Alejandro for coming back and not letting me go. I missed you so much."

We held each other for a long while, soaking each other in until we really had to find a bed or embarrass ourselves in front of everyone.

We barely made it inside her house, we were so desperate for each other. I'd never expected this kind of passion. Sure, I had sex. I liked sex, but it was always something I could take or leave. But with Maria, it was a sweet madness. That she was just as eager as me made the sex hotter.

I had her against her front door, her dress hiked up. Her panties were somewhere on her floor.

"I can't wait," I groaned and drove into her.

Her legs were wrapped around my waist, and she held me close. I felt like I was home. I moved slowly within her, in and out, setting a rhythm as I kissed her, my tongue mimicking my cock.

"I love you," she whispered in my ear and that's all it took. I came inside her, embarrassingly before she did.

I carried her to her...*our* bed without pulling out of her.

"You make me behave like a teenage boy, losing control like that."

She laughed and damn me if I didn't hear it again,

the tinkling of bells. "It makes me feel...powerful."

"To make me come before I'm ready?" I asked as I nudged her thighs apart.

"Yes." Her eyes were serious now. "It makes me feel...like..."

"Like you have just as much control over me as I have over you?"

"Exactly—" She whimpered when her swollen pussy made room for me. "Don't stop."

I rammed into her, and we both felt the pleasure rip into us. "I'm not stopping, *mi amor*, I'm never stopping. I love you, Maria."

THE END

BONUS CHAPTER

Keep this story going with the bonue chapter, ***Alejandro & Maria's Wedding*** on my website. Click here and read on.

READ THE SERIES

Meet the characters you fell in love with in the Golden Knights series. Esme, Raya and Daisy have their own stories that are poignant; and about redemption and forgiveness; and above all, the power of love.

A REQUEST FROM MAYA

Thank you so much for reading **Golden Promises**. If you liked this book, I request you to leave a review and/or a rating on Amazon so other readers can find this book.

NOT *a love* MARRIAGE

A SECOND CHANCE ROMANCE

MAYA ALDEN

Excerpt: Not A Love Marriage

Chapter 10: Daisy

"Fuckity, fuck, fuck, fuckity fuck." I held a pregnancy test in my hand and the news was still the same after five tests from different brands. I was pregnant.

I picked up my phone with shaking hands and called Raya. "I need you. Come home."

She came home and brought Esme along, who brought her baby Mireya along. And since Maria was visiting Esme, she tagged along. Seeing the baby made me feel both excited and anxious.

"I'm pregnant," I told the women.

Esme jumped up, baby and all from the couch she was sitting on and hugged me. "Congratulations. Does Forest know? He'll be so excited."

Esme was tiny, just five feet two but a bundle of energy. Her dark hair was tied up in a ponytail and she looked like the earth mother holding the adorable Mireya. Esme was an elegant woman, incredibly feminine with a core of steel. I adored her.

Raya, who was more careful, came up to me and

put a hand on my shoulder. "All okay on the bodily functions front?"

Unlike Esme, Raya was five feet ten inches tall, nearly two inches taller than me. Unlike my waist-long red hair, hers was blonde and cropped. She rode a Ducati and was most comfortable in a pair of jeans, a T-shirt, military-style boots, and a leather jacket when the weather warranted it. Of all my friends, I was closest to Raya.

I looked up at her. "I don't know how I feel. But the body is good.

"This is Forest's baby?" Raya, the practical one asked.

"Raya," Maria protested. "She's in love with him."

Maria had become part of our group over the past year since Esme and Dec married. As had her brother Mark who was doing a residency in neurosurgery at UCLA—which meant we didn't see him that often and when we did, he was either of a double shift or on his way to one.

Maria was the CEO of the Caruso Investment Bank and was doing a better job than her father had running it. Nearly as tall as Raya, Maria was a brunette bombshell. I always wished I could be more like her—soft and sweet, sophisticated—but I was half Irish and half Creole—I was loud and emotional. My hair was red and my eyes green. I was loud and took up a lot of space. Soon I'd be taking up a lot more with being pregnant. I still couldn't believe it.

"She has a lot of sex, Esme," Raya retorted. "But you've not been sleeping with anyone but Forest for the past…I don't know several months now, right?"

I sat down, still holding the five pregnancy tests. "Forest *is* the father of the baby. Holy fuck! I'm a sensible smart woman, how did I get pregnant?"

"Well, you know when a penis meets a vagina," Raya grinned. "Come on, Daisy, you love babies and you've always wanted one."

"But I'd hope that I'd be like Esme and have a husband to go with the baby. You know, like matching bags and shoes."

"Why can't Forest be that husband?" Esme asked.

"Because when we were fucking and made this baby, he said we'd scratch the itch," I shuddered when I remembered.

"Mateo said something similar to me," Raya remembered.

"And look at you now," I looked pointedly at Raya's engagement and wedding rings. The engagement ring was a stunner with an amber gemstone as a centerpiece.

"You love Forest, Daisy, why not see this as a way to—"

"Trap him?" I offered sullenly. "I don't want him like this. I want him…like…you know we used to be."

"Can you tell us what happened five years ago?" Maria asked, using a tissue to take the pregnancy tests from me and throwing them into the trash in the kitchen.

No one knew. I hadn't told anyone except my brother; and Forest had confessed his sins to no one but his. River had reached out to me after Forest, and I broke up. He let me know that Forest was in bad shape—but then so was I and I wasn't ready to pull my heart out of my body and hand it over to a man who had gone and fucked an acquaintance of mine the first minute we had a problem.

"He's the first and only man I ever loved. The only man I said *the words* to, and then he got some pictures of me...fake pictures of me in bed with Mad Chase." I shook my head as the memories assailed me.

I told them everything. What he said, what I said and how he'd come to apologize but I couldn't forgive him, couldn't risk it.

"Who sent those pictures?" Raya wondered. "Did you guys ever find out?"

I shrugged. "What the heck does that matter? It's how he behaved that does. It could be anyone. I mean, I work in Hollywood, making shit up is the lifeblood."

Esme rocked Mireya to sleep. "I think it does matter. And I wonder..."

"What?" Raya asked.

"You know Nina Knight, Dec's mother didn't like me and tried everything she could to break us up. What does Lena Knight think of you, Daisy?"

I couldn't believe that Lena Knight would go this distance—not only because it was a bit extreme but also because I didn't think she was smart enough to pull something like this off. Lena Knight was a society butterfly.

"I doubt it was her."

Raya and Esme looked at each other and I groaned. "Oh, come on. What are you both communicating with that look?"

"Don't worry about it," Raya said. "Let us handle the investigation part of your story. You handle being pregnant."

Esme put Mireya down in her bassinet and pulled out her phone. "You need to get some vitamins and asap."

"I already ordered online," Maria told them and put her phone aside. "How is the nausea? Any morning sickness?"

I gaped at the women. "I'm pregnant."

"She's in shock," Raya commented.

"No shit, Sherlock. Damn, I need to tell Forest now. He's going to flip." I was certain of it. Would he think I trapped him? Got pregnant on purpose? God, I hoped not. This is the last thing I wanted with him. No, that's not true. I always wanted to marry him and have his babies; I'd just hoped he'd be madly in love with me and not asking me to help scratch his itch.

"I'm going to ask him to come over," I decided.

"Do you need us here with you?" Raya asked.

I shook my head. "No. I think we need to do this together. Because once the baby is here, we'll have to co-parent, so we better learn to get along."

"You're sure you want to keep the baby?" Esme asked. With her background in social service, it was obvious she'd suggest the option without judgment.

"I want the baby." My hand instinctively was on my belly as if to protect it. "I've always wanted a baby or two or three." I smiled. "This may not be the ideal way to do this but I'm absolutely sure that I want to be a mother. I may be a complete shit mother. Speaking of shit mothers...I'll have to call mine and tell her. She's going to lose her shit."

My mother had been raised Irish Catholic though she was now lapsed. A baby out of wedlock would not make her happy. My father, who was Creole, would have absolutely no issue whatsoever and would simply look forward to performing the duties of a grandfather. Dom would be thrilled to be an uncle. They'd all want to know if Forest was going to do the right thing. I fucking hoped not. Getting knocked up was no reason to tie a knot with a man for the rest of your life.

I wondered how Forest's family would feel about my having his baby. Probably not great.

After the girls left, I texted Forest: *Can you come over? Urgent.*

Forest was not a texting kinda guy as he still had a Nokia flip phone that he barely knew how to use to send text messages though he'd become surprisingly good at receiving messages.

He called instead of texting. "Baby, you alright?" he asked.

"Yeah," I didn't want to do this over the phone. I needed to see his face when I told him. "I need you to come over."

"I'm on my way. Are you sure you're, okay?"

"Yes." I felt miserable. I didn't know how Forest would react and it made me jittery.

∞∞∞

Chapter 11: Forest

I drove like a madman to get to her. Daisy wasn't the type who'd send a message saying urgent if it wasn't a firestorm.

She opened the door before I could ring the doorbell. She was in denim shorts and a t-shirt. Her hair was tied up in a messy bun. She looked absolutely gorgeous and worried as hell.

"Baby, what's wrong?" I took her in my arms, and she hugged me back.

She led me inside the house and we into her brightly lit kitchen.

"You want coffee?" she asked.

I shook my head. "Honey, what's going on?"

"Sit," she instructed and pushed me onto the white bench in the breakfast nook. She sat across from me, looking nervous.

I took her hands in mine and moved my thighs to hold hers between mine.

She smiled uneasily. "Forest, I...I'm pregnant."

Thunder fucking bolt! "I don't know if I heard you correctly. Did you say you are pregnant?" My heart was falling all over itself beating like a mother fucker. *Finally, finally, the fucking universe was giving me a break. Fucking yes!!!!!!*

"Yeah. I just found out. Took five pregnancy tests. I need to make an appointment with my gyno. And... Forest?"

I couldn't stop beaming. "You're pregnant?"

"Yeah."

I got up and pulled out of the breakfast nook and hugged her. "Fucking A, DeeDee."

She pulled away so she could see my face. "You're not upset?"

"Upset? Why the hell would I be upset? Nah. This is...wow, DeeDee. We're going to be parents."

She smiled, but she was confused. "I'm so...it's great that you're so positive. We'll obviously come up with a...you know custody agreement and all that."

My heart sank, but I refused to let go of her. Of

course, she'd assume that we'd continue as we were. Fuck that. She was mine now. DeeDee and the baby inside her.

I did some fast thinking—well, I was known to think on my feet and be creative. I gradated top of my class in Harvard, and I was a fucking Judge. "DeeDee, sweetheart, you know I'm up for the judgeship of the Ninth Circuit."

She nodded.

"Baby, we can't...you know...you can't have a baby without us being married. It's going to mess up my chances." I had no idea whether that was true or not; and if this were any other woman than DeeDee I'd be all about a custody agreement and the hell with the world. But this was my Daisy, and I was going to marry her. Sure, I was trapping her, using a bogus reason, but once she was mine, I'd make it my life's work to keep her there.

She looked stricken, and I kissed her on her forehead. *Poor DeeDee.* This was all too much for her. But I was here now, and I'd take care of her.

"We have to get married?"

"I'm afraid so." *Thank you, UNIVERSE!!*

"Married?" If she got any paler, I'd have to call 911, I thought.

"But Forest—"

"DeeDee this is a once in a lifetime opportunity for me."

"Then we tell no one," she said steadily. "And… once you get confirmed—"

I hugged her tighter and kissed her to stop her from talking. "You know it's going to be near impossible to keep it a secret. I want to come to all your doctor's appointments. I want to hold your hand through this and be there with you. Please, DeeDee."

"Christ, Forest." She pulled away from me. "This isn't like you asking me to come to some party with you as a date. This is a marriage."

Think, Forest, think before she convinces herself that this is a bad idea.

"I know. How about we say we'll remain married for eighteen months and then we can revisit our status."

"Why eighteen months?" she asked suspiciously.

Fuck if I know! It just seemed like a good number.

"You know how these hearings go; they can take long. You'll need help once the baby is born. We should be together for all of that."

"Eighteen months is doable," she said, and I breathed a sigh of relief. "But we have to live here. I can't live in Venice."

"Not a problem. This is closer to the court, anyway." I'd give up surfing if she asked me to. "We'll have to have an airtight prenup. I don't want anyone to think that I want anything from you."

I grinned. The world may think Daisy was marrying into the Knight family for money, but the truth would be that she'd make sure the prenup protected me. I didn't need protection. I didn't even want a prenup. The hell with it. I was never going to let her go.

"Of course. I'm sure we can get that in place. Stop thinking so hard, baby." I opened my arms. "Come here."

She took two steps, and she was in my embrace. I held her close.

"I don't want us to keep fighting, Forest. It's too stressful."

"I promise I will be the most agreeable husband you could ever imagine." *As long as you didn't want to leave me, then I'd be damned disagreeable.*

She chuckled.

"What?" I asked.

"Looks like you and I will get married in the courthouse like Esme and Dec; and Mateo and Raya did. Too bad you can't marry us. Then we'd just put a "get married here" sign outside your chambers."

"If you want a Church wedding..."

"It feels wrong when we know this is temporary."

She was killing me with this wall she had built around her. "Anything you want."

"My parents, Forest. I have to tell them."

"We'll do it together." She would never have to do anything difficult alone again.

She nodded. "*And* your parents, how will they react?"

"Let me prep them first and then it should be fine; and if it isn't they can go fuck themselves. If they can't be happy about a grandchild, the hell with them." But my mother was a sweetheart, I knew I would be able to turn her around. She didn't like Daisy, but she'd like a pregnant Daisy, her only chance of having grandchildren, considering River didn't sit still long enough to get a woman pregnant.

I stayed the night with her.

There was no way I was going to give her time and space to think about us. She'd convince herself the marriage was a bad idea. She lay with her head on my shoulder, and I had an arm around her with my hand on her stomach. A slightly curved stomach—but that wasn't the baby, not yet, just Daisy, lush and lovely.

My phone vibrated, and I saw that it was River who tended to call at all times of day and night. I had called him earlier in the evening and left him a voicemail to call me back.

I disentangled from Daisy and left her bedroom with my phone. I stood naked in her kitchen when I answered the phone.

"Who's dead?" River asked.

"Daisy and I are having a baby." I couldn't believe I'd just said those amazing words.

"No shit."

"She's pregnant, River. She's fucking pregnant."

"All that fucking probably got her in her situation. You're obviously thrilled. How does she feel about being *enceinte*?"

"Confused, scared, happy, afraid, thrilled."

"All the feels."

I heard loud popping sounds on River's end. "Where the fuck are you, River?"

"Somewhere in the East."

"That's a rather large mass of land. And what I hear is a HIMARS." I had been in LAPD for a hot minute and knew my weapons.

"A what?"

"A High Mobility Artillery Rocket System, asshole."

"No? Really?" River chuckled and then somberly said, "Congratulations, brother. This is awesome news. What's next? What can I do for you?"

I told him quickly (because he was *literally* in a war zone) about the upcoming wedding and how I'd sort of emotionally blackmailed Daisy into agreeing to it. I had absolutely no moral issues with it. She just needed to start believing in me and us; and know I'd not fuck up the way I had.

"Please tell me you didn't get her pregnant on purpose," River laughed.

"I would have if I'd thought about it...but this is

the universe smiling at me. You think you'll be back stateside in a week or two? I'd like for you, Dec, and Mateo to be witnesses."

"You know Mom is going to lose her shit." *No shit!*

"I know. I'm meeting her for Saturday lunch tomorrow. I'll calm her down. Daisy is going to be my wife and the mother of my child, the sooner she comes to terms with it, the better."

"Good luck. Send me date information and I'll try to make it. No guarantees."

The sounds around River seemed closer than before.

"Okay, dude, I got to get the hell out of here. I'll talk to you—" His line was cut off. I wanted to call him back to make sure he was okay, but I knew that wouldn't assuage my concerns. I worried about River all the time; it was like a low-level hum in my brain.

River loved his job, so I supported him no matter what. That was the *job* of a brother; and he did the same for me. Sure, he'd kick my ass when he thought I screwed up—but he was always on my side. As River once said, "If you murdered someone, I'll help you move the body, but try not to kill anyone if you can help it. If you can't help yourself, try to do it when I'm in the country."

Keep reading...

Author's Note

Hey there, awesome Reader!

I just wanted to drop you a line to say a big thank you for picking up my book. I really hope you had a blast flipping through the pages and diving into the adventure. But hey, I've got a little confession – the idea of our connection coming to an end with that last chapter is a bit of a bummer.

So, here's the scoop – I'm throwing out an invite to you, yes, YOU! How about we keep this bookish party going? You're totally invited to hang with me beyond the pages. How, you ask? Well, I've got this rad newsletter and some social media shenanigans that you can join in on.

Picture this: juicy behind-the-scenes tidbits, sneak peeks of what's cookin' for my next literary escapade, and oh yeah, exclusive giveaways that you won't find anywhere else! You'll be in the know before anyone else, like a VIP for all things bookish.

I'm seriously stoked about the idea of us staying connected. So, don't be a stranger – let's keep the book love alive! Looking forward to more bookish adventures together.

Happy Reading!

Maya

Website: www.MayaAlden.com

Newsletter: Sign Up

Facebook: @authormayaalden

Instagram: @MayaAlden_Romance

Email: maya@mayaalden.com

Books In This Series

Golden Knights

The Golden Knights Series takes place in the vibrant City of Los Angeles, where we delve into the intricate lives and heartfelt romances of individuals associated with Knight Technologies, a prominent cyber security company. You will also meet the Santos family! They own and run Golden Valley, one of the larges farms in California. The patriarch of the family Arsenio and his wife Paloma have a bad habit of micromanaging the love lives (and lives in general) of their three children.

My stories center around the powerful themes of forgiveness and self-acceptance. As we navigate through the challenges of life, both forgiving others and ourselves, we uncover the path to becoming the best version of ourselves and embracing love with all our hearts.

The Wrong Wife: An Arranged Marriage Romance

Bad Boss: An Office Romance

Not A Love Marriage: A Second Chance Surprise Pregnancy Romance

Golden Promises: A Single Father Romance

Twisted Hearts: An Enemies To Lovers Second Chance Romance

A Golden Christmas: An Age-Gap Holiday Romance

Made in United States
Troutdale, OR
09/21/2024

23008170R00206